MW00779483

Death Comes
at Night

James Dalrymple

BLACK ✿ ROSE
writing™

© 2015 by James Dalrymple

All rights reserved. No part of this book may be reproduced, stored in a retrieval system or transmitted in any form or by any means without the prior written permission of the publishers, except by a reviewer who may quote brief passages in a review to be printed in a newspaper, magazine or journal.

The final approval for this literary material is granted by the author.

First printing

This is a work of fiction. Names, characters, businesses, places, events and incidents are either the products of the author's imagination or used in a fictitious manner. Any resemblance to actual persons, living or dead, or actual events is purely coincidental.

ISBN: 978-1-61296-564-2

PUBLISHED BY BLACK ROSE WRITING

www.blackrosewriting.com

Printed in the United States of America

Suggested retail price $17.95

Death Comes at Night is printed in Adobe Garamond Pro

To Marla, who died at night.

Acknowledgements

I can't begin to tell you how incredibly helpful it is to belong to a writing group. Somehow I have been able to convince two very good groups to allow me to participate. I'm not very good at critique, although, I love to read. And, I love to read what my group members, friends, write. Fortunately for me, they are very good at providing valuable, insightful feedback. My writing is better for them. With gratitude I acknowledge Ginger Churchill, Brooklyn Evans, Matthew Evans, Meagan Langer, Jeni Lee, Dene Low, Steph Lineback, Scott Livingston, Allison Merrill, Janiel Miller, Melissa Hernandez Seron Richardson, Loraine Scott, Marlene Scoville, Cally Stephens, Eric James Stone, Nicki Trionfo and Charmayne Gubler Warnock for their talent, encouragement and words of wisdom.

There is one more member of our group that deserves more credit than I could possibly give, Caleb Warnock. Caleb got tired of the monthly read and critique thing and asked for my manuscript. He provided great feedback and helped with problem areas. He followed me through the extensive and frustrating query process, baffled that I did not have a contract. He encouraged me to keep going, many times when I set the manuscript on the shelf. I knew, when I went to our writers group that Caleb would demand that I be accountable for getting published. So, Caleb, here it is, in book form. Thank you!

I would also be remiss if I did not thank Reagan Rothe of Blackrose Writing for taking a chance on me. I am grateful for this opportunity and for Reagan's concern for me as a writer.

Lastly, I must thank my family. Writing is a solitary, somewhat schizophrenic occupation. It is easy to walk around, living in two worlds, not fully in either one. Occasionally I am able to return to the real world and realize just how lucky I am to be surrounded by a family who love me, and, rely on me to remain here, in this world.

To my wife, Anne, you are my hero. You bless my life every single day. I love you.

Death Comes at Night

Chapter 1

The sun sets early in the Pacific Northwest in late fall. Even though it was only 4:00 pm it was nearly dark. And it was raining. Daniel Monson was driving State Road 92 from Mount Si toward Carnation, Washington. He'd been meeting with his boss's favorite client, doing discovery work for her current divorce. He didn't like what he was discovering. His boss would love it. They might add his name to the long list of names that would probably never fit on the office marquee, no matter how small the type.

As he drove, Daniel liked to think his Honda was a sports car. It handled like a sports car. At least Daniel liked to think it did, even though he'd never actually driven a sports car. State Road 92 was a great road to drive. It only had two lanes. It had lots of curves. And it was in the middle of nowhere.

Garth brooks was singing Thunder Rolls. Daniel switched the windshield wipers from delay to constant and turned up the music. He didn't particularly like Garth Brooks, but the rain made it hard to hear. Lately, he'd been listening to country music because he liked the stories they told, most of them depressing. Julie didn't like country music. Their ten-year marriage was fractured–not completely broken–yet. Jenny, their six-year-old silver lining, was the cast setting a difficult break. Daniel didn't know if it was going to heal.

Douglas firs deepened a deepening gloom as Daniel drove beneath their outstretched limbs. He felt as if he were in a lengthening tunnel with the light switched off at the other end. He shivered involuntarily and turned the heater up. As he drove out of the deepest part of the Snoqualmie forest, he couldn't help thinking the evergreens were reaching for him. Sometimes, he could be overly dramatic, Julie said. And, paranoid.

There was just enough light left for Daniel to see the "Welcome to Carnation" sign. A smiling, happy cow, holding a bottle of milk, welcomed passersby to the main and only street in downtown Carnation. California's happy cows must have never met Carnation's bovine ambassador or they would easily concede the crown for the world's happiest cows.

Carnation wasn't an interesting town—with just a few exceptions. Set deep in the forest of the Snoqualmie Mountains, there were more dairy cows than people in Carnation and there really weren't that many dairy cows. You could get really good ice cream at the Carnation dairy. Daniel liked ice cream. Really good vanilla.

Even though he was amused by the happy hoofed welcome, Daniel didn't stop. He wanted to get home. He needed to be home. He promised Julie he'd be there—Jenny's school play.

Driving out of the town, Daniel stepped on the gas, passing acres of well-maintained white-slat fences protecting rain-blackened pastureland. The fences seemed to iridesce in the dim ambience as a gray sky dripped to black. Occasionally, a ghostly light would flicker through the trees and mist, suggesting some phantasmagoric guardian of distant cottages. "Riders on the Storm" began to play. Daniel pressed the accelerator a little harder.

As he drove, he was thinking about chicken soup with soda crackers—Campbell's Chicken Soup. This was a perfect chicken soup night. He could almost taste it, although he hadn't had chicken soup since he was a boy. His mother used to make it on nights like this. He hadn't thought about his mother in years. She had passed away long ago. Julie never made chicken soup.

Anxious to get home, to be there for them like he promised, Daniel could feel the tension pulling on him, stretching him out like salt water taffy. He checked the rear-view mirror, not sure he even looked like himself. He wanted to make things work, put things right, save their marriage. He just didn't know how. He felt like he couldn't breathe, desperation rising. He pushed the accelerator even harder.

There she was.

As Daniel rounded a corner, thinking about Tokyo Drift, she was just there, standing in the middle of the road. At first he thought it was Julie. Was he dreaming? What is she doing?

It wasn't Julie.

He wasn't breathing. Was she?

Daniel slammed on the brakes. The gray Honda groaned but didn't stop. Now he was drifting for real, hydroplaning. The woman didn't move. She just stood there. Daniel turned the steering wheel. The car slid. He turned the wheel again. He remembered riding the racecars at the carnival when he was a kid. His Dad rode in the car with him. His Dad "let him" drive. He felt like he was in control. He wasn't. It didn't matter which way you turned the steering wheel. The car was on a track. It didn't matter if you turned the wheel at all. It didn't matter if you even held on.

Did it?

His car spun off the pavement, into the muddy moat separating the glistening road from the pressing evergreen sentinels. Daniel's brief case slammed into the windshield and popped open. Papers flew everywhere. The sucking mud sucked at the Honda's wheels and the car stalled. He hadn't stepped on the clutch.

I'm not going to make it.

The windshield wipers were still flapping. The headlights shone on the woman, standing in the road. She looked lost. Daniel sat there, breathing hard. When he felt his heart rate drop below 200 bpm he opened the door and got out, into the mud. Florsheim shoes weren't designed for mud. It was raining, hard. Daniel's overcoat was in the backseat. He had forgotten to put it on. With sucking resistance, he pulled his feet out of the mud and stepped onto the road. Mud squished inside his shoes.

"ARE YOU CRAZY?" Daniel said in his most understated yell. "What are you doing standing in the middle of the road? You could get killed."

The woman turned slowly toward Daniel, arms at her side. She was barefoot, wearing a black cocktail dress, soaked to the skin. She was slender. Her hair was long and dark and very wet. She could have been swimming. Her eyes looked empty somehow, vacant. Daniel couldn't tell if she could even see him, or hear him.

He took a step toward her.

"Are you O.K?"

She looked right at him.

Then, she SCREAMED.

A blood-curdling scream.

She backed away from Daniel, pulling her arms across her chest. She convulsed in a gag, bending over.

Daniel took another step toward her.

"NO!" she sobbed. "Don't touch me. Don't come near me."

Daniel backed off. Holding his hands out, to show her he meant no harm.

"It's O.K. I won't hurt you. I can help you."

"Help me?" she sobbed. "Help me, please," she repeated, desperately.

Daniel took a step toward her.

"No, don't," she backed up.

Daniel stopped.

"I won't," he said. "What's wrong? What's happened?"

Her sobs continued.

"I…don't…know. Something…happened."

"What? Where?"

She pointed down a muddy road, into the dark woods. Drizzling diamonds glistened in the yellowing headlights from Daniel's car, still on. All Daniel could see was mud, trees and rain.

"It's so cold."

Daniel looked at the woman. She didn't look crazy, just wet. He was the crazy one.

"Here, take my jacket." Daniel slipped off his soggy sports jacket and held it out to her.

"Hurry," she said. She turned and began to run down the muddy road, into the darkness, barefoot. That was crazy.

In horror films, the hero or heroine always goes into the attic, or up the stairs, or into the garage. No matter how stupid you think they are, or how bad the acting is, or how much they know something bad is going to happen to them, they do it anyway. The writer and director know that even though we say that we would never do that, secretly we want them to. We need them to. If they didn't, we would have to. We would have to run the gauntlet, or drink from the crucible, or bleed in Gethsemane.

Raindrops danced on the blacktop. Daniel looked back at his car. The wipers were still flapping. The headlights were still on. He stepped back into the mud and followed the crazy woman into the darkness.

Slogging through the mud, he could barely see the gliding shape of the woman up ahead. He began a jog along the muddy road. It was nearly impossible to keep the woman in sight. It was nearly as difficult to pick out a path on the sloppy road. He kept slipping. He thought he would go down, more than once. The farther down the road he got, the harder it was to see her. Then, he couldn't see her.

He rounded a muddy bend in the blackness. There she was, again. He could see a glimmering light and the shape of the woman seemed to float quickly along. He kept going. It was too late to turn back.

It's never too late to turn around.

He rounded another bend and saw a barn. A light was on inside. The barn door was open. The woman was standing still, silhouetted in the open barn door. The shape of the barn blended into the blackness pressing upon it. He slowed down, then stopped, breathing hard.

The woman was staring into the barn. He couldn't see inside. She turned to him and pointed inside with her left hand.

She had the most compelling eyes he had ever seen. He was surprised that he could see them in the darkness. She was backlit by the yellow light escaping from the barn. Yet, her eyes seemed to glow. Deep pools. He couldn't look away.

When he was a boy, Daniel had been hiking in the Cascades with the Boy Scouts. He was usually the last one into camp. Most of the boys liked to run ahead. Daniel liked to take his time. He thought a lot about the trees, their size and majesty. He loved the smell of the deep woods, and the quiet. He was alone. He wasn't afraid of the deep forest. Not then.

The trail he was on climbed out of the forest, onto a ridge. As he climbed a ridge, he could see two small lakes down below. Mirror Lakes. He had never seen such deep blue water, until now. He was being pulled in. The water was cold.

"In there," she said.

Daniel shivered.

"What is it? What's in there?"

She didn't answer. She turned back to stare inside.

Now I must be crazy.

Daniel Monson had never really done anything crazy in his life. He lived a normal life, a perfect life, sort of.

Good things don't last.

Shut up.

Go home.

What are you doing here?

Against his better judgment, Daniel stepped around the woman, into the barn.

The light was blinding. He had stepped out of the blackness into a light much darker.

There she was.

The black cocktail dress was torn from her shoulder revealing pearl white skin. A trickle of blood dripped from the corner or her ruby lips. Her arms were above her head as if she were lounging. Her legs were skewed and her black dress was pushed too far up her hips. She had the bluest eyes he had ever seen. She was staring up at him, pleading. He shouldn't be here. He shouldn't see this. Who did this?

Run.

He couldn't run. His arms and legs felt very heavy. He hadn't realized it, but his teeth were chattering.

So cold. So very cold.

He heard footsteps.

Running.

He turned to look at the woman in the doorframe. She was bleeding on the floor of the barn.

Chapter 2

"Why don't you tell it to me one more time," Sheriff Jasper Clawson drawled. Daniel couldn't tell if the Sheriff was from the south or if he just liked to talk that way.

Flash.

A deputy was taking pictures of the woman. Daniel turned away.

"Come on, Sheriff. I'm cold and wet, and I'm not going to change my story."

"So it's a story, is it?"

"No, it's not a story."

"Then that's not your story?"

"No…Yes…I'm telling you the truth. I'm an attorney, for heaven's sake."

"Well, Son, I'd like to believe you, but what you're telling me don't put you in the best light. You being an attorney and all, I'm sure you know what your rights are."

"I'm a family lawyer, not a criminal lawyer."

Sheriff Clawson was a large man, tall and round. Daniel stared at the handcuffs on the Sheriff's belt.

It must take a lot of leather to hold those pants up.

"You got a family?" the Sheriff asked.

"Yes, why?" Daniel said.

"You just might want to get yourself a criminal lawyer, then."

"Come on, Sheriff, you're not going to arrest me, are you?"

"Not until we're done investigating this here crime scene. But, I'm not letting you go no where's either."

"My wife and daughter must be worried sick by now."

"Would you like me to call them for you? That might be interesting."

Daniel pulled the police issue wool blanket tighter around his shoulders. His teeth wouldn't stop chattering.

"The 911 operator said you sounded sorta panicky like. She said, you said, the dead woman brought you in here. Was she dead before she brought you in here, or after."

"She wasn't dead at all. I told you, she was standing in the road. I swerved to miss her."

"Was that before, or after you killed her?"

Daniel exploded.

"I DIDN'T KILL HER."

"Listen, boy, there's been a lot of folks dying around these parts of late. You're the first good candidate we got. I'm not gonna let you go till I know Damn sure you didn't do it."

Flash.

Daniel winced. The deputy taking pictures looked at him.

"A little jumpy, aren't you?" the sheriff said. The deputy smirked.

"Come on, sheriff. Why would I call 911 if I did it?"

"I don't know. Why did you?"

"I didn't do it."

"Come on now, boy, we've got the tapes to prove it."

"Not 911. I didn't kill this woman," Daniel said with exasperation.

"You said, the last time you saw her, she was standing outside this here barn. That makes you the last person to see her alive. You sounded crazy on the 911 tapes. You said she was outside the barn. Then you said she was dead. Why'd you do it?"

Daniel was cold and wet and tired. He didn't know what had happened. It didn't make a lot of sense to him, either. Maybe he was crazy. He didn't think he was crazy. But, if you were really crazy, would you know it? Didn't wondering about whether you were crazy or not mean you weren't really crazy?

"I didn't do it," Daniel said.

"Looks like strangulation, chief," the deputy said. "Hematomas about the neck. And, she's got some skin under her fingernails."

"Let me see your hands, boy," Sheriff Clawson said.

Reluctantly, Daniel held out his hands.

"You ever worked a day in your life?" the Sheriff asked.

"What?"

"Got any scratches we can't see?"

"No."

"You come here to have sex with this girl?"

"Are you crazy?"

"What's her name?"

"How should I know?"

"You said she brought you here."

"I was trying to help her."

"She don't need your kind of help."

"I couldn't agree more."

A dripping deputy stepped into the barn.

"Coroner's here, Chief."

"About time," Sheriff Clawson growled. "Alright Mr. Monson, I'm going to let you get. But if you cross the county line my boys'll hunt you down. You'll not have one night of sleep again, until it's your last one."

"I haven't been sleeping much lately anyway."

"That a fact."

"So, I can go?"

"Give me your shoes."

"My shoes?"

"That's right, your shoes."

"I'm not going to run away barefoot in this mud and rain."

"My boys'll give you a ride to your car."

"It's against the law to drive barefoot in the State of Washington," Daniel said.

18

"Learn something new everyday. Howdy Frank."

"Howdy J.C."

The coroner came into the barn with vulture like excitement.

"What we got, now."

The sheriff was done with Daniel, for now. Daniel wrapped the olive-drab blanket around his shoulders and shuffled toward the door.

"I'll be watching you, Monson," the sheriff said. "Give this SOB a ride out to the highway, Bert." The big deputy gave a nod and motioned for Daniel to follow him.

When Daniel finally made it out to the highway, he could see that his car was still in the exact same spot he had left it, stuck in the mud. The windshield wipers were still moving, in slow motion. His headlights were casting a dim yellow on the mud.

The big deputy was kind enough to hook up his winch and pull Daniel out of the mud. The deputy then got out jumper cables and gave Daniel a jump. By this time, his socks were completely worn through. His toes were sticking through the holes in the toes. Daniel climbed in the front seat, soaking the upholstery. He cranked the heat up and took a breath.

Not my best day ever.

The big deputy just stood beside his patrol car, watching. The plastic wrap covering his hat was beaded and dripping.

Daniel put the car in gear, stepped on the gas pedal and drove away. He looked in the rear view mirror at the deputy, still watching.

There she was.

She sat up in the back seat. The woman in black.

Daniel screamed.

It was a terrible, frightened scream. He could feel the scream, involuntarily, coming from the coldness in his bones. He slammed on the brakes and the Honda skidded, slid, to a stop, not more that 100 yards from where he had started.

"Are you going to help me?" she said, the woman in black.

Daniel yelled again. Panic. Fear.

Breathe.

This can't be happening.

Daniel turned around to look at her.

The woman in black sat patiently. Quietly.

"Are you going to help me?" she said again.

"What do you want from me," Daniel stammered.

Rap. Rap. Rap.

Daniel jumped, hollering.

"Everything alright in there?" the Deputy had come to see what was going on.

Daniel looked up at the deputy through the rain-dappled windshield with a wildness in his eyes. He turned to look back at the woman.

Where'd she go?

Daniel looked back at the deputy. He motioned for Daniel to roll down the window. Daniel obeyed.

"Fine. Everything's fine," he said, breathlessly.

"You don't look so good," the Deputy said.

"It's, uh, it's nothing…my foot just slipped off the gas pedal and hit the brake. That's all. You know, it's against the law to drive barefoot in the State of Washington."

Lame.

"I did not know that," the deputy said.

"It's a fact," Daniel said. "Look it up for yourself."

"I'll just take your word for it."

"Well, I, uh, I'll just be on my way," Daniel said.

"You be safe, you hear," the Deputy said.

Daniel rolled up the window and stepped on the accelerator.

"That's my goal," Daniel said, and drove away.

Chapter 3

Daniel opened the car door and swung his feet out of the car as the garage door closed behind him. He was soggy, sticky and tired. The heat from his Honda, even on high all the way home didn't dry him out, or warm him up. The garage floor was cold on his toes, protruding through his worn out, muddy socks.

Why did he take my shoes?

Daniel peeled the wet, threadbare socks off his feet. Wet, blistered skin stuck to the muddy material. The door to the kitchen opened and Julie stood, silhouetted in the doorframe; her slender form visible through her nightgown.

I'm home.

A wave of relief washed over him.

"Daniel, what happened? Where were you? I tried your cell. I've been worried sick. You promised you'd be there." A stream of questions gushed from Julie.

Daniel hobbled across the cold garage floor and gathered Julie in his arms. Julie recoiled from his wetness. He didn't smell very good. But, he held her tight, enjoying her warmth and the feel of her body against his.

"Daniel?" She pushed him back.

He released her and tossed his muddy socks at the trash.

"You won't believe what happened tonight," Daniel said. They stepped through the kitchen door into warmth and light. The door, on its own, closed behind them.

***

Daniel was shivering. It was cold. He was walking along a rocky path, in the dark. He couldn't see very far ahead, and, he couldn't see where he'd come from. He felt like he had been walking for hours, alone. He felt like he was surrounded. Dense black trees were reaching for him, pressing in upon him. Suddenly, he came to what he perceived was a large body of water.

A lake.

A river.

He couldn't tell.

The air was still. He looked up at the sky.

Black.

A sound.

Thrashing.

Splashing.

Someone was in the water.

"Help me, please."

A woman's voice.

He could see her. She was drowning.

Daniel jumped in. He gasped. The coldness took his breath away. He struggled for the surface.

Which way is up?

The water was thick, thicker, thickening. His lungs began to burn. "Help me, please."

He could hear her voice, clearly, under the surface. He struggled. He fought. He couldn't find his way up. He had to breathe. He couldn't breathe. He kicked and thrashed. His feet hit bottom. He tried to push up. His feet went deeper into the mud, the sucking mud. He couldn't get out.

"Will you help me?"

He would, if he could. He had to breathe. With one last effort, he pushed and kicked. All was going black. All was black. He broke the surface.

With thrashing arms and a great gasp, Daniel sat up in bed. His lungs filled with air. His heart was racing.

A dream?

So real.

The room was dark. The green light from the smoke detector made a small circle on the floor. Julie was breathing quietly beside him. The digital clock on the nightstand was flashing, 12:01.

The power must have gone out.

Daniel threw the covers off and swung his legs out of bed.

"Will you help me?"

Daniel jumped to his feet. The bed creaked. Julie sighed.

"What are you doing here? Who are you?" he whispered.

The woman was standing near the window. Moonlight shadows through mini-blinds played just enough visual tricks that Daniel wasn't sure she was really there.

Was she there?

"You can't be here," Daniel said. He had just purchased an alarm system for their house. The kid selling alarms door-to-door thought he won the lottery. Daniel purchased the deluxe package—motion sensors, noise detectors, doors, windows, attic, basement, everything. No one could get in to their house, uninvited.

"How'd you get in here?" Daniel had made sure the new alarm was set.

"I don't know," the woman said. She spoke in a whisper, but Daniel could hear her in his bones. "Will you help me?"

"Help you...how...with what?" Daniel asked.

The woman turned away from the window and looked right at Daniel. In the dark, he could see her eyes. They were penetrating, cool. He realized he was standing there, talking to her, in his underwear. He always slept in his underwear. He didn't like the cumbersomeness of pajamas. And, they made him too hot, even when it was cold. He was glad, at that moment, that he didn't sleep naked. Although, he felt like this woman could see inside of him. He shivered.

"Help me...stop him," she said. She seemed to be watching a horrific scene, from a distance.

This just keeps getting weirder.

"Stop him? Stop who, from doing what?"

"I...he...something horrible...I don't understand...I don't remember."

"Listen, Miss..." Daniel waited for the woman to tell him her name. She didn't. "Whatever your name is, you have to leave. Right now. I can't help you. I don't know who you are. I don't know how you got in here. I don't know what happened. I don't want to know what happened. I'm pretty sure I can't help you."

Daniel took a step toward the woman. It was time to get her out of here. He reached out to guide her out of his room. She recoiled. Her hands closed in fists.

"Don't touch me!" she shouted. Daniel could feel the force of her voice moving the air around him. He jumped back. Julie stirred and felt for Daniel. He turned toward her. His vacant spot in the bed brought her out of sleep. She sat up and brushed her hair back. She could see him standing by the window.

"Daniel, what is it?"

He was frozen. His heart was racing. How was he going to explain this to Julie? He couldn't explain it to himself.

Daniel looked back at the woman.

Gone.

He looked at Julie. He looked back to where the woman was.

"Daniel?" Julie questioned.

"I thought I heard something," Daniel said, near breathless.

He pulled open the blinds and looked out the window.

"What was it?" Julie said sleepily.

Daniel had no idea how to answer her. "Go back to sleep, babe. Just a bad dream." He tried to sound calm.

"You O.K."

"Yeah, sure. Go back to sleep. I'll be there in a bit."

"Don't be long."

"I won't."

Julie lay back on the pillow and was out. Daniel wished it was that easy. He pulled the blinds all the way open and stared into the night. The moon was bright. It seemed brighter than normal. He was glad for the light, the lesser light. As he stood there in front of the window, he was sure he was being watched, and he was glad, again, that he didn't sleep naked.

Who was the crazy woman?

Was she a ghost?

Was he going crazy?

He shivered, again. He closed the blinds and returned to his bed. When he climbed into bed, he slid next to Julie. She moved her body to fit his. He put his arm around her and thought about the possibility of sleeping naked. She rolled over, away from him and he stared up at the ceiling, frustrated.

Chapter 4

Daniel was late for work. This wasn't unusual. He frequently had early morning depositions or meetings offsite. He was on a senior partner track and the partners trusted him to keep his own calendar. His billable hours told them he was working more than most. This morning, though, Daniel was late because he was exhausted.

He pulled into the underground parking below the Seafirst building and parked his car in a reserved spot. He looked in his rearview mirror.

Nothing.

Good.

Maybe I was just imagining.

He pulled his keys out of the ignition, grabbed his briefcase and got out of the Civic. The car still smelled like mud, or wet dog, or both.

Daniel stepped into the parking garage elevator and pressed the button for the 21st floor.

There she was. Or at least he thought she was.

The woman in black was standing next to his car. Watching him. The elevator doors closed. Daniel was alone in the elevator. His heart was racing. His muscles felt like he'd been working out for hours. His ears popped. The floor bells chimed in rhythm to the pounding in his head. The elevator stopped. The doors soughed open. Daniel breathed.

Across the hall, he could see Lady Justice, holding her scales in an eternal bronze balancing act. The Senior Partners believed in justice. They demanded justice. Lady Justice was their lover and logo. She was etched into the double glass doors he would have to pass through. She floated, in all her oversized glory, atop the wire frame world map above the curved reception counter he would have to pass by.

The elevator spoke, "Going down."

Literally.

The doors began to close. Daniel slid his briefcase between the collapsing steel. The doors rebounded. He stepped out of the elevator. He was sweating. He got a drink from the fountain next to the elevator and approached the glass doors. He took a deep breath and entered.

The girl behind the counter, this week's temp, perfectly sculpted, bobbed hair, ruby lipped Venus, smiled, then quickly averted her eyes. Normally, Daniel could manage a 'good morning.' But, today he couldn't speak. He walked stiffly past her and headed toward his office.

At least I have an office.

He walked unsteadily past the cubicles confining the paralegals. Normally, he would say good morning and smile. Most of the women would return his smile with a warm 'good morning.' This morning, in spite of his desire to get to his own office quickly, he couldn't help noticing that as he passed by, the girl's heads would crest then fall as if they were a wave and he was riding the curl. No one would look at him. No one said a word to him.

Daniel reached his office and stepped inside. He was closing the door.

I made it.

Donna, the team secretary stuck her foot in the door. She did that, a lot. She gave orders. She got things done. She was retired army, now filling a functional place in society, working for a law firm.

"Don't get too comfortable," she said, unusually cheery.

"Should I stand at attention?"

Donna did not smile. "Mr. Beck would like to see you, right now."

"Do I finally get my corner office?" Daniel said, trying to sound casual. Donna ignored him.

Mr. Beck was the big B on the firm letterhead. Beck, Strom, Bough, Tem, Feller, Rich and Associates. There were a lot of associates. Daniel didn't like associating with most of them.

"I've got the papers Mr. Strom wanted on the Morrissey divorce," Daniel said.

"You can give them to me," Donna said.

"I don't think so," Daniel said.

"You will," she said.

Donna spoke in absolutes, black or white.

"I think I'll just give them to him myself."

"Mr. Beck is waiting," she said. "Bring your things."

Donna spun around and left his office. Daniel resisted the urge to click his heels together and salute. He followed her out into the hallway. Heads were bobbing. He could see the next set of waves curling through the cubicles as Donna towed him into deep water.

Mr. Beck's office was big. It was The corner office. He had an expansive view of Elliot Bay. He could watch the ferries come and go as he pleased. The other walls were lined with law books and case histories Daniel was sure were from a time before English common law was accepted.

Daniel stepped into Mr. Beck's office immediately behind Donna. Mr. Beck was sitting behind his massive wooden desk, barely visible. The desk was huge. Mr. Beck wasn't.

"Monson to see you, sir," Donna said.

"Approach." Mr. Beck had aspirations to the Supreme Court.

Donna stepped aside, making way for Daniel. He approached the bench. A small bronze lady justice on the desk corner was weighing him in the balance. Mr. Beck was reading something.

Daniel waited.

Mr. Beck put the papers down and turned to look out over Puget Sound. Steel gray storm clouds were swallowing the bay. Without looking at Daniel, Mr. Beck spoke in his kindly, mentoring voice.

"I got a call from the sheriff's office this morning," Mr. Beck said, not turning around.

Daniel waited for more. He knew there would be more. Beck would make him wait. Beck was carefully preparing a summation. And, Daniel knew, his summation would be careful.

"When I heard what they had to say, I was shocked," Beck said. He sounded shocked.

He's good.

"I had the sheriff's report faxed over to me immediately." Mr. Beck turned around to face Daniel, but didn't look him in the eye. Daniel waited for the scales to tip. Donna was scowling at him.

"You must understand, Daniel, our first responsibility is to protect the reputation of this firm."

Donna's head reminded Daniel of a bobble-head doll. The image was disturbing. He reached up to loosen his tie just a bit. It seemed to be particularly tight all of a sudden.

"When any of our associates are accused of wrong doing, our first course of action is to place them on administrative leave, pending a full investigation. If we determine there was no basis for the accusation, we offer the full resources of our legal staff, in their behalf, at a fraction of the normal hourly rate. Of course, the associate may assist in their own investigation, but their hours will also be charged to the case billings."

Daniel had the impression that Mr. Beck had recently created this addendum to the firm HR manual.

"To that end, Daniel," Mr. Beck's voice was no longer kindly, or mentoring, "I would ask that you place all active case files with Donna. She will assign them to the appropriate associates. Please complete your current billings sheet, clean out your desk, turn in your badge and exit the building. You will be notified, upon completion of our investigation, whether you will be allowed to return to the firm. But, I must say, Daniel," the kindliness had not returned to Beck's voice, "this doesn't look good. It doesn't look good, at all."

The scales of injustice were tipping his way. Daniel was being weighed in the balance.

"What are you talking about?" Daniel said.

Donna gasped. Associates didn't question senior partners, especially not The senior partner.

Mr. Beck picked up the fax papers he had been reading. They appeared to be very heavy. "It seems," he said, carefully, "that you are a 'person of interest' in a major serial killing investigation."

Donna's jaw dropped. Not even she had known about this.

"Oh that," Daniel began. Beck held up his hand.

"This is not the time, nor the place for explanation or defense, Daniel. Please follow procedure."

Donna reached out for the papers Daniel was carrying. Incredulously, he handed them over.

"Don't you want to at least hear my side of the story?" Daniel knew the pitch of his voice was rising.

"You will be notified as to when to appear for your deposition," Beck said.

"Deposition?" Daniel questioned. "For what?"

"Company policy," Mr. Beck monotoned.

"What if I don't show up?" Daniel said.

"Then you have little hope for mercy," Beck said.

"Mercy?" Daniel said. "I haven't done anything wrong."

Donna placed her icy fingers on Daniel's upper arm and moved him out of Mr. Beck's office.

"I had high hopes for you, Daniel." Beck's voice bounced off the glass-brick walls as Daniel passed through his portal.

With Donna's vice grip attached to his arm, Daniel felt like he was living a scene from "The Green Mile." The girls in the cubicles were no longer bobbing on waves, but were trapped in cells, as Daniel was passing them, for the last time. He could hear the drummer playing. He could see the electric chair. He imagined the firing squad. He could see the woman in black, the beautiful woman in black, offering him a final cigarette.

I don't smoke.

"C'est la vie," she said, mournfully, and kissed him on the lips.

"Wait here," Donna practically shoved Daniel into one of the many conference rooms available to Beck, Strom, Bough, Tem, Feller, Rich and Associates. "We'll bring you your things."

"What, I can't even return to my own office."

"Company policy," Donna said, as she disappeared around a corner.

Chapter 5

Daniel sat in his Honda Civic, still inside the underground parking garage of the Sea First building. He was trying to make sense out of the last twenty-four hours.

He couldn't.

It didn't.

He held his keys in one hand, but didn't put them in the ignition. He didn't know where to go.

Home.

He wasn't sure what Julie would think when he told her he was a 'person of interest' in a murder investigation. Not just a murder investigation, a serial killer murder investigation. Well, that wasn't quite true, he did know what she would think. She would think he was innocent. She would think it was absurd. She would stand by him. She would want to fight. She would tell them all it was a terrible mistake. Of course Daniel wasn't a serial killer. He couldn't even kill flies or spiders in their home. She would be sure he had an alibi. They would ask her if she knew where Daniel had been last night. They would ask her if he was having an affair with the woman in black. They would ask her how often Daniel went out to Carnation on 'case work.'

Daniel leaned his head back against the headrest and closed his eyes.

"Hello, Daniel."

He jumped.

The woman in black.

Who else.

She was sitting in the back seat.

"I know more about you now, than I did before," she said. Daniel Shivered.

How?

"Who are you? What do you want?" Why are you stalking me?"

"I need your help."

"For what?"

"Will you help me?"

She's persistent.

Daniel sighed, then took a deep breath and blew it out slowly.

"If I do help you," he began, "will you leave me alone?"

"Don't you understand, Daniel?"

"Understand what?"

The woman in black leaned forward and put her arm on the back of his seat. She had slender arms. Her black dress was still torn, the material falling down across her breast, almost as if it was supposed to be that way. Her shoulder was bare. Daniel starred in the rearview mirror at the very white skin of her shoulder. He turned around in his seat for a better look.

"We're connected, Daniel. You and I."

The conversation seemed to be in slow motion. Daniel couldn't seem to catch up.

"Connected? How?"

The woman looked at Daniel. She looked in his eyes. He remembered his dream.

Am I drowning?

"You were there," she said. "You were the first person to greet me."

Daniel couldn't look away. He was barely breathing. She was beautiful.

"I don't understand," Daniel whispered.

"Last night," she said, "when I died."

The hair stood up on the back of his neck. He turned away from her.

Maybe I'm still dreaming.

"No, you're not," she said.

Daniel suddenly felt claustrophobic. There didn't seem to be as much air in the car.

"What, now you can read my mind?"

"I told you," she said, "I know a lot more about you now than I did before."

"For instance?"

"I know it wasn't a coincidence that you were there."

"Right."

"I know you are supposed to help me."

"Help you do what?"

"Stop the killings."

"Apparently, I'm too late," Daniel said. "From what you've told me, you're already dead."

The woman looked sad. Her countenance had changed. Daniel could feel her sadness. It nearly overwhelmed him. His heart hurt. She lifted her hand to look at it. She turned her palm over and looked at the back of her hand. She turned it over again. Her lifeline was gone. Tears began to form in the corners of her eyes. Daniel could feel them in the corners of his eyes.

"I am dead," she said, mostly to herself. "But I'm still here."

Daniel sensed that she wasn't talking to him. She had a faraway look in her eyes. He needed to say something.

"What's your name?"

She didn't move. He could see her, but she didn't appear to be there with him. He watched her eyes. His neck was getting sore from turning around to talk with her. Slowly, her eyes started to focus. She looked at him.

"Sarah," she said, then repeated more surely, "Sarah Blackmore."

"Hi Sarah," he said. "I'm Daniel Monson."

Daniel reached back to shake her hand. Quickly, she pulled her hand away and leaned back.

"Do you believe in life after death, Daniel?"

Now, Daniel had a faraway look in his eyes. He could see Julie, and Jenny. They were alive. He was waiting for death. And now, here she was. His alarm system couldn't keep her away.

"I don't know," Daniel said. "I guess so. I want to believe. Hell, here I am talking to a dead person."

Sarah cringed when he said that word. Suddenly, she was afraid. She began to fade away.

"Sarah, wait. Come back."

"Help me, Daniel."

Now, Daniel became desperate.

"How? How do I help you?"

Daniel was trying to scramble over the seat. He was reaching for Sarah. She was almost gone.

"Find my killer. Stop him."

"How? Who?"

He could see Sarah mouth some words, but he couldn't understand them. She was gone.

He found himself nearly wedged between the front seats. He had been reaching for her and she was gone.

Slowly, he slid back into the driver's seat.

What is happening to me?

"Do you believe in life after death, Daniel?" He could still hear her words. They penetrated his soul.

That makes sense. She's dead.

He thought about life after death. All the time. But, he'd never really thought about what life would be like after death. When he did think about it, he had to admit he did believe in life after death. He couldn't imagine life after death without Julie and Jenny. But, what exactly that life, after death, would be, or be like, he had no clue.

Like life here, only better. Maybe. Hopefully.

And, he did want to see his Father again. His Dad had passed away unexpectedly, when he was 27. A phone call, the night before had been his only chance to say goodbye, and he had missed it. But that had been years ago. He still missed his Dad, terribly, but he never thought about dying, then.

Sarah Blackmore.

"We're connected, Daniel, you and I."

He did feel something. There was something about her. Her eyes. Her skin. Her face. He did feel something, for her.

In the ten years that he and Julie had been married, he'd never thought about another woman. He was in love, with Julie. He hadn't needed to.

He put the key in the ignition, buckled his seat and started the car. He would drive a while, just until he could get straight in his mind what he would tell Julie.

Maybe she is gone.

"Help me, Daniel."

He looked in the rear view mirror as he pulled out of the parking stall. He could see a short stocky man, badly dressed, watching him. One of the firm's private investigators.

I guess they all watch Colombo on Hulu.

It didn't take the firm long to begin their investigation. Daniel was thinking he'd like to see Mr. Beck's face when he reads the P.I. report. He suspected he wouldn't be coming back to the firm, anyway.

Chapter 6

As Daniel pulled into his driveway, he noticed a plain, unmarked police car parked in front of his house. He hit the garage door opener and waited for the door to open. Pulling in, he hit the button to close the door before his car stopped moving.

Homicide detectives.

He got out and went inside. Julie met him in the kitchen.

"Daniel, where have you been? What's going on? Those detectives, they're investigating a murder."

Where to begin?

"What did they say?"

"They're looking for you. I told them you were at work. They said they'd wait."

Daniel could see the worry in her eyes, and the questioning. He saw the worry quite often, but not the questioning.

"Sit down, Hun."

Julie slid onto a barstool at the kitchen island. Daniel took off his jacket and hung it on the banister.

He took a deep breath.

"I'm a person of interest in a murder investigation."

"What?"

"I told you what happened last night. I think they think I did it."

"Daniel?"

"Mr. Beck put me on administrative leave. Essentially, I'm out of a job, and under investigation for murder."

Julie, who normally had something to say about everything, didn't say anything.

That's not good.

He could see the moisture in her eyes. She didn't cry very often, either.

"I saw her today," Daniel said.

He couldn't tell if Julie was breathing. She seemed to be completely still. These waters were deep. Her eyes were about to spill over.

"She told me her name."

The doorbell rang.

They looked at each other. No words were spoken. It was as if Daniel could speak with the dead, but could not communicate with his wife. There was a new wall between them. He could feel it.

Sarah.

Life was always trying to build walls between Daniel and Julie. Sometimes they built the walls themselves. A careless word, a thoughtless action.

Other times, the walls were built by others. Pressures at work. Stress about money. Headaches at bedtime.

The trick was to take down each brick in the wall, one by one, as they were put up. If you didn't, you could wall up your heart and find, at some point, the person you love the most in life couldn't get in.

That's what Hell is. Maybe, death.

Daniel's wall had grown, since yesterday. More bricks. He was pretty good at taking down the bricks, usually. He was pretty good at climbing over walls. So was Julie. But, over time, you put a brick in place, made a wall, a small one that you don't want to take down or climb over, a place in your heart where you won't go, or where you keep score. And now this.

Our marriage is good, strong.

Julie didn't know about Daniel's obsession with death. He'd tried to build a wall around it. What he didn't know, was the wall he built was bigger, and taller then he realized. What he also didn't know was that Julie knew he had built it. She just didn't know why.

"I'll get it," he said. Julie didn't say anything. Daniel left the kitchen.

***

"I'm Detective Sears."

"I'm Detective Schwartz."

"Seattle, P.D." they said together.

Beavis and Butthead. Do they match them up alphabetically?

They held up badges, in unison.

"May we come in?" the brown suit on the left said.

"Why?" Daniel said, uncharacteristically abrupt.

"We have, some, questions, to ask you," the senior brown suit on the right said, like William Shatner from his overly theatrical days as Captain Kirk.

"What kind of questions?" Daniel asked. Julie stood behind him. He could feel her there, knew she was there, her warmth. His heart rate slowed just a bit. She did that to him, when he needed it, slowed his heart rate. Other times, when she did that, his heart raced.

"Look," Sears said, "we can ask you some questions, friendly like, or, we can take you downtown and ask the questions, not so friendly like."

Either these guys watch way too much T.V. or, they've read one too many Raymond Chandler novels.

Julie put her hand on Daniels arm.

Daniel stepped back to give the detectives access to his home. They stepped in, uninvited. Julie stepped forward.

"Ma'am." Both detectives tipped none existent hats to Julie.

"Right this way, detectives." Julie led the two brown suits into their living room.

Daniel watched her. He saw the way she moved. He knew she didn't want these men in her house. But, they would never know it. She was filled with grace, and, graciousness. Daniel loved her so much. He just couldn't tell her. It made his heart hurt. It made him afraid.

He followed the men into the living room. They sat down on the couch, side by side. Julie and Daniel stood. The men leaned back, making themselves at home.

"Nice house," one of them said.

"Thank you," Julie said.

"Listen, guys, let's get to the point, O.K," Daniel said.

"Maybe you don't want the Missus to hear all this," the other one said.

"Go for it," Julie said. "I can handle it."

The two suits looked at each other and smiled.

"It's not my divorce," one suit said.

"This is a no-fault state," the other one said.

"He's an attorney, for God sakes," suit one said.

"Cards are stacked in his favor, for sure," the other one said.

"What's she see in him anyway," suit one said.

"Listen, Detective Sears," Daniel interrupted.

"I'm Sears," the other detective said.

"I'm Schwartz."

"I'm sorry, Detective Schwartz, maybe it would be better if we go downtown," Daniel said.

"Funny guy," Sears said.

"Can I get you something to drink, detectives?" Julie said.

"Yeah, sure," Schwartz said. "I'll take a beer."

"Me too," Sears said.

"How about water," Julie said.

"Beer's better," Schwartz said.

"You're on duty," Julie said.

The two men laughed.

"She watches too much T.V." Sears said.

The air in the room got significantly colder as Julie left. The two men looked at each other again, but did not smile this time. Daniel sat down in the chair opposite the couch.

"So you like girls, huh," Sears said.

"Why'd you do it," Schwartz said.

40

"How many others have you killed?"

"How long have you been doin' it?"

"Did you screw 'em first?"

"Stop!" Daniel nearly shouted. "You two are insane."

"Maybe," Sears said, and they both laughed.

"It wasn't funny," Daniel said. "Do you want to ask me some questions or did you just come here to practice your obscene duet?"

"O.K. smart guy," Schwartz said, "you were at the scene of a murder, last night." Both detectives took out note pads and pencils.

"You're first on the scene," Sears said.

"You're the only one on the scene," Schwartz said.

"What happened?" they both said.

"You read the report," Daniel said.

"It don't make much sense," Sears said.

"Not to me," Schwartz said.

"Me neither," Sears said.

"Makes me wonder," Schwartz said.

"Kinda suspicious," Sears said.

"Here's your water," Julie reentered the room and handed water glasses to the detectives.

"Beer's better," Schwartz said.

"Guys," Daniel said, "I saw this girl, screaming, in the middle of the road. I swerved to miss her and slid into a ditch. She led me to a barn, where I found her, dead."

Both detectives were writing, furiously.

"You know her name?" Sears asked.

Daniel hesitated. Julie was watching him.

"Sarah Blackmore."

The two detectives stopped writing and exchanged glances.

"How'd you know her name?" Sears asked.

"I didn't," Daniel said.

"You knew her name," Sears said.

"She told me her name," Daniel said.

"Oh really, when'd she do that?" Schwartz said.

41

Daniel looked at Julie. He was hoping that she could help him, telepathically, with an answer. Some couples who had been married a really long time didn't need to speak to communicate. A meaningful glance. A subtle movement was all that was necessary. Daniel had not been married long enough. Most of the time, he realized, he had no clue what she was thinking. She was an enigma, wrapped in a most interesting conundrum. Occasionally, when they touched, he had a glorious epiphany. She called it something else. It didn't last long. He was hoping for a lifetime of research, exploration and epiphany, if he didn't screw it up. He just didn't know how long that lifetime would be. This time, she just shook her head no. Against her better judgment, he answered.

"This morning."

The two detectives looked at each.

"This morning," they both said in unison.

"That's right," Daniel said.

"He sees dead people," Schwartz said, smiling.

"Good movie," Sears said.

"Looney tunes," Schwartz said.

"How long you been seeing dead people?" Sears asked, smirking.

"You were right," Daniel said to Julie.

"Right about what?" Sears asked.

"I'm not crazy," Daniel said. "And I didn't kill her. If you guys were any good at your job, it would take you about 2 minutes to figure that out."

"Did you know this Sarah Blackmore?" Schwartz asked Julie.

"No," Julie said.

"Does your husband...fool around?" Sears asked.

"No," Julie said again.

The two detectives smirked knowingly.

"So, Danny boy," Schwartz began, "You seen the dead broad this morning. How's that work?"

"I don't know," Daniel said. "She was just...there...in my car, when I got in."

"What'd she say?" Sears asked.

"She asked me to help her find her killer."

Sears and Schwartz exchanged glances.

"And, she told you her name," Schwartz said.

"Yes."

"Why you?"

"I don't know."

"She say anything else?"

"No."

"You sure?"

"Yes."

"How come she don't know who her killer is? She was there, wasn't she?"

"I don't know."

"You expect us to believe you talked with a dead girl this morning?" Sears said.

"Since last night, I'm beginning to expect the unexpected," Daniel said.

"Expect that you're in serious trouble," Schwartz said.

"I told you, I didn't kill her," Daniel said.

"Anyone else see you talk to the dead girl?" Sears asked.

"The firm's P.I. was watching me. He may have seen something."

The detective's pagers buzzed. They both checked them in unison.

"We gotta go," Schwartz said.

They both got up.

"Don't go no where's?" Schwartz said, as they left the room.

"He sees dead people," Sears said, and they both laughed. The front door closed. The sun came out sending shafts of light back into the room.

Chapter 7

Bertrum Alexander Davis was photographing the crime scene. He was not a C.S.I. photographer, but he took pride in his art. Composition was his forte. The creative use of light, exposure, composition and line set his photographs apart from the average professional. His photographs were to be treasured, savored, studied, enjoyed. Bertrum would share his pictures with the department, but mostly, he took them for himself. His gallery. Bertrum was an artist. And, he was developing quite a collection.

Outside the dilapidated warehouse, Bertrum Alexander Davis heard two cars drive up. He took one last picture and then just gazed at the scene. He had an intense appreciation for the art direction, and, for the subject matter. It was incredibly erotic.

Sheriff Jasper Clawson filled the open man-door of the warehouse roll-up. The shaft of light highlighting Bertrum's subject disappeared. Floating dust mites vanished. Bertrum was annoyed.

"What do we got, Bert," Sheriff Clawson said, stepping over the threshold.

Bertrum cringed slightly, as he always did, at the use of his nickname. He preferred to be called by his full name, Bertrum, or, by his initials B.A.D. which, since his 14th birthday, he felt he had achieved. They still hadn't found the girl next door. But, since then B.A.D. had learned so much more about female anatomy.

"Same M.O. boss," Bertrum said, holding up his own personal Nikon D-800. "I got the scene photographed,"

"Good work, Bert," the Sheriff said, surveying the scene.

Bertrum smiled. His boss obviously recognized his artistic talent. Bertrum could forgive the use of his nickname.

Two brown suits followed Sheriff Clawson into the warehouse.

"This here's Schwartz and Sears, Seattle P.D." Sheriff Clawson said. "They've agreed to help us with the investigation."

This could be B.A.D., Bertrum thought, warmly, as he shook the two men's hands. He would have to be at the top of his game.

"Sheriff said you drove Monson out to the highway last night," Sears said.

"Notice anything unusual?" Schwartz asked.

"Any behaviors out of the ordinary?" Sears said.

"Yeah," Bertrum said. "Strange dude. Slammed on the brakes right after driving away. He was screaming like a girl when I rapped on his window. Looked like he'd seen a ghost."

"Had he?" Schwartz asked.

"How the hell should I know," Bertrum said.

"Did you?" Sears asked.

"Did I what?" Bertrum asked.

"See a ghost," Schwartz said.

Bertrum laughed, uncomfortably. "Good one," he said.

"How long's she been dead?" Sears asked.

Bertrum scrutinized the detectives. He wondered what kind of game these two were playing.

"Ask the Coroner," Bertrum said. "He'll be here in a few minutes."

Sears and Schwartz squatted down next to Sheriff Clawson who was kneeling by the dead woman.

"Don't look dead to me," Sears said.

"Not long dead," the Sheriff said. He touched his fingers to her neck. "She's still warm."

"She's a babe," Schwartz said.

"You're sick," Sears said.

"Not a mark on her," Schwartz said.

"Not a stitch of clothes, either," Sears said.

"I hadn't noticed," Schwartz said.

"That's why you're staring," Sears said.

"Looks posed," Schwartz said.

"Like for a photograph," Sears said.

"Perv's would pay for a shot like this," Schwartz said.

"You boys talk too much," Sheriff Clawson said, standing up. The detectives stood up, also.

"Strangled?" Sears said.

"Looks like it," the Sheriff said.

"Raped?" Schwartz said.

"Don't know," the Sheriff said. "See for yourself. Some of these girls have had semen inside and some haven't. None of them have shown any signs of forcible rape, except the Blackmore girl last night. All the rest appear to be untouched."

Flash.

Bertrum took a picture. Sheriff Clawson and the two detectives shielded their eyes.

"Can we get copies of those pics?" Sears asked.

To Bertrum, these weren't pics. They were photographs. Gallery quality photographs.

"Of course," Bertrum said.

Of course he would give them the pictures, the ones he had taken for them. But the photographs, the ones he had taken for his collection, he would keep for himself. He would thoroughly enjoy them as he pleasured himself. He could hardly wait. The photographs were better, for Bertrum, than the real thing.

Frank McPherson rumbled in with a couple of pathologist interns.

"Looks like the same M.O. Frank," Sheriff Clawson said.

"Damn," Frank said.

"Damn right," the Sheriff said.

"Got the DNA results in yet?" Schwartz asked.

"Not yet," Frank said. "A few more days."

"Send 'em to us," Sears said.

Frank looked to Sheriff Clawson.

"Please," Schwartz said.

The Sheriff nodded to Frank.

"You got to work on your manners," Schwartz said, to Sears. "We'll see you boys real soon," Schwartz continued, taking on a southern drawl.

The two detectives turned to walk out.

"Your Georgia accent's peeking through," Sears said.

"I'm not from Georgia," Schwartz said.

"You could have fooled me," Sears said.

Bertrum watched the two suits go. He was annoyed. They didn't appreciate his work. He'd have to do it again, soon.

The two detectives paused at the man-door and looked back at the dead, nude woman. Bertrum pointed his camera at them and took a picture.

Flash.

Chapter 8

Daniel climbed the stairs slowly. He was weary. He was worried. He opened his bedroom door and immediately, he felt different. Two candles were burning, one on his nightstand, one on Julie's nightstand. There was a pleasing scent of cinnamon in the air. And, most compellingly, Julie was lying on the bed in her very sheer nightgown, Daniel's favorite. She was propped up on one elbow and smiling, seductively. Daniel shivered, not because he was cold.

"Close the door," Julie said.

Daniel obeyed.

"I thought I might take your mind off your troubles," Julie said.

"What troubles?" Daniel said, taking off his shirt. He slid out of his sweatpants and climbed on the bed. Julie lay back, her blond hair fanning out on the pillow. Daniel smiled. This didn't happen very often, anymore. Julie's nightgown was smooth silk and was sheer enough to raise his expectations. He ran his hand over the smooth material covering the curves of her breasts. She exhaled slowly. He touched the smooth skin of her bare shoulders and leaned in to kiss her. Their lips touched. He felt her softness. This was connection. It pulsed through him. He could hear it. There was so much he meant to say in that kiss.

I'm sorry.

Julie broke the contact.

"Daniel," she said.

Somewhat dazed, he said, "What?"

"The door."

Now he really could hear it, a soft knocking on their bedroom door, a soft whimper outside their room. He threw the sheet over them.

"Come in, sweetheart," he said.

Six-year-old Jenny padded into their bedroom in her feet pajamas. She liked to sleep in feet pajamas, even in the summer. The northwest summers were cool enough that Jenny rarely slept in anything else. And, Jenny liked to sleep in Daniel and Julie's room. She didn't like to be alone. She had been doing better for a while, but lately, especially since Daniel bought the alarm system, she had been trying to come in every night. This made love making somewhat problematic for Daniel and Julie. When they did make love, it was usually with one eye on the door. It was hard to get in the mood when you expected to be interrupted, at any moment, usually the most dramatic moment, by a six-year-old in feet pajamas. Tonight, they were both in the mood. Daniel sighed.

Jenny climbed onto the bed, over Daniel and snuggled in between them. She was shivering.

"Another bad dream, sweetie?" Julie said.

Jenny shook her head.

"Can you tell me about it?" Julie asked.

Jenny nodded. "There was a bad man watching me and you, Mommy. He was trying to get us. He wanted to do bad things to us. He looked in my window."

"Your window's on the second floor, honey. No one was looking in your window," Julie said, soothingly.

"He was, Mommy. I know he was," Jenny said. She was obviously frightened.

"It's alright, Jenny," Daniel said. "No one can get in our house. Remember, I turned on the force field."

"The nice lady in the black dress told me to run and tell you," Jenny said.

Daniel sat bolt upright.

"What?" he said.

"She said she would watch out for me, if you would help her," Jenny said. "Will you, Daddy?"

Daniel jumped out of bed. All he had one were his boxers. He began to pace.

"This is too weird," he said.

Jenny began to cry, again.

"Daniel, calm down. You're scaring Jenny." Julie held the tiny girl tighter.

"You heard what she said, Jules. Now it's not just my nightmare."

"Stop it, Daniel. Now's not the time," Julie said, shielding Jenny.

"I can't stop it," Daniel said, desperately.

There was an energy in the room. He could feel it. Not a good energy. He had goose bumps. If he could feel it, he knew Julie could feel it. And, he especially knew Jenny could feel it. She was sensitive in the extreme to other people's emotions. She was like an emotional amplifier. She took in other people's emotions and sent them back, bigger, stronger, louder. He felt like he was under attack. He felt like his family was under attack. He had to do something. He switched on the overhead light.

"Come on," he said.

"What?" Julie questioned.

"Come with me," he said. "Let's check this out."

He could sense a definite change.

It's not just my nightmare, anymore.

Daniel didn't understand who or what Sarah Blackmore was. He didn't know if she was dead or alive.

Mostly dead.

If Jenny had seen her, she must be real, or at least must occupy some level of reality. She wanted him to do something, help her, stop a killer, something. He didn't know if he could. But, his life had taken a dramatic left turn. It was rather disorienting. One minute, his life was completely planned out. He knew, or at least he thought he knew who he was, faults and all. He knew where he was going, or at least, where he wanted to go. But, in one unforeseen moment, things changed. Life was different. He didn't understand it. He didn't like it. Now he had to live with it.

Daniel scooped Jenny up and winked at Julie. She got out of bed, put on her robe and followed Daniel into the hall. He noted that she still had her sheer nightgown on underneath.

"Let's take a look in your room," Daniel said to Jenny.

He made the trek down the hall in seconds. Her nightlight was still on. Daniel flipped on the overhead light and surveyed the room.

"See, honey," he said, "there's no one in here."

Daniel set Jenny down on her bed and opened the window blinds.

"No one could possibly see in your window, sweetheart. We're on the second floor and your blinds were closed," Julie said.

"Maybe it was just a dream," Daniel said.

"It wasn't a dream, Daddy," Jenny said.

"There's nobody outside, now," Julie said.

"How do you know?" Jenny asked.

Julie looked at Daniel for help.

"I'll go outside and check," Daniel said.

"Are you going to help the lady in black?" Jenny asked.

Daniel looked at Julie. He was hoping she would answer for him. She looked back at him, but he couldn't read her expression. He desperately wanted to know what she was thinking.

"Yes, honey, I'm going to help the lady in black," Daniel said.

He felt a huge weight pressing down on him. He hadn't felt so much weight on his shoulders since hiking in the Olympic Mountains, two summers before. He and Julie had left Jenny with grandma and spent 5 days hiking in the Olympic rain forest. It had been the experience of a lifetime. But, he had tried to carry everything. Julie's pack only weighed 20 lbs. His weighed 75. Julie had insisted that he let her carry some of the load. For the first two days, he'd tried to be macho. By the third day, he could tell his back was going out. He'd been forced to let her carry some of the burden. It made the trip so much more enjoyable, for him. Julie never complained. Now, he felt that same weight pressing down on him. His back was already hurting. But, he didn't know how to share this burden.

Julie sat down on the bed as Daniel left the room. He started down the stairs when he realized he was still in his boxers. He looked at his legs.

Shinny white beacons.

He hadn't seen enough sun, lately. His legs hadn't seen any sun, lately.

The neighbors might complain about the glare.

Retrieving his sweats from the bedroom, he went downstairs and out the door. He stopped immediately. There on the front porch steps were his shoes. The ones he had given to the sheriff's deputy. Jenny wasn't dreaming. He was, badly.

He picked up the shoes and stepped down the porch. He looked up at the front of the house. He could see the yellow light coming from the master bedroom. Unfulfilled expectations. It was pretty clear. He wasn't where he wanted to be in his life.

Am I where I'm supposed to be?

He didn't know.

He stepped onto the grass and made his way around the side of the house. The cold, wet grass made his ankles hurt. He didn't have a lot of padding on his white beacons.

He looked up at Jenny's room.

It must have been a dream.

The warm light coming from Jenny's room was different. He could feel it. His feet were no longer cold.

"There's no way," he said, out loud. No one could get into Jenny's room without a ladder. The alarm would prevent that.

What if there's a fire?

How would Jenny get out? How would they all get out?

He looked around the base of the house for signs of a voyeur. Directly under Jenny's window, he could see footprints. Someone had been there. He pulled the shrubbery back to look closer. It was dark. He couldn't be sure. He took his shoes and set them down in the footprints. They matched.

"He's watching you," Sarah said. "He's watching her, too."

Chapter 9

Bertrum Alexander Davis was sitting in a Volvo station wagon, watching the Monson's house. He chose the Volvo because he could blend in with all the other Volvos in all the other driveways of all the other families concerned about the safety of their children. Safety was just an illusion. BAD could enter their houses anytime he wanted.

Bertrum had been planning to enter the Monson's house, when he had heard their little girl scream. This was most unusual. He was sure he hadn't been detected. Yet, somehow, someway, she had known. Bertrum could feel it. It wasn't a good feeling. Yet, it was a premonition. Bertrum believed in premonitions. He believed it was possible to know about things, before they happened. He had done a great deal of reading on the ancient practice of soothsaying. He could not yet predict the future, but he felt like he was making progress in the art. Maybe this was part of it.

The front door of the Monson's house opened. Daniel came out. He stopped short and quickly picked up the shoes. Bertrum smiled. Nice touch, he thought. Bertrum hoped Daniel got the message. He was now being hunted, tracked, stalked.

BAD things happen.

Wrong place.

Wrong time.

Bertrum would kill Daniel. But not quickly, and not first. He was, after all, an artist. He had to maintain artistic integrity. He had to understand his subject before he could capture the essence of his subject. And, killing Monson would be a first for BAD. He preferred to kill women. He had never even considered a male subject. He would not have considered a male subject this time if Monson had not interrupted his plans, his process, his art. He wondered what his followers would think about this. Would they be offended? Would they imply some kind of sexual confusion?

Bertrum was not confused. He knew who he was. He knew what he was. He definitely preferred women.

Family.

That's it.

He would do a composition on the fallen state of the modern family. He knew he would kill the woman, and the child. But his victim was clearly the man. This troubled Bertrum, until he understood the artistic implications of this family.

Father, Mother, Child. Nude. Limbs entwined. Erotic. Dead.

Bertrum could feel his arousal. He knew his artistic vision was inspired when the visions became physical. He unzipped his pants.

He could see Monson looking at the footprints by the side of the house.

Yes.

Bertrum's breathing was becoming shallow.

Suddenly, he could see Monson jump, startled.

Who's he talking to?

Electricity shot through Bertrum's body and out his hand. The hair on the back of his neck stood up. His hand recoiled from his groin. He felt like he'd been burned.

She's looking at me!

Bertrum couldn't see anyone but Monson.

"Who's he talking to?" he said out loud.

She's looking at me!

"She's looking at me."

Bertrum was sweating. He was hyperventilating. He jammed the key in the ignition and started the car. He could feel her presence. He slammed his foot down on the accelerator. The Volvo jumped. The tires squealed.

She's dead!

"She's dead."

He flew past the Monson's house. He knew they could see him.

"There all dead," Bertrum said as an oath. He could barely see where he was going, so strong was the vision of the dead woman before him. He was undone. His art had a life of its own. His erotic graphic images were staring back at him. He looked down. His pants were still unzipped.

**

"Who is it?" Daniel asked, as the Volvo sped past.

"He's a very BAD man," Sarah replied.

The wet grass under his feet, the cold night air, the specter before him, the speeding Volvo, the very BAD man, the darkness and shadows, his shoes, the footprints, Daniel trembled violently. His teeth chattered.

"The end is coming," Sarah said. The air before Daniel shimmered. Sarah was gone.

"Help me help you," Daniel said, to the darkness.

Chapter 10

Daniel had plenty of time to think as he navigated through morning rush hour traffic. He was driving on the floating bridge over Lake Washington, leaving the city. The sky was gray. The water was gray. It was raining. He was in a dark mood. He was heading back to the crime scene. He was going to figure this whole thing out. Carnation. To the East.

The East Wind is blowing.

He looked in the rear view mirror, expecting to see a ghost. There she was.

"Good morning," she said. "Sleep well?"

She smiled. She was beautiful.

"Not really," he said.

"Me neither," she said, laughing. Her laugh was like music.

"I thought death was like, I don't know, the big sleep, eternal rest," he didn't know how to put it.

"When you die, you're not really…dead," she said. "I'm still the same person I used to be. I just don't…have…a body."

Daniel looked at her in the mirror, regretfully. She seemed incredibly sad, but he could tell she had a beautiful body.

"Since I don't have a body, I don't need to sleep. I don't want to sleep. It's like it's always daytime and I don't get tired. But, for me, it's never really daylight. I can't rest."

Daniel was listening intently. It was as if all the cars and all the traffic in all the world had disappeared. It was just Daniel and Sarah. Her voice was like music. He didn't know if she was speaking out loud, or if she was speaking to his mind, or his spirit. He didn't know if he was going crazy, seeing ghosts or hearing voices in his head.

"Why do you always sit in the back seat?"

Instantly, she was in the front seat.

He jumped, startled. The car swerved. The car next to him honked. The driver flipped him off. Daniel recovered, ignoring the insult. Sarah laughed, again.

"You think that's funny?" Daniel said, feigning anger.

"I'm still learning what I can and can't do," she said.

"So am I," Daniel said.

Silence.

Silence between them. But it wasn't an uncomfortable silence. Daniel thought about Julie. When they were first married, they would talk, non-stop. Whenever they went somewhere together they were talking. There was always something to talk about. He would tell her about everything that happened when she wasn't with him. She would do the same. It was on a long drive to visit the in-laws when he first realized the silence. He hadn't wanted to go. She wanted him to want to go. He was driving, but he was miles away. They hadn't said a word for an hour. He hadn't noticed. She had. It became a very uncomfortable silence. He tried to break the silence, but it was hard. It was the first time he understood that there were things he couldn't say to her. He had a place in his heart she couldn't go. He didn't want to build the wall. It just happened.

"It's not as high as you think," Sarah said.

Daniel was back. Julie was not sitting beside him. It was Sarah.

"What?"

"The wall," she said.

Daniel shivered.

Can dead people hear your thoughts?

"I'm not dead," she said.

"Yeah, right," he said. "Then what are you?"

57

Daniel reached over to touch her hand. Alarmed, she pulled away.

"Don't do that," she said.

"Why not? Are you afraid of being touched?"

Sarah shivered. Daniel could see her tremble.

"No," she said. "You can't touch me."

She looked him directly in the eyes. She was…vulnerable, somehow. He wanted to touch her. He wanted to put his arm around her. Protect her.

This is insane.

"I'm dead," she said.

"No you're not," he said.

The car left the floating bridge, climbing the steep grade off the lake to eastbound I-90. He let up on the gas. Things were moving way too fast.

"Yes, I am," she said. "I just can't move on yet."

"Move on?" he said.

"You know, go towards the light, heaven, the pearly gates, the place of peace and rest, all that stuff you hear when you're alive," she said. Her mood had darkened considerably.

"Why not?"

"I don't think I qualify," she said.

"What, they won't let you in?" he sounded incredulous. "What'd you do, kill someone?"

"No," she said.

"Then what?" he said. "Why?"

She stared out the window. "I have to save your life."

"My life? I thought I was supposed to help you."

Sarah smiled. "Maybe we can help each other."

Daniel smiled back. Sarah looked away.

"Last night, Jenny said she saw you," he said.

Sarah didn't respond.

Daniel continued. "She said you told her that if I would help you, you would look out for her. Why?"

She still didn't respond. Daniel switched on the radio.

"Don't," she said.

"Why not?" he said.

No answer.

He turned off the radio. She continued to stare out the window.

"Fine," he said. "You're dead, anyway."

"Restitution," she said, quietly.

"Restitution?" Daniel said. He wasn't sure he had heard her right. "For what?"

"Let's just say, I didn't always make the best decisions in my life."

"I didn't think you had the opportunity to make restitution, once you were dead."

"I have to try. At least until they tell me I can't anymore."

"How come you get to do this?" Daniel asked. "It's not like I see a lot of dead people walking around, trying to make amends for all the bad stuff they did in this life."

"Most people can't see dead people," Sarah said. "But, that doesn't mean they're not here."

Daniel shivered again.

The here after.

"Right," Sarah said.

"Stop doing that," Daniel said.

"Doing what?" Sarah said.

"Reading my mind."

"I didn't," Sarah said.

"I did not say, 'the here after' out loud."

Smiling, Sarah said, "I read your spirit."

What does that mean?

It means we can speak spirit to spirit. There are some things we just know.

Daniel's mind was filled with a multitude of thoughts. None of which he wanted to speak out loud. Most of which he didn't want Sarah to know. He was thinking of Julie. This was the kind of connection, the kind of intimacy he wanted with her. Now, he had it with another woman. An attractive, intelligent, dead woman. And, he hadn't done anything to create it. He didn't want an intimate relationship with another woman. Somehow, he felt wrong about this. He was definitely attracted to Sarah. He fully intended to help her. He enjoyed talking with her. On one level, he liked that she knew what he was thinking. On another level, he didn't want her to know how conflicted he was. In an impossibly short time he had developed feelings for her.

Not good.

"Why not?" she asked.

"Because I'm married," he said. "And, I love my wife."

"And I'm dead," she said.

"I was not interested in having an affair," he said. "Especially a necromantic affair."

She laughed. "Impossible."

"Why not?" Daniel asked, disappointed.

"Because," Sarah said, "I'm not here to do more damage. I'm here to pay for damage already done."

Daniel took the exit for North Bend in the foothills of Snoqualmie pass and headed north, for Carnation. He was silent. But he could feel Sarah listening to his 'spirit'.

"So, what are we going to do?" he asked.

"I don't know," she said, "yet. Really, there's not much I can do. Mostly, it's up to you."

"Why do I have to make restitution for your sins?" Daniel asked, angrily.

"You don't," Sarah said.

"So, if I told you to go away, you would?"

"I can't compel you to do this…against your will."

"Would you…? Would you leave me alone?"

Sarah stared out the window. She seemed, thinner, somehow, less opaque. She turned back to look at Daniel. There were tears.

"Yes," she said, "I would."

Daniel was silent.

Sarah was silent.

The windshield wipers kept time. Daniel drove into the dark woods.

Maybe in another life.

"How come Jenny can see you?"

"I don't know, I'll ask?"

"You'll ask. Who will you ask?"

"The others," she said.

"There are others?"

"I told you," she said. "They're all around us."

Daniel felt claustrophobic. He was breathing harder. They were getting closer. He drove past the welcoming Carnation Cow. He didn't feel welcomed. He turned onto Carnation Main Street, passed the post office, passed the fire station and pulled into the sheriff's office. He switched off the engine.

"How come I can't see the others?" Daniel asked.

"I don't know," Sarah said.

"You don't know much about being dead, do you?" Daniel said.

"I'm learning," Sarah said.

"You going in with me?" Daniel asked.

Sarah nodded. Daniel reached under the seat, picked up his shoes and got out of the car. He walked around the car, out of habit, to open the door for her. She wasn't in the car.

"What are you doing?" Sarah said.

Daniel jumped.

"Don't do that," he said.

She laughed. He liked to hear her laugh.

Daniel said, "For your information, I was going to open the door for you."

"That's sweet," she said, genuinely, "but totally unnecessary."

"I can see that," Daniel said.

He walked up the cement steps and opened the glass door to the sheriff's office. He looked back for Sarah. She wasn't there. He looked inside. She was smiling at him.

"That's going to take some getting used to," Daniel said, opening the door.

Tiny bells above the door jingled. Sarah looked up at them, intently.

"What is it?" Daniel asked.

The dispatch officer sitting at the counter gave him an odd look.

"The bells," Sarah said, smiling.

"Can I help you?" the dispatch officer asked.

Daniel looked from Sarah to the dispatcher and back.

"He can't see me," she said.

"We're looking for Sheriff Clawson," Daniel said.

"Who's we?" the dispatcher asked with attitude.

"Daniel Monson," Daniel said.

"Got that multiple personality thing going on, huh," the dispatcher said. He pressed a button on the desk mic. "Hey boss, the perp's here."

Sheriff Clawson's voice boomed out of the radio shack speaker above the desk. "If there's a perp here, Wazulsky, arrest him."

"He's not actually a perp, Chief, he's the poi," Wazulsky said.

"Poi, ain't that some Hawaiian mush?" Sheriff Clawson said.

"Not poi, Cap, P.O.I. Person of Interest," Wazulsky said.

"You mean Monson?" Sheriff Clawson asked.

"He's good," Wazulsky said to Daniel. "That's what he says," Wazulsky said in the mic.

The office door next to the desk opened. Sheriff Clawson filled the frame.

"Monson, what in the Sam-hill are you doing here?" Sheriff Clawson drawled.

Daniel looked at Sarah. Sheriff Clawson followed his eyes to empty space. Daniel held up his shoes.

"Could use some polish," Sheriff Clawson said.

"They've been through a lot, lately," Daniel said.

"I ain't going to shine 'em for you," Clawson said.

"Someone left them on my doorstep, last night, after making tracks with them under my daughter's bedroom window," Daniel said.

Sheriff Clawson stared at the shoes.

"If you remember, you took them from me the other night," Daniel said, sarcastically.

Sheriff Clawson turned sideways in the doorframe.

"Step into my office," he said.

Daniel looked for Sarah. She was already in Sheriff Clawson's office. The Sheriff turned sideways in the doorframe and motioned for Daniel to enter. Daniel tried to pass the Sheriff, but there was not enough room between his belly and the doorframe. The Sheriff huffed and led the way in. Sarah was already behind his desk, reading a report. Sheriff Clawson walked around the desk and sat down, motioning for Daniel to sit across from him. Sarah stepped back to let the Sheriff pass, but she was intent on what she was reading.

Daniel whispered intently, "What are you doing?"

"I was going to ask you the same thing," Sheriff Clawson said.

"There's been two more killings," Sarah said.

"How do you know?" Daniel asked.

"How do I know what?" Sheriff Clawson said.

"It's in the report." Sarah said.

"I mean," Daniel corrected, "do you know who did it?"

"Did what?" the Sheriff asked. He turned around to see who was behind him. Satisfied, he turned back to Daniel.

"The two murders," Daniel said. "In the report."

Sarah tried to turn the page of the report. Unable to do so, she moved to the other side of the Sheriff to look at papers in his in-box.

"How do you know about them murders?" Sheriff Clawson squinted at Daniel.

"Mutt and Jeff, I mean, Sears and Schwartz," Daniel lied.

"I said those two dicks talk too much," Clawson muttered. "What else you know about it?"

"Two women, about my size, nude, raped, strangled and posed," Sarah said.

Daniel repeated, "posed?"

"Damn," Sheriff Clawson said.

"Just like me," Sarah said, looking up, "like for a photograph."

"You sure that's all you know," Sheriff Clawson studied Daniel.

"Just like you?" Daniel said.

"What'd you say?" Sheriff Clawson stood up and looked behind him again.

"Listen Sheriff, you know I didn't do it," Daniel said.

"I don't know nuthin'," Clawson said.

The Sheriff's office door opened. Deputy Bertrum Alexander Davis strode in, camera in hand, with a manila envelop filled with pictures.

"Got some more shots…" BAD stopped, frozen in place.

"It's you," Sarah gasped. The hair on Daniel's neck stood up. He turned to see who it was. Bertrum couldn't speak. He couldn't move. Daniel stood up, still holding his shoes.

"Bert, give me that folder," Sheriff Clawson said. "What's the matter with you? You look like you've seen a ghost."

A shudder passed through the deputy. Mechanically, Bertrum handed the folder to Sheriff Clawson. Daniel looked back at Sarah. She wasn't there. He looked back at the deputy. Bertrum looked blankly at the spot Sarah was standing.

"I don't know what's going on here, but I better get some answers," Sheriff Clawson growled. "Bert, you know anything about how Monson's shoes got back to his porch last night."

Slowly, Bertrum turned his gaze on Daniel. His eyes were black. Daniel could feel a darkness, an oppressive weight fall on him. The deputy's jaw tightened. The veins in his temples were pulsing. He unsnapped his gun. Daniel thought the deputy was going to explode, or kill him.

"Can't say I do," Bertrum said, fingering his gun.

The tension in the room was tangible. Sheriff Clawson rumbled around his desk and stepped between Daniel and the deputy.

"That's fine, Bert," the Sheriff said. "Why don't you check in with dispatch? Danny and I are gonna have a heart to heart."

Daniel cringed at the contraction of his name. He hadn't been called that since the 7th grade. Bertrum refastened the strap on his gun, never taking his eyes off Daniel. Daniel could feel his rage.

"You got it boss," Bertrum said. He backed out of the room.

Sheriff Clawson closed the door.

"O.K. Monson, what was that all about?"

Chapter 11

Daniel pulled out of the Carnation Sheriff's Department parking lot. He was alone. He hadn't seen Sarah since the strange incident in the Sheriff's office, an hour ago.

Where did she go?

He couldn't imagine what dead people did in their spare time. He could feel her absence. He could feel the silence of her absence. He could feel the distance of her absence.

She's dead.

He could never feel her.

She's gone.

He had never felt her. But he had an incredible, profound sense of loss. He had a hole in his heart where Sarah had never been.

A siren squawked behind him. Daniel looked in the rear view mirror. A Sheriff's car, blue lights flashing, was riding on his tail. Daniel pulled off the two-lane highway, coming to rest under the happy Carnation Cow. He rolled down the window, even though it was still drizzling. He took his driver's license in his left hand and his registration in his right hand and held them against the steering wheel. He knew what cops liked to see. He didn't want any more trouble with the Carnation County Sheriff's Department.

Bertrum Alexander Davis approached the car carefully. His weapon was unfastened.

"We've got two stop signs in Carnation," Bertrum said, "one coming and one going. You didn't stop at either one."

Daniel couldn't remember seeing a stop sign, although he was sure that if he had, he would have stopped. He didn't mention that he couldn't really see a reason for anyone to stop in Carnation. He handed over his license and registration.

"Proof of insurance," Bertrum said.

Daniel fumbled through the glove box. There were a bunch of papers inside, the owner's manual to the Honda, Jenny's parent/teacher conference report, Costco receipt for new tires, but no insurance card. He closed the glove box and reached into the console for his wallet. He remembered that Julie had given him the new insurance cards. He could see them clearly, sitting next to their computer, by the phone. They were still there.

"I have insurance, officer," Daniel said, "but I left the card at home. We just renewed our policy…"

"Get out of the car," Bertrum commanded.

"What? Why?" Daniel said.

Bertrum took a step back and put his hand on his gun. "I said, get out of the car."

Daniel complied.

"But officer, I can call my wife and get the policy number," Daniel said, reaching for his cell phone.

Bertrum drew his gun. "Put your hands above your head."

"What are you doing? You're going to arrest me for not having my insurance card?"

"Shut up," Bertrum exploded. "Turn around, put your hands on the vehicle and spread your legs."

"You're kidding," Daniel said.

Bertrum, without warning, slammed Daniel's head into the Honda. Lights flashed in his brain, behind his eyes. His knees buckled. He was suddenly inside his head, looking out. The line between conscious and unconscious was much closer than it had been moments ago. He could see himself, face-tackling a future NFL running back, his senior year in high school. He was lying on his back and the coach was shouting, 'Get in the game'.

Bertrum was shouting, "Get in the car."

He didn't understand why the coach was shouting that. He was already in the game. He didn't understand why the deputy was shouting that. He was already in the back of the patrol car. He couldn't move his hands. They had strapped him down to a backboard gurney. It hurt to move his wrists. They had handcuffs on.

Chapter 12

On the days when Julie worked, Jenny Monson walked the three blocks home from her 1st grade class at Mar Vista Elementary. Now that Jenny was in 1st grad, Julie felt she could work a couple days a week. She had a degree in business management, but she had a real talent for flower arranging. Her friend Cindy Beasley owned a local flower shop. Julie helped her until Jenny got out of school. She would hurry home and meet Jenny in the driveway. Besides, when she was a girl, Julie would walk to school, over a mile, in all kinds of weather. Daniel kidded her that it was uphill, both ways. He didn't like having Jenny walk. Daniel would give her a ride to school on his way to work.

Daniel didn't like having Julie work. He wanted to be the provider. But, it wasn't about his not being the provider. Julie needed to do something, important. Not that raising Jenny wasn't important, it was. It was just the time when Jenny was in school. And, it wasn't like flower arranging was that important. Mostly, Julie just enjoyed the time with Cindy. She had a gift with color and design. Since Julie had been helping her, Cindy had landed some important accounts with some downtown hotels and a local mortuary. Death could be big business for flower shops. Besides, it was only three blocks.

Chapter 13

The flashing lights, the visual distortions, the sense of floating began to fade. Daniel realized where he was. His head hurt.

"Where are you taking me?" Daniel asked.

Deputy Davis was driving. He didn't acknowledge Daniel's question. Daniel tapped the safety glass between the front and back seats of the patrol car.

"Where are you taking me?" he demanded.

"Someplace safe," Bertrum said through the back seat speakers.

"Safe from what?" Daniel said.

Carnation was a one street town. They weren't on that street. Daniel looked for door handles. There weren't any. He slid down on the molded-plastic seats and tried to get his feet in position to kick at the windows. He couldn't do it. He slammed the handcuffs into the safety glass partition. The plastic scuffed. His wrists began to bleed.

Bad Idea.

Deputy Davis agreed. "Shut up and sit still."

"You realize that I'm an attorney," Daniel began.

No response.

"I know my rights."

No response.

"You're going to be in a great deal of trouble."

No response.

"I'm going to sue the crap out of you."

Crap?

Daniel knew there was a much stronger, better word than crap. His undergraduate degree was in English. He knew what the word was. He loved words. He hated that word. Post Modernist literature was filled with it. Crap was understatement. It happens. In some situations, he might consider using that word.

The patrol car rolled to a stop. Deputy Davis got out and opened the door for Daniel.

"Get out of the car," the Deputy said, "and don't try anything."

Daniel got out.

They were deep in the Snoqualmie forest. The Douglas firs were tall and thick, dripping with moisture. Moss hung heavy from branches. The air was thick with evergreen scent, mixed with decay and rot. Wind and rain didn't descend this deep into the forest, except by proxy.

"Take a walk," Bertrum said, pointing into black olive forest depths.

When he was a boy, Daniel had been on scout hikes in these mountains. He remembered the smell. He remembered the wetness and the stillness beneath the towering conifers. He had not been afraid, then.

"Where are we going?" Daniel asked, stalling.

"Home," Bertrum said, "now move."

"I don't live here," Daniel said.

"No one does," Bertrum said.

Daniel's wrists were handcuffed in front of him. He knew this wasn't police academy procedure. He didn't think Deputy Davis had actually attended the police academy. He was grateful for this small freedom. With his hands and arms extended, Daniel spun around like an Olympic hammer thrower and slammed his wrists and handcuffs into the Deputy's face. Bertrum's nose erupted. A red river streamed down his face. Bertrum swore, loudly.

Something clicked.

Ozone smell.

Fireworks exploded in Daniel's head, again, behind his eyes. The fireworks were ripping his body apart. Earthquake drill. Fire drill. He

70

tried to roll. Somehow, he'd already completed the first two steps. The trees above were shaking their fists at him. The ground below was sifting him through it. Bertrum Alexander Davis was glaring at him, blood dripping from his nose into Daniel's eyes. The fireworks were red.

Bertrum shoved the clicking thing into Daniel's ribs.

Clear!

Daniel's body jumped and shook. He watched it, shocked.

Strange. I didn't feel that.

Blinding, flashing, light. Fire inside. His body was exploding from the inside out.

"It would have been easier to walk," Bertrum said, zapping him a third time.

Daniel heard the thunderclap. He was riding the lightning bolt. He could see Jenny walking home from school. Julie was driving in the Escalade to meet her. But the elements were out of order. The sky was gray. The earth was gray. He wasn't where he needed to be. And he didn't know how to get there.

Chapter 14

Daniel was lying on his back, staring at the clouds, large fluffy white ones. The sky was deep blue. The grass was cool. He was ten and it was summer. He was amazed at how fast the clouds could move when he didn't. He wanted to stop the clouds, keep them from moving. If he could, maybe summer wouldn't end. He wouldn't have to go back to school.

But the shapes in the sky kept changing. The sea turtle chasing the mallard became a knight riding a horse, questing. Slowly, very slowly, the knight was raising an arm. He was holding a long sword. Nearby clouds began to form faces. The faces were looking to the knight for protection. The faces were familiar. He knew those faces.

A dog barked.

He heard a lawnmower startup, in the distance.

Julie.

Jenny.

He could see their faces.

The sun came out, blinding him. He raised his hands to shield his face, but his arms wouldn't move. His muscles were tingling. They must have gone to sleep. Pins and needles were poking him from the inside out. He closed his eyes. The blinding light was still there, penetrating. It hurt. It made his head hurt. His whole body hurt. His body was shaking, trembling, stinging. His teeth were chattering. He could hear a metallic rattling. And, he could still hear the lawnmower. Groaning, he turned his face away from the light. He couldn't move the rest of his body.

"If you live through it, the burning sensation will pass," Bertrum said.

Daniel remembered. "Why are you doing this?"

"It's a talent," Bertrum said. "A gift."

"Where am I?" Daniel asked opening his eyes.

"My studio," Bertrum said.

Daniel looked around. He was naked, chained, hands and feet to a bed. His body was shaking. He was cold. Very cold.

Flash.

Bertrum took a picture. The bed was surrounded by strobes.

"I wanted to wait until you were awake, to start the photo shoot. I've never done men before, so don't get the wrong impression. I don't enjoy looking at men. But, I've found there is interest among my clients. Significant interest."

Flash.

"You're insane," Daniel said.

"I don't think so," Bertrum said. "By definition, insanity is doing the same thing over and over and expecting different results. I on the other hand, do the same thing over and over and expect the same results. I'm usually quite right."

Daniel tugged, violently, at the manacles chaining him to the bed. The chains rattled. The bedposts rattled. His wrists and ankles bled.

Flash.

"That's good," Bertrum said, "better than I thought it would be."

"What do you want from me?" Daniel asked.

"Just what you're giving me," Bertrum said. "I'll call this series, 'Naked struggle in futility'."

Daniel ceased to struggle. He didn't know what Deputy Davis was trying to do, but he would not cooperate with him. Right now, he didn't have his freedom, but no one could take away his agency. He would choose. And, he would choose not to cooperate.

"Why me?" Daniel said.

"Coincidence, fate, right place, right time, I don't know," Bertrum said. He continued taking pictures. "There's something strange about you. Bad vibes." Bertrum started to laugh. "BAD vibes. Get it?"

"No," Daniel said.

"You will," Bertrum said, still laughing. He stopped laughing, "It was better when you were struggling."

"Where are my clothes?" Daniel asked.

"You're not struggling," Bertrum said again.

"I'm cold," Daniel said.

"YOU'RE NOT STRUGGLING," Bertrum shouted. He pulled the taser from his belt. Daniel began to struggle.

"Too late," Bertrum said. He jammed the taser into Daniel's thigh.

Flash.

The lights.

The fire.

The pain.

Daniel's body began an epileptic like seizure. He was frothing at the mouth. His body was shaking, uncontrollably.

"That's better," Bertrum said.

Daniel lost consciousness.

Chapter 15

Sheriff Jasper Clawson was deep in thought. He folded his arms across his barrel chest. He was staring at Daniel's car. Detectives Sears and Schwartz matched his pose, on purpose. They looked like stooges in a cops and robbers movie.

The Honda's driver's side window was shattered. Safety glass bits were scattered on the ground. Shattered bits still hung from the rubber window frame. There were blood drips on the glass. There were blood drips on the car.

Sears looked up at the welcoming Carnation Cow.

"I guess Monson wasn't welcome," he said.

"It's a happy cow," Schwartz said.

"No it isn't," Sears said. "Happy cows are from Wisconsin."

"Washington," Schwartz said.

"California," Sheriff Clawson said.

The two detectives looked at him.

"Then what's it doing here?" Schwartz said.

"It's not a happy cow," Sheriff Clawson said.

"You can say that again," Sears said.

"It's not a happy cow," Schwartz said.

"Don't you two ever shut up?" Sheriff Clawson said.

"He doesn't," Sears said.

"Neither does he," Schwartz said.

"I resemble that remark," Sears said.

"Shut the hell up," Sheriff Clawson said.

"I think J.C.'s got some problems he can't handle," Schwartz said.

"That's why we're here," Sears said.

"Ain't no problem we can't handle," Schwartz said.

"This might be one," Sheriff Clawson said.

"Maybe you better start by telling us what Daniel Monson was doing back here in Carnation," Sears said.

"He wasn't visiting the welcoming committee," Schwartz said.

"Are you boys gonna help, or not?" Sheriff Clawson said.

"I think we're helpful," Sears said.

"Definitely," Schwartz said.

"Then make it quick," Sheriff Clawson said. "This has got to stop."

"Get the boys from forensics out here," Sears said.

"At least this'll give 'em something to do," Schwartz said.

Detective Schwartz pulled out his cell phone and ambled away from the trio.

Sheriff Clawson pulled out his cell phone. "Wazulsky, get Bert on the radio. I want to know if he's seen Monson wandering around our fair town."

Chapter 16

BAD was snapping pictures, nearly as fast as the Nikon D-800 could take them, which was pretty fast. Daniel was writhing on the bed. Bertrum had to admit that these images were going to be good. There was definitely something erotic about the human body, writhing in pain. He began to get aroused. That was bad. He stopped shooting. He didn't want to get aroused shooting pictures of a man. He didn't have time for that. He had work to do.

Bertrum set down his camera and put on a pair of rubber gloves. He didn't want any of his subject's blood or skin getting on him. Carefully, he selected a three-pronged gardening hand rake from among an eclectic assortment of tools on the steel surgical table next to the bed. He especially liked this tool, not because he liked to garden, but because it reminded him of a falcon's claw-like talons. Bertrum pressed the prongs into the skin of Daniel's cheek. He pressed harder. A shiver ran through his body. He was definitely enjoying this. He broke the skin. Blood began to trickle down Daniel's face. Daniel tried to scream, but didn't have enough control of his body to make much more than a gurgling sound. Bertrum pulled the metal prongs down the side of Daniel's face, tearing the skin. Daniel was thrashing and moaning and blood was streaming down the side of his face and reddening the tattered bedding.

Bertrum pulled the hand rake away from Daniels torn face and admired his work. As Daniel lost consciousness Bertrum's belt radio squawked.

"Bert, you there, come in." Wazulsky's thin voice broke the silence of Bertrum's sexually violent reverie. Bert could feel his arousal fade. This annoyed him.

"What?" he responded, angrily.

"That time of the month, is it?" Wazulsky shot back.

"What do you need, Wazulsky? I'm kinda busy here," Bertrum said.

"Really? Whatcha doing?" Wazulsky said, cheerfully.

Bertrum held the radio in his hand and stared hard at it. He hoped that Wazulsky could feel his psychic power painfully punishing him for interrupting the shoot.

"Are you using the department channel just to chat, or do you have something specific to tell me?" Bertrum barked.

"Monson's car's been abandoned by the cow. Looks like there's some foul play involved. Chief wants you to check it out. See if you can find him."

Bertrum swore. He wasn't finished here. He pressed the talkback button on the radio.

"I'm 20 minutes out," he said.

"Roger that," Wazulsky said. "I'll tell the boss."

"Idiot," Bertrum said, putting the radio back on his belt. He looked carefully at the ends of the hand-rake prongs.

"That should do it," he said.

Bertrum took a Petri dish from off the steel table and scraped the skin residue from Daniel's face into the dish. He put the Petri dish into an insulated bag, switched off the light next to the bed and left the room. Stepping outside of the corrugated metal doublewide, Bertrum switched off the small generator and hiked into the foggy gloom.

Chapter 17

Daniel could feel himself returning to consciousness, gradually. It was dark and cold. At first, he couldn't tell if his eyes were open, or closed. His body was exhausted. He felt as if he had just run a marathon. His face hurt. He reached with his hand to feel his face and the chains holding him in place jangled and caught. Pain shot up his arms, beginning at his wrists. Daniel remembered.

Nightmare.

He knew there was evil in the world. It had just never touched him. He'd never done anything really bad. But, had he ever done anything really good.

Julie. And Jenny.

Maybe they didn't count. Maybe he had just been lucky. At the right place at the right time. Maybe it was all just luck, or fate, or destiny. Some people said it was God. He didn't know. He wanted to know. But, he didn't know how to know. If it was just fate, or luck, or whatever, maybe the pendulum had swung the other way. He'd had his share of the good. Now it was his turn for the bad.

Why Me?

There is no why. Bad things happen to good people. If there is a God, where is he? Why does he let these things happen?

"I didn't do anything."

Sudden realization shook him in a wave of self-condemnation.

"I didn't do anything."

His voice sounded hollow, raspy. His throat was dry. The sound disappeared into the darkness without as much as a ripple. It hurt to speak. He decided he would do something. He would break these chains. He pulled and thrashed. Arms and legs. Chains rattling. Bed creaking. Pain shot up his arms and legs as the shackles peeled away more layers of skin. In the blackness he could feel the warm moisture of blood oozing from his shackle wounds. He couldn't do it.

No way out.

"God," Daniel spoke out loud, "if there is a God." For years, Daniel had been ambivalent about God. He knew his mother believed in God. His father? He wasn't sure. He didn't know. Now, he hoped. "Help me," he cried out.

Radio Static.

Bertrum's voice filled the blackness. "I hear you," he said, through the thinness of hidden speakers. "What do you want?"

"I have to go to the bathroom," Daniel said.

Static.

"Go ahead," Bertrum said.

In that moment, Daniel did something he had hadn't done in years. He cried.

Chapter 18

Monson wasn't going anywhere, anytime soon. BAD was off duty. He chuckled to himself. It was only when he was off duty that Bad was really on duty. He was on duty now, searching for a subject. It used to be that he could take his time and plan his shoots. He would research his subjects so he was prepared to capture the essence of their souls. Now, his clients were increasingly demanding. They wanted new material, all the time. He was required to satisfy their insatiable hunger, or they would move on. He would no longer be of use. That wouldn't happen. That couldn't happen. He was BAD. And, he was good, at what he did.

Bertrum pulled into the parking lot of a rundown bar on the outskirts of Tacoma. He parked in the back. No streetlights. It was dark and it was late. He sat in his Volvo station wagon and closed his eyes. He had not yet mastered the ancient art of soothsaying, but he was getting better. He tried visualizing the inside of the bar. He thought he could see a jukebox, a pool table, the bartender and a woman. Sometimes he wasn't sure if he was just making it up, or if he could really see, remotely. Sometimes the images were so clear, so real. Sometimes he would confuse the images with his photography. Sometimes he was just confused. Sometimes, he was just lucky. Most of the time, all the bars looked alike.

Bertrum stepped out of the Volvo and walked around the back of the cinderblock building. Dirt, mud and gravel crunched and squished under his feet as he navigated the potholes in the unpaved parking lot. As he came around the front of the building, the neon sign flickered randomly, preparing to die. Red and blue neon proclaimed 'My Place' as anything but.

Perfect, Bertrum thought. He opened the worn wood door and stepped in. The room reeked of stale beer and tobacco smoke. Draft beer neon cut through the heavy smoke. Bertrum didn't smoke. He disliked tobacco smoke. He believed that second hand smoke was bad for you. But he also knew that in order to catch bottom feeders, you had to fish the bottom.

Country music was playing, something twangy, with steel guitar. Bertrum disliked country music, with a passion. He preferred head banging heavy metal. He had been a grunge fan for a while, when grunge was new in Seattle. But grunge had become too mainstream. Metal never changed. It was just raw thrashing power. Power. That's what Bertrum was seeking for, among other things.

The bar tender, fat and balding, was wiping down the counter. Bertrum was pretty sure this was the same guy he had seen remotely. So was the pool table. Two guys were sitting at a table, smoking.

Where's the woman?

Juke box.

There she is?

Her eyes were closed, she was holding a beer mug and she was swaying softly with an invisible partner to a sappy love song. She had on cowboy boots, tight jeans, and a very tight t-shirt. From across the dimly lit, smoky bar, she was quite attractive.

Bertrum crossed the empty six-by-six dance floor to the jukebox. He approached the woman from behind. Stepping right behind her, just barely touching her, he reached around and put a quarter in the jukebox. He matched her gentle sway. Without missing a beat, she pressed E-7 on the jukebox, put down her beer and leaned back against Bertrum. Her long brown hair fell softly on his shoulder. He closed his arms around her and pulled her against him. She responded with the familiarity of a lover. They'd both done this before.

"Lonely?" Bertrum said, softly.

"I was," she said. Her eyes were still closed.

"Now?" Bertrum asked.

The woman opened her eyes, turned to face Bertrum and put her arms around his neck. Bertrum had his arms around her waist and held her close. They were moving in the way couples move when they're not really interested in dancing.

"What's your name?" she asked.

"Bertrum," he said.

"Where've you been all my life, Bert?" she said, then giggled. Bertrum cringed slightly. She was drunk. He preferred to be called Bertrum. But, he knew where this game was going, so he'd keep playing. He wasn't concerned about giving out his real name. This woman would never pass it on. She leaned her head on his shoulder.

"What's your name?" he asked.

"Elizabeth," she said.

"Nice to meet you, Lizzy," he said. She giggled. "Can I buy you a drink?"

"Just one," she said, giggling again.

Bertrum thought that she might have been cute, if she wasn't drunk. He knew, from experience, however, that neon lights and cigarette smoke usually hid most flaws. So, he reserved judgment until he could see her in the lights of his studio. He didn't think he would have to use any of his pharmaceuticals on this one. She was already quite compliant. Alcohol alone should be enough.

They sat down at a booth on the same side and Bertrum motioned to the bar tender. The fat man brought them two beers. Bertrum also asked for a whiskey. Elizabeth took a drink and smiled. Bertrum smiled back. This was the part of the evening he disliked most.

"Tell me about yourself," he said, with all the warmth of a serpent.

Elizabeth began to tell Bertrum her own particular tale of woe. The story was pretty familiar. Bad decisions in life. Bad decisions in love. Bertrum listened to her and smiled and nodded and encouraged her to take another drink, especially in the emotional parts. And, there were emotional parts. She'd been abused, abandoned. She couldn't believe she was telling him all of this.

"Tell me about you," she would say.

"How do you do it?" he would say. "It must be rough, just getting through the day."

He put his arm around her. She put her hand on his thigh.

"Not really," she would lie taking another drink.

Bertrum slid his beer in front of her. She drank the whiskey, then his beer. As her story unfolded, Bertrum detested all the men who abused and mistreated such vulnerable women. She appreciated his compassionate understanding. She began to run her hand along his thigh. She thought he was strong and brave and noble and good. She had no idea.

He wondered why some women so willingly gave themselves away. He detested her weakness. He detested her neediness. He detested her drunkenness. But, he thought she would be good on camera.

"Would you like to get out of here?" he asked.

"Desperately," she said. Her consonants were noticeably slurring.

He stood up and held out his hand to her.

"My prince," she said, giggling. She took his hand and stood up, woozily. "My, My, I think I'm a bit tipsy." Bertrum put a twenty on the table. She leaned into him for support. He held her up with tender care. They walked to the exit glued to each other.

When they stepped outside into the cool lateness, Bertrum was afraid the fresh, damp air would sober her up. Instead, she leaned closer and tighter.

"Your place, or mine?" he asked, innocently. He knew where he was going, either way. She looked up at the 'My Place' neon glow and laughed.

"Yours," she said.

"So be it," he said.

Together, arms around each other, they awkwardly made their way toward Bertrum's car. She stumbled over the uneven, rocky ground.

Bertrum held her tighter for support. She slipped a hand into his back pocket and squeezed, then giggled.

"Nice glutes," she slurred.

Bertrum smiled. He did have nice glutes. He worked hard to keep them that way. He didn't mind the attention to them either. He wondered why it was that some men felt compelled to pay for sex. With a little attention, very little attention, many women would give it away for free. Although, he did have to admit that the true professionals could do things that the freebies would never even dream about. That's why he liked to enhance his experiences chemically. Under the influence of certain drugs, even the most inexperienced would do things that gave Bertrum the satisfaction he craved.

When the evening began, Bertrum wasn't looking for sex. He was just looking for a subject for his next photo shoot. He'd found his subject, quite easily. But, she was so willing, and she needed it so much, Bertrum wouldn't pass up the sex. He might even enjoy it. In her afterglow, he'd give her the drugs that would make his photo shoot spectacular.

Bertrum helped Elizabeth into his car. She looked up at him with gratitude. He could tell she hadn't been treated very well by the men in her life. She'd never have to worry about that again. Bertrum sat behind the driver's seat. She smiled at him. He smiled at her. He knew she'd give him everything he wanted. She had no idea what he was about to do.

Chapter 19

Daniel was wet, and cold. It was pitch black. He was miserable. He was pretty sure there was no heat in the room he was imprisoned in. It had to be close to freezing outside. It wasn't much warmer inside.

He tried to remember details from his surroundings from when the deputy had been there. Deputy Davis had used modeling lights while taking pictures of Daniel. In between the strobe flashes there had been enough light for Daniel to see. But, he had been in so much pain from the tasering that he hadn't been able to concentrate on the environment. Now, in the blackness, he tried to think. He remembered the lights. There had been two, with umbrellas, at forty-five degree angles from the end of the bed. There had been another light, behind some thin material, directly above him. The room seemed small. He remembered seeing a steel table with surgical instruments on it, next to the bed and a table with a computer not far from the bed. The memories began to come back to him, vividly. He just didn't know what to do with them.

He closed his eyes.

Blackness.

He opened his eyes.

Blackness.

He'd never been in such a dark place.

Hell?

He couldn't tell. He didn't know. It didn't matter if his eyes were opened or closed. He left them open. He heard rattling noises, then realized that he was trembling. His shackles were rattling against the metallic bed frame. He tried to lie still. He couldn't. His body was responding to the temperature.

Hypothermia?

He thought about his scout training as a boy. Shared body heat and an emergency blanket were not going to help him now. He thought about all the ways he was going to die.

I knew it.

He felt justified, in a weird sort of way, for his obsession. He knew Julie would never understand. He certainly didn't choose to die. But, he had felt death coming for quite some time.

His eyes began to play tricks on him. He thought he could see a faint glow beginning to form at the foot of the bed. It wasn't a bright light. It didn't illuminate anything else in the room. It was just there.

"Hello, Daniel."

Sarah.

"I'm so sorry," she said. "I didn't understand what was happening. I would never have gotten you into this."

She stood by the bedside. In the darkness, he could see her quite clearly. The dim glow seemed to emanate from her. She was very beautiful.

"I'm naked," he said. His voice croaked, barely above a whisper.

She smiled. "I'm not looking."

"Help me," he rasped.

Sarah closed her eyes. Her face took on a most serene calmness. She was translucent. Daniel could see through her, yet, he felt he could see into her. He heard a slight metal clanking. He turned his face toward the sound. Surgical scissors slowly rose from the steel table near the bedside. The scissors floated in the air toward him. Daniel tensed. The scissors floated to the chains holding his left arm in place. They were thin enough that they fit into one of the links. Suddenly, as if an invisible hand twisted them, they violently wrenched against the chain link. The link snapped.

A metal fragment ricocheted across the room and clinked to the floor. The scissors fell to the bed. Daniel's left arm was free.

Sarah opened her eyes. She didn't look well.

"I didn't know you could do that," Daniel said.

"Neither did I," Sarah said.

She looked like she was going to collapse. The effort had obviously been great. The light surrounding her seemed to withdraw. She was falling, then, she was gone.

"Sarah," he groaned.

Now, the coldness he had been feeling reached deep. While she was there, he hadn't noticed it, as much. Now, it overwhelmed him. The darkness pressed upon him. But, his left arm was free. The shackle was still attached to his wrist, but, there was hope.

He groped for the scissors, and nearly knocked them onto the floor. Carefully, he picked them up and reached across to his right arm. In the darkness, it wasn't easy to get them in between the chain link. After a few tries, he got them inside one of the links.

Like threading a needle in the dark.

He twisted the scissors, the way he had seen them move when Sarah was there. Nothing.

He pulled the chain taught. The shackles tore into his already bloody wrists. The pain shot up his arms. He yanked. He twisted. He pulled. With one great effort he twisted the metal scissors as far as he could. The pain in his wrist was nearly unbearable. He twisted even harder.

The chain link broke. It sounded like a gunshot. The broken link shot into the wall and rattled against the outer metal. Daniel's right arm was free.

It looked a lot easier when she did it.

He sat up. His body resisted. His legs were still chained spread eagle to the metal bedposts. He felt light headed. He felt for the metal chain holding his right leg and slid the scissors into a link. He twisted, twisted, snap. He did it again with his left leg. He pulled his legs together. His hips and muscles hurt from being stretched in position for so long. He still had the shackles on his wrists and ankles, but he was free. He rolled off the bed and onto the floor. He had no idea where his clothes were.

Daniel stood up. There was no light in the room. From memory, he groped his way toward the door. Finding the doorknob, he opened the door to a much larger darkness. He took a few steps into the room and stood still. Either his eyes were beginning to adjust, or there was a faint light in the room. He could see curtains. He pulled them back. It was dimly dark outside. Enough light entered that he could tell he was in the living room of a doublewide trailer. He flipped a light switch. It clicked in the darkness but brought no light.

No Power.

Daniel needed to find clothes. He proceeded down a narrow hallway. Opening a door on the right, he found the bathroom. Opening a door on the left, he found a bedroom.

His room.

Daniel went in. He pulled the drapes open. The dim light from outside seemed to be a bit brighter. He pulled open a sliding closet door.

Eureka.

Daniel pulled a flannel shirt from the rack and put it on. It smelled of cologne. He didn't know what kind, but it was heavy. Images of tortured young people frolicking on the beach entered his mind. The black and white images created by a twisted Madison Avenue ad exec had become the reality for Deputy Davis.

Daniel buttoned the shirt. The warmth made up for the smell.

He pulled some Levis off a hanger.

Who hangs up their Levis?

Daniel considered searching for some underwear, but then thought better of it. It was bad enough wearing a psycho's clothes. Wearing his underwear would be just a little too weird.

The pants were too long. The shirt was too big. Daniel was glad. They covered his shackles.

Shoes.

There was a whole row of shoes, organized below the hanging clothes.

Neat freak.

Daniel selected a pair of Nike running shoes. He figured he could wear them without socks and still be O.K. Although, he would have preferred that they be Assex. The shoes pressed against the shackles on his ankles causing constant pain. He figured he could get used to it. He'd gotten used to everything else.

He heard a sound.

An engine.

He ran back to the living room and grasped at the door. It was locked. The sound was louder. Closer.

He fumbled with the flimsy lock. The door opened. He slipped out onto the wooden steps. He could see headlights through the trees. He jumped off the steps and ran around to the back of the rusted metal trailer as the headlights broke through the trees.

Did he see me?

Daniel slid under the visqueen skirting and held still. He was breathing hard. His heart was beating fast.

The Volvo stopped. The lights went out. The door shut. The generator engine chugged. Creaky steps. Light leaks through the floorboards.

"I'm back," Bertrum said, enthusiastically.

Rattling. Footsteps above him ran through the trailer shaking dust down upon him. Doors slammed. The front door of the trailer opened. Daniel could hear Bertrum standing on the front steps. He could see a flashlight beam darting back and forth.

Then, Bertrum SCREAMED.

Daniel jumped. It was a blood curdling, animal-like primal scream. The hair on the back of Daniel's neck stood up. Shivers ran through him. He shook where he was, rattling his shackles.

The scream stopped.

Stillness.

Daniel tried to hold still.

The flashlight beacon darted back and forth.

Bertrum jumped off the trailer steps. Daniel could hear his boots crunching in the dirt and gravel.

"WHERE ARE YOU, DANIEL?"

Daniel held his breath. He tried not to move. He tried not to make a sound. He crunched his teeth together to keep them from chattering.

The flashlight beacon swept past. Bertrum's boots crunched close. Stopped.

Silence.

"DAMN," Bertrum shouted. "DAMN IT TO HELL."

Bertrum crunched around to the front of the trailer and was inside the Volvo in a moment. He fired up the engine and threw it into reverse. He spun around and floored the engine. The tires spun in the muddy soil and then gained purchase. Rocks and mud splattered the trailer and the Volvo jumped forward, raced down the service road and was gone. Echoes of the straining engine faded into silence.

Relief flooded through Daniel.

He's gone.

He began to shake, uncontrollably.

Daniel climbed out from under the doublewide and stood up. Unleaded gas fumes mingled with the loamy scent of the deep woods. The gas fumes dissipated. The rich moist evergreen scent remained. The sun was coming up. The light below the dense trees was dull and directionless.

Now what?

Daniel stood there for a moment breathing the cool damp air. Then, he went back inside the trailer. The lights were still on. The generator was chugging away. Daniel went into the room he was held captive in and turned on Bertrum's computer. He hoped the deputy had an internet connection. He hoped it wasn't password protected. It was. He needed to find a phone. He needed help. He needed to let Julie know where he was.

Daniel walked back through the trailer looking for anything that could be of help. He was hungry and tired and was probably not thinking clearly. He couldn't find anything useful, so he went outside the trailer. He stared down the fire service road Bertrum had come and gone from. The road looked ill-used. He stared at the deer path leading into the woods. He thought they had come that way, through the forest. He didn't think it could be that far.

To where?

He wasn't sure. It was better than here. He trudged into the deep woods. His shackles couldn't have been that heavy, but they made his arms and legs feel like dead weight. He also realized he needed to eat and drink something. He almost went back to the trailer, but thought better of it and kept going.

This isn't going to be easy.

Chapter 20

In all of Bertrum Alexander Davis' 34 years, he had never had one victim get away. He preferred to think of them as subjects. But, in Monson's case, he was a victim. He would be a victim. His family would be victimized. He would terrorize them. He would do things to them that would amaze, possibly even sicken his clients. They would love it. Monson would scream. His wife would die. Their little girl would be sold. Bertrum's anger poured out in vicious, sickening, angry, violent, and demented thoughts. He let them flow. He reveled in the intensity. He languished in the anger. His heart was racing. He was speeding.

Control.

Control over his emotions had given him the ability to walk undetected through the world. He was a genius. He would be famous among those for whom fame was unnecessary. He would do what he wanted, as long as he did what they wanted, first.

This might be an exception.

He would have his vengeance. But he had to act fast. He did not know how Monson had escaped. This was troubling. He did not know where Monson was. This was disconcerting. He did not know who had helped Monson. This was infuriating. He slammed his hand on the steering wheel. He was speeding, dangerously.

Slow down. Breathe.

Death Comes at Night

Bertrum felt like he had set up Monson so that Sears and Schwartz would think he had gone on the run, underground. J.C., as Bertrum liked to call him, would have no clue. He never did. No one would figure out who was killing these women. He was too smart. He had too many people counting on him. He was invincible. They would blame Monson.

He began to slow down. Somewhere, in the back of his brain, there was a nagging feeling that he should be more careful. He knew he had spent too much time with Elizabeth. But, he had enjoyed himself. The sex had been amazing. She had been so needy, and, so very good. He hadn't given her the drugs, until after. She probably would have posed for him without the drugs. But, someone so good had to suffer more than most, more than all. Elizabeth, Lizzy, was his best work yet. And, they would think Monson had done it. Bertrum smiled. He put one hand on his crotch. Just thinking about it made him want to pull over and touch himself.

Not now.

He thought about Monson's wife. He could barely contain himself. He was doing things to her he had never done to anyone, or anything. He was making Monson watch. Both hands were on his crotch. He was controlling the steering wheel with his knees. He was weaving across the two-lane highway. He felt incredibly good. He could see it. He could feel it. He would do it. Do it. Do it.

A logging truck blasted past, its horn blaring. The Volvo rocked from the air pressure and spun out of control. Bertrum grabbed the wheel and held on. Spinning. Slowing. Slow.

The Volvo slid into the muddy shoulder and came to rest.

What just happened?

He looked around. He wasn't in his studio. He wasn't in his trailer. He was in his car. He zipped up his pants.

Stay focused.

He'd been awake all night.

Working.

He popped a little white pill. It was still early, 5:30 am. He had two hours before his shift started. They wouldn't find Lizzy for another couple of hours. The call would come from Seattle PD.

Sears and Schwartz.

He'd left her body just so they would find it, just so they'd think Monson had done it. That made a lot more sense when Monson was missing. Now, Monson was a wild card. He needed to find him before they did.

Where is he?

The pill kicked in. Bertrum floored it. He could feel it coursing through his veins. He could see for miles. He could hear the drizzle on the car roof. His reactions were quick. His senses were sharp. His thoughts were quick. He was invincible.

He knew what to do.

Control the things you can control.

Monson would go home. She wouldn't be there when he got there. BAD would be.

Drive.

Two hours to shift start. He'd call in sick. He never called in sick. He was sick. He laughed.

Faster.

He couldn't quite see the outcome, but, he could taste it. It tasted metallic. Maybe that was the drugs. Drugs did enhance his soothsaying abilities. If he could taste the outcome, then soon, he would see the outcome. The Volvo broke 100 miles-per-hour. BAD would be there soon. He put his hand on his crotch.

Chapter 21

Daniel had no idea where he was. The trail he was hiking didn't seem like it was used very often. The forest was dense. It was raining, up above. But down below the massive evergreens it was still relatively dry.

The trail led down hill. That was good. Daniel hadn't eaten anything in over twenty-four hours. He'd been tased more times than he could remember. He hadn't slept. He was sure he didn't have the strength to hike up a mountain. He wasn't thrilled to be hiking at all. When he came to a small stream, he knelt down and cupped the cold water into his mouth. It had a pure, sweet taste he could feel all the way down his throat. It felt good. He had to fight a nearly overwhelming urge to lie down under protective branches of the Douglas firs, the Cedars, the hemlocks, especially the hemlocks.

He fought the urge. Rising to his feet, he crossed the narrow stream and continued down the trail. Wisps of fog began to weave in and out among the thick tree trunks. Moss hung heavy on the branches. High above, he could hear the giants sigh. Delicate tresses of fog began to coalesce into shapes. The shapes into forms. The forms into bodies.

Spirits.

They turned to look at him.

Daniel stopped walking.

For an instant, the spirits waited. They watched. He felt them. He felt them all. Moisture. Soil. Life. And death. The spirits of men, women, children. Here, among the trees. At one with the trees. Tending the trees. Tending the giants. They nodded. He moved on. The shapes dissipated around him, wafting on the subtle air currents beneath the living pillars. The veil was thin here. The experience was rich, sacred.

The trail was there, and then it wasn't. Daniel stepped onto a paved logging road. The forest was still thick, but the road cut through the trees. Branches reached across to companions separated by the asphalt scar. He stood on the road wondering which way he should go. It was still quite early. Clouds sat atop the brooding giants. Here, on the road, their protection was strained. Heavy drops of water fell around him, on him. Drizzle floated up and down and around, penetrating his clothing completely. Light beads of water sat on his hair. His teeth began to chatter. A heavy diesel engine echoed through the woods. He couldn't tell how far away it was. It sounded quite close. He could hear it shifting gears, down shifting for greater purchase on the steepening grade. Fingers of following fog reached across the narrow road as headlights revealed their tenuous nature. A Mack Truck penetrated the wispy veil between earth and spirits with a growling grind of gears.

Daniel was standing in the road, in the way. He began waving his arms, jumping. Air brakes sighed, rpms dropped. The truck slowed, then stopped. The driver's window slowly slid open.

"What in the hell are you doing here," the driver barked.

All Daniel could see was a large reddish beard and baseball cap.

"Lost," Daniel said. "I could use a ride."

"I ain't goin' anywhere you want to go," the Driver said.

"Got a cell phone?" Daniel asked.

"No reception," the Driver said.

"CB?" Daniel asked.

"Short range," the Driver said.

"I'm cold and I'm wet and I haven't eaten since I don't know when. I could use a ride."

The giant engine rumbled. The beard stared down at Daniel. He felt like he was being weighed in the balance. He waited for his life to flash before his eyes.

"Get in," the Driver finally said.

Daniel walked around the front of the massive truck. The steal grill dripped moisture hungrily as he walked past. Daniel's stomach growled back. He grabbed a handrail and hoisted himself up onto the elevated running board of the truck. The truck door swung open as he did. The truck driver was spreading a thick Indian blanket out on the richly appointed leather seat. Daniel slid into the cab and sat on the blanket.

"Thanks," Daniel said.

"Name's Caleb," the Driver said. He was big, and burley, and hairy. If Santa Clause had a lumberjack brother, Caleb could be him.

"Daniel," Daniel said.

Caleb reached a large hand over to Daniel. Daniel grabbed the hand and shook it. His sleeve pulled back to reveal his shackle. Daniel tried to pull his hand back. Caleb didn't let go. He held on tight, looking at the manacle curiously. With his left hand, Caleb pulled a 9mm Smith and Wesson semi-automatic pistol from under the seat and pointed it in Daniel's face

Chapter 22

Snatch and grab.

Simple.

Bertrum figured he could be in and out of Monson's house in two minutes, with the Broad.

Easy.

He'd recently been reading Raymond Chandler novels. He liked to picture himself as a tough guy from a much tougher time. When he took the drugs, he saw everything in black and white, with much higher contrast. Sometimes, he also heard voices.

"Hello loverboy." A women's voice caressed his mind, soft, sensual.

Bertrum smiled.

"Hiya Doll," he said.

"Thanks," she said, "for," she hesitated, "last night."

Bertrum felt a shiver run through him, beginning in his mid-section. He heard the shy, blushing, gratitude in her voice. He was BAD. But, last night he had been very good. He had given her what she wanted, what she needed.

She giggled.

The shiver Bertrum felt continued up the back of his neck. He recognized that giggle.

"You're a very naughty boy," she said.

Bertrum felt cold, thin fingers around his neck. He looked in the rearview mirror.

"Lizzy," he gasped. He would have said more, but he couldn't breathe.

"Elizabeth," she said, less seductively. "You weren't there this morning, when I woke up, so, naturally, I came looking for you."

Bertrum's black and white worldview was turning purple. The Volvo was flying down the highway, much too fast. Bertrum took his foot off the gas.

"You were so kind, so tender, so noble. My knight in shining armor. I knew you wouldn't love me and leave me like that. I knew that we were meant to be together, forever. We're connected, Bert. We're connected."

The Volvo was coasting.

She was angry. She was shouting. Her face was distorted.

"You weren't there, Bert. That was bad. You're bad. You are BAD. I'm going to do you BAD." She giggled. The sound was more of a gross gurgle. Bertrum could no longer see. Icy fingers were locked around his throat.

The Volvo rolled to a stop, still in the lane. Bertrum couldn't move. He couldn't see. He couldn't breathe. He felt cold. The coldness spread from her fingers to his neck and then throughout his body. He could feel the coldness flowing through his veins.

"I did BAD," he heard her say. She giggled again. "And it felt so very good."

Chapter 23

There was only one gas station in Fall City. In fact, Fall City wasn't really a city at all. It was a wide spot in a narrow logging road on the Green River. The falls were more of a trip. Caleb pulled the big-rig logging truck into the B.P. gas station and stopped with airbrake flatulence.

"Hassan's a friend of mine. He'll let you use the phone." Caleb hopped out of the cab with a lot more nimbleness than Daniel would have expected from someone as large as he was. Daniel opened the rig door. It was quite a ways down. He felt lightheaded climbing down. He still hadn't eaten.

Caleb was already inside the office. Daniel followed him in. When Daniel stepped inside, Caleb wasn't. Hassan, wearing greasy coveralls was behind the counter.

"Caleb tells me you want to use the phone," Hassan said.

"If it's not too much trouble," Daniel said.

"What happened to your face?" Hassan asked.

Daniel put his hand to his check. His face stung, but there were so many other places that hurt, he had forgotten about his face. He realized he must look pretty bad.

"Bad scratch," Daniel said.

Caleb came through the garage door carrying bolt cutters.

"Hold out your wrists," Caleb said.

Daniel complied. Caleb cut the shackles from Daniel's wrists, then did the same for his ankles. The metal shackles popped off and clanked on the dirty floor. Hassan looked on indifferently.

Daniel held his wrists. They hurt. The skin was raw. But, they felt so much lighter. It wasn't that the shackles had been that heavy. It was more like Tolkien's ring effect. They were heaviest when the 'great eye' was watching. What a relief to have them removed. He felt like dancing.

"Could I use the phone?" Daniel asked Hassan.

Hassan slid the dirty black rotary dial phone across the counter to Daniel.

Caleb slapped Daniel on the back with a heavy thud.

"Well, that should do it and I'm late," Caleb growled.

"You owe me one," Hassan said.

"Put it on my tab," Caleb said.

"Your tab," Hassan protested, "your tab. I do not keep a tab in these days."

Caleb laughed. "Hassan'll take care of you."

Daniel shook the big man's hand.

"Thank you," Daniel said.

"Catch the bastard," Caleb said over his shoulder. Tiny bells tinkled as he walked out the door.

Daniel could hear her voice. "Hurry, Daniel."

Voices in my head?

He dialed his number on the dirty black phone. It rang. And rang.

"Hi, you've reached Daniel," his voice, "and Julie," her voice, "and Jenny," high and squeaky. "We're not here right now, but if you leave a message we'll call you back."

BEEP.

"Hi hon," Daniel didn't know what to say. "I'll try your cell. Love you." He pressed the button down, held it and dialed again. The number seemed to resist his effort. It rang, once.

"Hi, this is Julie. Leave me a message and have a most excellent day."

BEEP.

He smiled. The Wild Stallions hadn't yet changed the world, but Julie had changed his.

"Hey, babe, where are you? I know you're worried. Me, too. Deputy Davis is a psychopath—torture, murder, the works. Be careful. Get Jenny and go to Cindy's. I'll call when I can. I'm on my way."

Daniel put the receiver down. Hassan had large brown eyes. They looked at the phone and then at Daniel, but Hassan didn't speak. Daniel couldn't read his expression.

"I need a car," Daniel said.

"How much?" Hassan said.

"I don't want to buy a car, I want to rent one," Daniel said.

"You want to rent my car?" Hassan said.

"Yes, I want to rent your car," Daniel said, slowly, letting frustration creep into his voice.

"You think if you speak slowly, I understand?" Hassan said.

"No. Yes. I don't know," Daniel said. "You heard me on the phone."

"Do I look like Enterprise Rent-a-car? Do I look like Hertz?" Hassan said.

"Please," Daniel said. Frustration was giving way to desperation. Hassan didn't miss a beat.

"O.K. For you, I rent car." Hassan pulled some papers out from under the counter; they were gummed together in triplicate.

"I thought you said you don't rent cars," Daniel said.

"No," Hassan said, emphatically. "I not Enterprise. I not Hertz." Hassan slid a dirty black pen with plastic palm tree leaves taped to the top over to Daniel. "I need driver's license and credit card. Initial here, here, here and here. Sign here." Hassan circled the various places on the form. Daniel noted the form had coffee stains on it. Daniel looked up from the form, at Hassan.

"I don't have my driver's license or credit card," Daniel said.

"Then you not rent car," Hassan said.

Daniel slammed his hands down on the counter. "I need a car,"

"I need. I want. What you think I am, Santa Claus. You want me to give you car?"

Daniel looked down at his hands.

"No," he said, defeated.

His gold wedding ring glinted in morning light. Daniel remembered how it felt when Julie had slid it on his finger. He didn't like rings. He had never worn rings. He didn't like how they felt. But, when Julie slipped that ring on, it was different. It felt warm. He had never taken it off. He joked with Jenny that if he did take his ring off, he would become invisible. She would grab his hand and try to pull it off. They would play and laugh and Julie would smile.

Daniel slid the ring off his finger. It came off with remarkable ease. He'd been losing weight.

"Here," Daniel said, holding the ring out to Hassan. "When I bring the car back, I'll pay you in cash."

Hassan picked a jewelers lens up from beneath the counter and took the ring. He examined it carefully.

"It's real," Daniel said.

"You bring cash when you come back," Hassan said.

Daniel knew it was only a symbol. He knew it had relatively little value in and of itself. But, he suddenly felt guilty. He felt lonely. He felt naked. The tan line around his finger was cold. This ring was his greatest, and at this point, his only possession.

Symbolically.

"I bring cash," Daniel repeated.

"Initial here, here, here, here and sign here."

Chapter 24

Bertrum was in a cold and dark place. He couldn't see more than a foot or two in front of him. He felt like he had been walking for hours. The path was rough, but well worn. He was thirsty and tired. He wanted to lie down and rest, but he couldn't. He could feel them all around him, presences, hiding, watching, waiting. He could hear the faint sound of water, trickling. The sound made his mouth dry. His lips were cracked. His tongue felt thick. He breathed through his mouth. The stench of this place was overwhelming, nauseating. He felt a slight breeze. At first, the breeze was welcome. It drove the stench away. But, it was a cold breeze. And, it got colder, icy, penetrating. As he walked, he began to hear voices, whispers at first, then laughter. Laughter without mirth. Vicious, scornful laughter. He felt naked. They were pointing at him. He couldn't see them, but he knew, they were pointing at him. He reached for his gun. It wasn't there. The laughter grew.

In the distance, he could see a faint flickering yellowish light. It wasn't on the path. He stopped walking. He didn't know what to do. For some reason he couldn't define, he didn't want to step off the path. Yet, he needed the light. He wanted the light. He would go mad in this enveloping, consuming darkness.

He stepped off the path. He heard rustling, then, the voices were silent. The ground was rough. He was walking on loose rock, shattered shale. The breeze was colder. He was shaking. His teeth were chattering.

Death Comes at Night

The effort was exhausting. He drew closer to the light, flickering yellow-orange. He could see it now. He could see beyond his own steps. It was a metal drum, with a fire inside, the kind a homeless person would use to keep warm. It cast an eerie light around, what, a cavern. Stalagmites hung from above. He couldn't see what they were attached to. All he could see were the jagged points hanging down. The floor of the cavern was smooth. He stepped off the broken shale and onto the smooth cavern floor.

"Hello, Bertrum," a woman's voice said, smoothly. "I'll be your guide for the evenings' festivities.

He knew that voice. She stepped out of the darkness, into the orange glow of the trashcan.

"Elizabeth," Bertrum breathed out.

"Call me Lizzy," she said, giggling. "You did last night." Bertrum heard other women's voices giggling behind her. Elizabeth was dressed in a red satin teddy. She didn't act like she was cold, but Bertrum could see she must be. He was.

"Come stand next to my fire," she said. She gave him a cute, come-hither smile.

Bertrum had no idea where he was. But he thought it couldn't be bad, with all these women. Maybe the Moslem's had it right. Maybe you did get 70 virgins when you die. Well, maybe he didn't qualify for the virgins, but, he'd take the women. He wondered if he could do them all at one time. He drew closer to the fire. Elizabeth giggled and turned around to look behind her. The other women, he couldn't see them, giggled in answer.

Geese. A whole gaggle of geese.

Bertrum thought Elizabeth was attractive, maybe even beautiful. In the glow of the trashcan firelight, he could see none of the hardness or wear around her eyes that he had seen last night. In fact, he couldn't see any signs of the wounds he had inflicted upon her.

"Take off your clothes, Bertie," She said, seductively. He could hear giggling behind him, but Elizabeth just smiled sweetly.

O.K. that's annoying.

"Bertrum," he said.

"Yes, I know. Bertrum Alexander Davis. You've been very…BAD.

She was close enough to touch. He thought he could feel her breath. He unbuttoned his shirt, slowly. She watched, appreciatively. He tossed the shirt aside, then slipped off his shoes and socks. She encouraged him with her eyes.

"Right here?" he said.

"Right now," she said.

He unbuckled his belt, then unzipped his pants. The unseen women giggled. Elizabeth smiled, then turned her head. The unseen women were silent, although, Bertrum thought he could hear them breathing. Elizabeth turned back to Bertrum.

"Go on," she said.

Bertrum let his pants drop to the smooth cavern floor. He stepped out of his pants. He was standing before her, in just his boxers. He wasn't embarrassed, just cold. He could tell she wanted him. She came close, closer. She reached out and grabbed the elastic band of his boxers and snapped them against his skin. The unseen women giggled. Elizabeth slid his shorts down. He moved his hips to help her. His shorts fell to the floor. He could hear the women behind her. He could hear their hunger. Elizabeth looked him in the eyes. He could see her desire.

"O.K. ladies," she said. Elizabeth stepped back. Thirty-eight women rushed from the darkness. He could see them coming at him. He thought he knew them. He thought he recognized them. These were the women he had raped and murdered and photographed. He tried to run. They crashed into him, clawing and scratching and pulling. He fell to the cavern floor. He felt clawing hands tearing his skin. He couldn't resist. He couldn't escape. They held his arms and legs. They stretched him out, spread eagle on the cavern floor and chained him down. The coldness chilled his flesh.

"I'll keep you warm." It was Elizabeth.

She reached into the glowing trashcan and pulled out a firebrand. One word was glowing orange-red, BAD. She held it above his chest. The women surrounded him in a large circle.

"No. Please." Bertrum tried to struggle. He tried to beg. He began to panic.

Elizabeth thrust the brand into the bare flesh of his chest.

Bertrum screamed.

His flesh sizzled like bacon.

Burned flesh-smoke rose off his chest like steam. He tried to struggle. The chains held him tight. He wept. He pleaded. The pain was unbearable.

Elizabeth removed the brand and put it back in the metal drum. Bertrum relaxed, crying.

"You are bad," she said.

Another woman stepped forward with a large scalpel. She kneeled down next to Bertrum and placed the scalpel against his genitals.

"No, not that. Don't do that. I'll do anything you want. What can I do?"

"What do you think, Ladies?" Elizabeth asked. "After all, there isn't much there."

The women surrounding Bertrum giggled.

"Please," Bertrum pleaded. "What do you want?"

"What do we want?" Elizabeth repeated.

"We want to live!"

Elizabeth nodded to the woman with the scalpel. She looked at Bertrum in the eyes. He recognized her. She was just a girl, fourteen.

Why had he done it?

She smiled at him.

The scream had been forming in his burned chest.

She needed it.

It came from his very core.

She wanted it.

It welled up and spewed out.

The flesh began to wither from her face. Her skeletal fingers held his greatest possession. There was nothing he could do but wail, a keening wail that was answered by 39 female skeletons.

She cut him off at the root.

***

Bertrum was screaming and crying. One hand held his crotch and the other was pressed against his chest. He was delirious with pain. He was writhing and wailing when a teenage boy tapped on the Volvo window. The car was stopped on the shoulder of the road. Bertrum opened his eyes. He could still see the female demons tearing at his flesh. His skin was crawling with them.

This new face was different. There was fear in the boy's eyes. Bertrum didn't care. The pain was too intense. But, he was alive. His hands were free. He could still fight back. He reached for his gun. He fired. The front windshield of the Volvo exploded. He fired at her. The passenger's side window exploded. He fired at him. The driver's side window exploded. He threw open the car door and leapt out. Safety glass tinkled and crunched. He fired at them, in the car, in the air, on the ground. He poured shots into the Volvo.

The boy was running. He was running into the woods. Bertrum fired at him.

Click.

Click. Click. Click.

The magazine was empty.

He threw the gun at the Monster. It bounced off the Volvo with a metallic clank. The sound woke him up.

He grabbed his crotch.

Still there.

He pressed his chest.

No pain.

The memory of the pain was still there, was still intense. He gagged. He fell to his hands and knees and retched. The vision was so real. His skin was on fire. He kneeled there, breathing hard. Gagging. Breathing slower. Slowly, breathing.

Bertrum leaned back on his haunches. He wiped his mouth and looked around. Not a single car had gone by.

Death Comes at Night

Drugs.

When Bertrum had taken drugs in the past, he had not had hallucinations. But, he thought, he'd been awake for too many hours. He'd been under a lot of stress.

It must have been the drugs.

Bertrum stood up, tenderly. He looked at his hands. They were bleeding. Chunks of safety glass were embedded in his palms.

Interesting.

He couldn't feel them.

He looked at his Volvo. It was filled with bullet holes. In his delirium, he'd shot out all the windows, except the back one.

He looked at his watch. The whole episode had only taken a few minutes. This surprised him. He felt like he had walked for hours through the darkness. He thought the torment and torture had taken all night. He still had time.

He needed a car. He couldn't drive his Volvo into the city without being noticed. Fortunately, the boy's car was parked 25 yards down the road. It was still running. He knew that eventually they would find his car. Hopefully, with the evidence he had planted on Elizabeth…

Elizabeth.

When he thought of her, his chest hurt. His groin hurt. A wave of nausea passed through his gut.

Elizabeth.

Drugs, hallucinations, revenge or eternal torment, he didn't know. He didn't want to find out. Whatever, it was bad. Not bad like BAD. He was BAD. But, he knew he was bad. From the girl next door, to the girl last night, it was bad. He knew when he touched them it was bad. He knew when he took their pictures it was bad. He knew when their rich red blood drained out it was bad. But, it felt so good. It looked so good. He had taken their lives. Apparently, he had collected their souls. He realized they would continue to torment him. He was BAD. But, if it is possible to torment the dead, he would find a way to torment them, too.

He climbed into the boy's orange, Ford Fiesta. It was dented, dinged and dirty inside.

What's wrong with teenagers these days?

The car offended him. But, it was available. The forces in the universe had combined, once again, to enable him to accomplish his goals. He took this as a good omen. He put the car in gear and drove away. In the rearview mirror, he could see the boy running out from the woods. The boy stood there looking bewildered.

"Yep," he said out loud, "I'm bad."

Chapter 25

"It looks like a scene from the X files," Schwartz said, watching the activity around him.

Men in plastic space suits hovered over a female body inside a quasi-sterile clear plastic room. The empty warehouse had been turned into a surgical science lab by a team of forensic technicians. An eerie glow filtered through the plastic draping.

"The movies or the TV series?" Sears asked.

"The series. The movies sucked," Schwartz said.

"I'm Mulder," Sears said.

"The hell you are," Schwartz said. "I'm Mulder."

"There's no way I'm going to be Scully," Sears said.

"Why not? You have gender issues?" Schwartz said.

A space suit stepped through the artificial barrier. Michael Wu, forensic biochemist, pulled the sealed cover from off his head. Sears gave Schwartz a dirty look.

"Elizabeth Watley," Michael said.

"You ID'd her that fast?" Sears asked.

"We're connected to Big Mamma," Michael said.

"Big Mamma?" Schwartz said.

"FBI's super computer back at Langley," Michael said.

"Mulder," Sears said, looking at Schwartz.

"Scully," Schwartz said.

Michael Wu looked confused.

"X files," Sears said.

"Oh. Right. I was even born when that was on," Michael said. Michael Wu was a genius, a very young genius. "My parent's didn't let me watch TV."

"Too bad," Schwartz said.

"Lots of good educational programming on TV," Sears said.

"Right," Michael said. "Anyway, Elizabeth had a blood alcohol level of .09."

"Drunk," Schwartz said.

"Barely," Sears said.

"In California," Schwartz said.

"We're in Washington," Sears said.

"Guys," Michael interrupted, "stay focused."

"Oh, we're focused," Schwartz said.

"The banter helps us think," Sears said.

"What are you thinking about?" Schwartz asked.

"Elizabeth," Michael cut in again, "also had traces of Rohypnol in her system." Sears and Schwartz looked at each other, but this time they didn't speak. "Rohypnol, as I am sure you guys know, is also called the 'date rape' drug."

"Was she on a date?" Sears asked.

"Was she raped?" Schwartz asked.

"No sign she did it against her will," Michael said. "Except…"

"Except what?" Schwartz asked.

"She had some skin under three fingernails on her left hand," Michael said.

"Scratched him, did she?" Sears said.

"Maybe," Michael said.

"What do you mean, maybe?" Schwartz asked.

"Well," Michael said, "it looks a bit like maybe the skin was put there to look like she scratched him."

"Do you have a DNA match?"

"Not yet, but soon," Michael said. "We also found one single pubic hair that didn't belong to her."

A space-suited technician came through the plastic barrier carrying a computer print out.

"Momma says," the technician said through a yellow ventilator, handing the paper to Michael. The technician smiled at Schwartz then turned and dissolved into the inner sanctum.

"I think she likes you," Sears said.

"She?" Schwartz said. "There was nothing about that alien that looked female to me."

"You do have gender issues," Sears said.

Michael looked up from the print out.

"The skin samples don't match the pubic hair," Michael said.

"Two different people?" Schwartz asked.

"The skin looks like it was put there," Michael said. "It doesn't have the kind of cohesion you would expect if she actually scratched him. Also, it contains traces of iron-oxide."

"Rust?" Sears said.

"That's right," Michael said.

"I took chemistry in High School," Sears said.

"You're a regular scholar," Schwartz said.

Sears smiled.

"Any names?" Sears asked.

"No matches," Michael said, "yet. But we will. It takes a while to search the billions of possibilities. Big Mamma's patient. She'll keep looking until she finds a match."

"How long?" Sears asked.

"Hard to say," Michael said. "Could be ten minutes. Could be ten hours. Could be ten days. One case recently took about a week. Big Mamma didn't find a match until some new data was entered, in Norway."

"Norway," Schwartz said.

"Big Mamma looks everywhere," Michael said. "And, she's watching all the time."

"Sounds like Big Brother," Sears said.

"Big Brother's just a baby," Michael said. "Big Mamma's watching him, too."

"That's comforting," Schwartz said.

"Very," Sears said.

"Isn't it?" Michael said. "Who do you think keeps our fragile society from collapsing?"

Sears looked at Schwartz. "I didn't think the Y generation believed in conspiracy theories."

"Maybe he's not Y generation," Sears said.

"It's not a conspiracy," Michael said.

"X generation," Sears said.

"I'm Mulder," Schwartz said.

"O.K." said Sears. "Then I'm the Smoking Man."

"You don't smoke," Schwartz said.

"I'm not going to be Scully," Sears said.

"Call us when Big Mamma makes up her mind," Schwartz said. The two detectives began to walk away. Sears turned back to Michael.

"Thanks, Mike," Sears said.

"I want to believe," Michael said.

"Alrighty then," Schwartz said. They quickened their pace.

"What's he want to believe?" Sears asked.

"You got me," Schwartz said.

"That's comforting," Sears said.

"You do have gender issues," Schwartz said.

Chapter 26

Daniel pulled into his driveway and jumped out of the rented Subaru. He ran through raindrops to the code box for the garage door. Punching in the code, he ran back to the Subaru as the door opened. He drove the car inside, jumped out and pressed the button to close the door. He opened the door to the kitchen and called out.

"Julie?"

Silence.

He knew she wasn't home, but he called out anyway. Hoping.

Running upstairs, he unbuttoned the deputy's shirt and threw it on the bedroom floor. He slipped out of the pants he'd been wearing and jumped when he saw his reflection in their full-length bedroom mirror.

He barely recognized himself. He looked old. His body had the thinness of old people. His skin looked gray, except for the scarlet wound marks on his face, wrists and ankles. The burn marks from direct taser to skin contact were brown. He had dark, drooping circles under his eyes, and his eyes seemed to have receded into his eye sockets. She put a hand on his shoulder. He shivered, though he couldn't feel it.

"Hello, Daniel," Sarah said.

"Don't you ever knock," Daniel said, shrugging her invisible hand off his shoulder and hurrying into the walk-in closet. "I'm naked."

She smiled. "I know." She followed him into the closet.

"Don't come in here," he said.

"Why not?" she said. "It's not like I haven't seen you naked before."

"And I don't want you to see me naked again," he said, putting on his underwear.

"Why not?" she smirked, rather seductively.

"You're nothing but trouble," he said.

"I know," she said.

"Who are you talking to?"

Julie stood in the closet doorway. Daniel was only partially dressed.

"Julie!" he said. "Am I glad to see you."

He rushed to hug her. She held up her hands.

"Don't touch me," she said.

"What? Why?" He was bewildered.

"Who were you talking to?" she said again.

"Julie…"

"It was her. Wasn't it?"

"Julie, let me explain." He sounded desperate.

"This should be interesting," Sarah said.

"Stay out of this," Daniel said.

"She's here right now, isn't she?" Julie said.

"I'm dead," Sarah said.

"She's dead," Daniel said.

"Were you with her last night?" Julie asked.

"No," Daniel said.

"Well, that's not entirely true," Sarah said.

Daniel looked at Sarah. Julie followed his gaze.

"Where is she?" Julie asked.

"Right there," Daniel said, pointing to the bathtub.

"Leave my husband alone," Julie said.

"I'm only trying to help," Sarah said.

"She's only trying to help," Daniel said.

"We don't need your kind of help," Julie said.

"But I need your help," Sarah said.

"She needs our help," Daniel said.

"Daniel!" Julie said. Tears began to form in her eyes.

"I'm sorry," Sarah said.

"She says she's sorry," Daniel said.

The tears spilled over. Julie wiped them away.

"What happened to your face?" she asked.

He touched the scrape marks on his face. When he thought about it, they stung. He was thinking about it now.

"You wouldn't believe what I've been through," he said, buttoning his shirt.

"Try me," Julie said.

"He's coming," Sarah said.

"What?" Daniel said, turning to Sarah.

"He's coming," Sarah said again, looking into the distance.

"Stop that," Julie said to Daniel. Turning to where she thought Sarah was, she said, "Leave us alone."

"He's coming," Daniel said.

"Who's coming?" Julie asked.

Sarah gasped. "He's not coming for you. He's coming for Jenny."

"Jenny!" Daniel exclaimed.

Sarah vanished.

Daniel zipped up his pants and fumbled through his chest-of-drawers.

"What about Jenny?" Julie asked.

"Sarah said he's coming for Jenny," Daniel said, still fumbling through the drawers. "Where is it?"

"Who's coming for Jenny?" Julie demanded.

"Deputy Davis. Psychopath. Murderer. BAD. That's where I was last night. He was trying to kill me. Here it is."

Daniel pulled a .38 special from the back of the top drawer.

"Daniel, what are you doing?" Julie asked.

"I'm telling you, Jules, this guy's nuts. Serial-killer nuts. He's crazy bad," Daniel said, still fumbling in the drawer. He pulled a box of shells from the drawer and began to load the gun.

"Come on, we've got to get Jenny. Then, we'll find someplace safe." Daniel stuffed the gun between his back and his belt and then ran past Julie. She looked bewildered, but she followed him.

Daniel raced through the bedroom, down the stairs, and through the kitchen with Julie right behind. He grabbed the keys to the escalade, ran into the garage and jumped into the SUV. Julie hurried around to the passenger side and climbed in. Daniel hit the garage door opener, started the Escalade and backed out, just barely clearing the ascending garage door. He hit the accelerator, looked in his rear view mirror and slammed on the brakes. Tires squealed. Daniel and Julie slammed back against the seats as the protesting Escalade rocked to a stop inches from an orange Ford Fiesta.

"Daniel, what are you doing?" Julie exclaimed.

Daniel didn't answer. He held onto the steering wheel with a vice grip, thinking.

"Stay in the car," he commanded, opening the door. Daniel jumped out of the Escalade and pointed the .38 special at the Fiesta.

"Take it easy, Monson," Bertrum said. "I've got your daughter." Deputy Davis slid out of the Fiesta and pointed his gun at Daniel, using the open driver's door as a shield.

"Get down, Jenny," Daniel shouted.

BOOM.

He fired a shot.

Daniel didn't have any formal weapons training. He was an attorney. Attorneys don't need guns, right? He only kept this gun in the house for an emergency. He hadn't fired it since he was a teenager. His Dad had taken him out shooting. They went to the mountains and shot cans off rocks. His Dad told him he was a good shot. He missed.

The front windshield of the Fiesta exploded.

"Bad decision," Bertrum said.

Daniel was running. He was running at the Fiesta. He was running to get Jenny. He heard screaming. His driveway felt remarkably like beach sand.

Bertrum fired a shot.

Daniel could see the bullet. It was heading right for his heart.

Sarah hollered.

"Daniel, look out!"

He could see Jenny. She looked so small. Her eyes were open, wide.

She shouldn't have to see this.

The bullet was getting bigger.

He wasn't going to make it.

I'd better get out of the way.

He twisted. Too late.

He watched as the bullet entered his body. It didn't ask for permission.

His forward progress was stopped. The bullet traveled a thousand miles through his chest, carrying him along with it. Daniel didn't want to go.

Sometimes, after a long journey with traveling companions, you may decide not to travel together again. Daniel and the bullet parted company. The bullet left through Daniel's right shoulder blade, leaving Daniel suspended in the air. He didn't appreciate the abrupt departure. He fell to the earth. He didn't realize he had been so high.

THUD.

Now, the pain started.

Daniel couldn't breathe. He felt like he had been ripped apart.

A thick red liquid trickled from underneath him, toward the driveway drain. The liquid gained speed and fluidity as it mixed with the dripping Northwest drizzle.

Julie was screaming. She kneeled down next to Daniel. He couldn't understand what she was saying.

"She's telling you she loves you," Sarah said.

"I love you too," Daniel said. It hurt to talk.

"She's telling you not to give up," Sarah said.

"I've failed," Daniel said.

"I've failed," Sarah said.

"You're pathetic," Bertrum said. He kicked Daniel in the side. Remarkably, it didn't hurt. Bertrum grabbed Julie by the hair and yanked her to her feet.

"Get in the car," he said.

"You're in a pretty tough spot this time, son."

Daniel turned toward the sound, the voice. He hadn't heard that voice in…

"Dad," Daniel said. His Dad held out his arms. Daniel stepped past Sarah, into his father's embrace. He felt warmth. He felt joy. He felt comfort.

When Daniel was a small boy, he used to get up in the mornings and find his Dad downstairs working. He would scurry down the stairs and sit on his Dad's lap. He didn't remember having anything really to worry about. But, he knew that while he was sitting on his Dad's lap, he didn't have anything to worry about. Everything would be all right. His Dad would make everything all right. His Dad would protect him. This was good timing.

"Dad, I'm so glad to see you."

"I'm so glad to see you too, son."

BAD had moved the Fiesta out of the way and was backing out of the driveway in Daniel's Escalade. Daniel turned around to watch. His body was lying on the cement driveway. He didn't seem to mind that. He knew his father would fix it.

"I'm sorry, Daniel," Sarah said.

"It's OK," Daniel said. "My Dad will take care of it." Sarah vanished.

The Escalade drove away from the house. Julie and Jenny were in the back. He did mind that. He began to run after the Escalade.

"Daniel," Daniel's Dad called out. Daniel stopped running. He looked back at his Dad, then looked after the vanishing Escalade, then noticed his bleeding body in the driveway.

"Daniel," Daniel's Dad said again, "there are some things we need to talk about."

"What things?" Daniel asked.

Chapter 27

When the first shot went off, Julie jumped out of the Escalade. She could see Daniel jump up and start to run. Julie started to run, too, and scream, and shout.

"No, Daniel! Don't."

The second shot went off. He wasn't that far away from her, yet it seemed like a thousand miles. She would never get there in time. Even if she could get there, there was nothing she could do. The bullet hit Daniel in the chest and knocked him down.

This is bad.

Julie screamed. She knelt down at his side.

"Daniel," she said, "I love you."

He smiled up at her. His mouth moved, but no words came out. Julie looked at the hole in his shirt where the bullet had gone in. Blood was washing away the burn marks.

"Daniel, stay with me," she said desperately. "Don't give up."

His eyes were open. He appeared to be conscious. But, he wasn't looking at her. He was looking through her.

She screamed at him and slammed her hands into the wound. She would stop the bleeding.

"Daniel, look at me."

He wasn't.

"Daniel, stay with me."

He smiled again.

"Don't give up," she commanded.

He reached out, but not for her.

Something yanked her hair. Her head snapped up and back. Her body followed involuntarily.

"You're pathetic," Bertrum said. He kicked Daniel in the side.

Julie swung at Bertrum. He had a firm grasp of her hair. She didn't have the angle, but she had the anger. She connected his nose with her bloody fist. His nose bloomed. Blood rushed out.

"Damn you, bitch," Bertrum shouted. He hit her in the face with his free hand. Her head would have snapped back except that he held her hair firmly in his other hand. Julie screamed furiously. She drove a knee into him, hoping to hit his sweet spot. He anticipated the move. Her knee missed the mark. He drove a fist into her stomach with such force she couldn't find air. She retched. Her body went limp. She gasped and gasped as air began to find its way back in. Bertrum hit her across the side of the head with the flat of his hand. Bright white lights flashed in her peripheral vision. He dragged her across the driveway and tossed her ragdoll body into the backseat of the Escalade.

"Mommy," Jenny screamed. Her eyes were wide with fear.

"Shut up," Bertrum commanded. He slammed the door of the Escalade.

"Mommy," Jenny said again, "Mommy?"

Julie shook her head. She was dazed, but she recovered quickly.

"I'm here, honey," she said. She pulled herself off the floor and onto the seat, trying to get out.

Darn those kiddie locks.

"Where's Daddy?" Jenny asked.

Julie was grateful Jenny hadn't seen what had happened to Daniel, but she didn't know what to say. Tears formed in her eyes. She would not let them out. She would not give her enemy the satisfaction of seeing her cry.

"He's coming," she lied.

Generally speaking, Julie considered herself to be an honest person. She tried to be a good person. She tried to teach Jenny to be a good person. She wanted to be an honest person. But, sometimes, she lied. Like when Daniel asked her if it was good for her too. He wanted so much to please her. He tried so hard. She had to lie. Didn't she?

"Is he OK?" Jenny asked.

The funny thing about lying to children is that even when they know you're lying, even when they know the truth, they'll accept what you say because they love you. It's that love that makes you better.

"No," Julie said. "He's not OK."

"Should I say a prayer for him" Jenny asked.

"Yes, sweetheart. And you'd better say one for us, too."

"What's happening to us?"

The driver's door of the Escalade flew open. BAD jumped in.

"A bad man's got us," Julie said.

"Damn right," he said. "Now shut up."

He put the Escalade in gear and drove away.

Chapter 28

Detectives Sears and Schwartz got out of the brown Ford Crown Victoria as the ambulance drove away.

"Just in time," Sears said.

"Day late, a dollar short," Schwartz said.

"Pessimist," Sears said.

"Realist," Schwartz said.

"What do we got, Max?" Sears asked.

Sergeant Max Bowin, Seattle P.D., was securing the crime scene.

"Monson took a shot to the chest from close range. Laid him out pretty good." Max Bowin was a veteran police officer. He'd seen worse.

"Did he say who did it?" Sears asked.

"He's not talking, if you know what I mean," Bowin said.

"Dead?" Schwartz said.

"Mostly dead," Bowin said.

"What we need is a miracle, Max," Sears said.

Schwartz chuckled. Sergeant Bowin looked confused.

"Any witnesses?" Schwartz asked.

"Neighbor lady, Mrs. Thorson, keeps pretty good tabs on the Monson's. She saw the whole thing."

The two detectives descended on a frumpy, middle-aged woman in a dingy housecoat. Mrs. Thorson spoke before the detectives could introduce themselves.

"I knew there'd be trouble," Mrs. Thorson said. The two detectives exchanged glances.

"How's that Ma'am?" Sears said.

"Appearances can be deceiving," Mrs. Thorson said.

"Ma'am?" Schwartz said.

"You know what I mean," Mrs. Thorson said.

"Maybe you could just tell us what you saw," Sears said.

Mrs. Thorson smiled, a sickeningly sweet smile.

"Certainly, gentleman," she said, preening. She brushed her limp dishwater blond hair back. "I think he was having an affair."

"Who was having an affair," Schwartz said.

"Mr. Monson, of course," Mrs. Thorson said.

"Why do you think that?" Sears asked.

"Well," Mrs. Thorson said, authoritatively, "he didn't come home last night."

"How do you know that," Schwartz asked.

"I'm on the neighborhood watch committee," she said. "It is my responsibility to know these things."

"Just the facts, Ma'am," Schwartz said, in his best Joe Friday voice. Sears smiled.

"Well," Mrs. Thorson said again, "he shot him!" She paused for emphasis. Sears and Schwartz leaned forward, anticipating that she would continue. She didn't.

"Who shot him?" Sears asked.

"Her lover, of course," Mrs. Thorson said. The detectives exchanged glances again. Mrs. Thorson continued. "Mr. Monson had been seeing his wife, or girlfriend. Wife, I think. I'm pretty sure. I am sure. It was his wife. Mr. Monson spent the night with her. They're not wealthy people, mind you. He works for the forest service. He can't compete with an attorney's salary. She was a legal secretary in Daniel's, I mean, Mr. Monson's office. They fell in love. Poor Julie. She didn't know a thing about it. Well, Daniel must have spent the night, I mean; he did spend the night with her while her husband was out surveying the forest. When he came home, Mr. Monson, Daniel, was just leaving. He followed him here in his old Ford Fiesta. She hated that car, by the way. His wife, I mean. But, poor dear, that was all they could afford on a Forest Ranger's salary. Anyway, he followed him here. Daniel must have told Julie about the whole thing. She was worried sick about her husband, the louse. Daniel must have told her about the affair, because she screamed. Daniel got out of the car and tried to shoot him. I'm sure he shot him in self-defense. It wasn't his fault."

Sears and Schwartz looked at each other. It was possible there was a kernel of truth in there somewhere. Finding it would be difficult.

"Then what happened?" Schwartz said in his best Joe Friday voice.

"She got in the car and left with him," Mrs. Thorson said.

"Just like that," Sears said.

"Just like that," Mrs. Thorson said.

"I thought you said Mr. Monson was having an affair," Sears said.

"I did," Mrs. Thorson said.

"Then why would she leave with the Forest Ranger?" Sears said.

"Well," Mrs. Thorson said. "He was obviously better looking."

"Where did they go?" Schwartz said.

"Now Detectives, how would I know that?" she said. "But, if you ask my opinion, I think they're running off together."

"What about the little girl?" Sears said.

"The little girl!" Mrs. Thorson said. "Jenny. Poor thing. Totally forgotten in this whole experience. I'm sure she'll end up being a ward of the court, or go into an abusive foster care situation. No one ever thinks of the children. It's all about me, me, me."

"What'd he look like?" Schwartz asked.

"Daniel's about six feet tall, brown wavy hair, brown eyes…dark brown eyes. You can get lost in those dark brown eyes…"

"I mean, the other guy," Schwartz said.

"Oh," she looked embarrassed. "He was big…taller than Daniel."

"How did you know he was a Forest Ranger?" Sears asked.

"He had on a green shirt," Mrs. Thorson said.

The detectives waited for more. There wasn't any. Schwartz's cell phone began to play the X Files theme. He flipped it open.

"Agent Mulder," Schwartz said.

"Scully," Sears said. Schwartz rolled his eyes. Mrs. Thorson looked annoyed that they weren't paying attention to her anymore.

"Hey Mike. How the hell are you?" Schwartz said. He nodded and began to drift away from the story lady. Now, Sears looked annoyed that he couldn't hear the other side of the conversation.

"I feel that it is imperative that I do my civic duty," Mrs. Thorson said.

"Commendable," Sears said. He was watching his partner, trying to read his lips.

"As Chairperson of the Neighborhood Watch Committee, I feel it my responsibility to know everything that goes on in my neighborhood."

"Admirable," Sears said.

"If I can't know what's going on, then I must infer what's going on from circumstantial evidence," She said.

Schwartz closed his flip phone. Sears walked away from Mrs. Thorson.

"Good news?" Sears said.

"The skin under Elizabeth Watley's fingernails belongs to Monson," Schwartz said.

"He's not having the very best of days, is he," Sears said.

"If he's still alive, let's go see if he can tell as good a story as Mrs. Thorson."

Chapter 29

Bertrum knew he didn't have much time. His life was unraveling. He had enjoyed the protection of his clients for many years. They protected him, he believed, because he was an artist. He did things they could only dream about, and then, he photographed them. He had been free to choose his subjects. He had been free to experiment. He had not worried about consequences. His clients were powerful. His clients were supportive. They encouraged him in his work. His work, he knew, would be his legacy. But, he wasn't ready yet to leave his legacy.

"Why not?" Elizabeth asked.

Bertrum jumped. The car swerved. He had to exercise his superior driving skills to keep it under control. His last experience with Elizabeth was still fresh in his mind.

"Why not what?" Bertrum responded. He looked over at the empty passenger seat. Why was she here? He hadn't taken any drugs. He also hadn't slept.

"Why not leave your legacy?" She said.

"What are you talking about?" Bertrum asked.

Julie and Jenny were riding in the back seat of the Escalade. They looked at each other. Bertrum was carrying on a one-sided conversation.

"Your legacy," she said. "Alive, you're just another demented serial killer. Dead, you'll be famous."

"Shut up bitch," Bertrum was angry with her. She had seemed so needy.

"I didn't say anything," Julie said.

"Not you, her," Bertrum said.

"Who?" Julie said.

"Lizzy," Bertrum said, looking over at the empty seat. He smiled. He knew she preferred to be called Elizabeth. He used his pet name for her, just to annoy her.

"Who's Lizzy?" Julie questioned.

Jenny looked up and pointed. Bertrum looked in the rear-view mirror. The girl was pointing at Elizabeth. Elizabeth turned and smiled at the girl. If the girl could see her, he wasn't crazy.

"Yes. You are," Elizabeth said.

"I said SHUT UP," Bertrum yelled. He slammed his fist against the passenger seat headrest. He meant to hit her. He meant to hit her in the face. He wanted to break her teeth, her nose. She giggled. The vehicle swerved. Julie screamed.

"Stop it," Julie yelled. "You're going to get us all killed."

"She's right, you know," Elizabeth said. "Oh, wait, I'm already dead." She giggled. She laughed. Her laughter changed to cackling.

"Stop it," Bertrum yelled.

She cackled harder.

He slammed on the brakes. Julie and Jenny flew against the seat backs then fell to the floor. The Escalade screeched and swerved to a stop. Bertrum jumped out of the vehicle. A car horn sounded in a rush of wind. Bertrum spun out of the way and slammed into the Escalade. Elizabeth, standing by his side, giggled innocently.

"Leave me alone," he shouted. He pulled out his gun and pointed it at her.

She stood behind him.

"Go ahead," she said. "Shoot me."

"Stay down," Elizabeth mouthed to Jenny. "Just in case."

Julie peered out the window as Bertrum spun around and pointed his gun at an invisible target.

"Stay down, Mommy," Jenny said.

Bertrum was nearly hyperventilating. He took a perfect three-point stance.

"You're a ghost. You can't hurt me," he said.

She giggled. "That's right, Bert. Remember what happened last time you pulled out that great big gun of yours." She put the emphasis on big, smiling seductively.

She was cute, he thought. It was a shame he had to kill her. She stepped closer, smiling. He fired his weapon. He fired again, and again, and again.

Julie pushed Jenny to the floor of the Escalade and covered her with her body. She didn't count the number of shots in his gun. The sound was swallowed up in thunder.

His gun clicked. Elizabeth was gone. He stood there, shaking. She giggled. He spun around. A car drove past and slowed down. An elderly couple stared at him. He pointed the gun at them. The car sped up and away. She was gone. For now.

His life was unraveling faster than he could ravel it. He would have to hurry.

Chapter 30

Detectives Sears and Schwartz stood at the large double doors to ICU. The doors weren't open. Sears pressed the button on the intercom next to the doors. No one answered. He pulled on the doors. They didn't open.

"What do you think they're doing in there?" Sears said.

"Injecting alien viruses into unsuspecting subjects," Schwartz said.

Sears looked at him, but didn't respond, this time. He pressed the button, again.

"Two bits says he did it," Sears said.

"Who?" Schwartz said.

"Who do you think?" Sears said.

"We got nothin' on the Forest Ranger," Schwartz said.

Sears pressed the intercom button, twice, with malice.

"Why can't you ever give me a straight answer?" Sears grumbled.

"Maybe you're not straight," Schwartz said.

Sears pounded the button.

"Hey, anybody home," he shouted.

A young girl in green scrubs quickly shuffled down the hall toward them.

"Can I help you," she said.

"Not him," Schwartz snickered, "but me, you bet."

"Shut up," Sears said. "We need to see a patient in ICU. It's an emergency," he added for emphasis, and flashed his badge.

"I'll see what I can do," she said. She swiped her badge and the double doors opened. She vanished behind them as the doors closed.

"It's an emergency?" Schwartz laughed. "Like, what kind of emergency?"

"Like, murder suspect emergency?" Sears said.

The intercom clicked.

"Yeah?" A thick brown voice with attitude assaulted their hearing.

"We need to see a patient in ICU," Sears said.

"What patient?" the voice demanded.

"Monson. Daniel Monson."

"You family?" the voice questioned.

"We're detectives," Sears said. "Seattle P.D."

"Go away," the voice said. The intercom clicked off.

"Whatever happened to good old customer service," Schwartz said.

The double doors opened. The girl in green scrubs came out.

"I'm sorry," she began. "He's..."

Sears went through the doors, before they closed.

"You can't go in there," she said, following after him.

"Tell that to a judge," Seers said over his shoulder.

The doors began to close. Schwartz jumped in front of the closing door, expecting that it would reopen like an elevator door. Instead, it pushed him through and closed with a sigh.

Sears was proceeding, with dispatch, down the hallway, when a formidable African-American woman dressed in white stepped out from the ICU nurses station to fill up the hallway.

"Where do you think you're going?" she said with her hands on her ample hips.

Sears flashed his badge. "We need to talk to Monson."

The girl in green and Schwartz accordianed up behind.

"I tried to stop him," the girl in green said.

The large nurse looked over the tiny black granny glasses on her nose at the younger nurse. "Uh huh," she said. Then, in an institutionally professional voice, she continued, "the patient is not able to speak with you at this time," she said. "You will have to come back tomorrow."

Sears could see around the large woman, barely, to the glass doors of the patient care rooms. He was not that far from his goal. He could see Monson in the room. At least he thought it was Monson. The patient, Monson, had an oxygen mask on. There were tubes and tubing running in and out of his face and arms. There were several green clad attendants, maybe doctors, maybe nurses, doing things to him.

"Is that Monson?" he asked.

"Uh huh," the nurse said.

"Is he awake," he asked.

"Not anymore," she said.

"I need…we need to talk to him," Sears looked back at his partner for moral support.

"Honey, he ain't talking to no one," she said, "at least not for awhile."

Sears pulled out a card and held it out to her.

"Will you call us when he wakes up?" Sears asked.

At first, the woman didn't move. Then, reluctantly she took the card.

"If he wakes up," she said.

Sears turned around and bumped into the girl in green.

"I'm sorry," she said. She smiled at him.

"I'm not," he said. She stepped out of his way.

The two detectives walked back down the hallway while the large nurse and the girl in green watched. The large nurse never took her hands off her hips.

When they were out of the ICU, Sears said, "You were remarkably quiet back there."

"Just watching your back," Schwartz said. The two men walked out of the hospital. Sears began to smile.

"The Seahawks could have used a lineman like her this year," he said.

"Substantial woman," Schwartz said, smiling. "Very substantial woman."

"Big Mammas got nothing on her."

The two men got in their brown Ford Crown Victoria and drove away.

Chapter 31

Bertrum pulled up to his studio-trailer and got out of the Escalade. He liked the Escalade. It was big and heavy and the four-wheel drive made it ideal for getting deep into the forest. He didn't think anyone could find him at his studio. But he knew it was time to move. He was going to have to obtain a new identity. With the help of his clients, he would set up a new studio in a small rural town in out-of-the-way America. Maybe in California this time. Maybe not. There was too much competition among serial killers there. He smiled. He still had a sense of humor. Then, he heard her giggle.

"Damn it," he said.

"You are," she said, and giggled again.

He couldn't believe he had thought she was cute.

"I'm flattered," she said.

"Shut up," he said.

She giggled again. It was beginning to sound like fingernails on a chalkboard. He pointed the gun at Julie and Jenny.

"Get out," he commanded.

They did.

"Her name is Elizabeth," Jenny said.

"Who?" Julie asked.

"Shut up, I said," Bertrum said.

"The lady by the door," Jenny said.

Bertrum didn't like children. He thought he would be a good father.

"You can see her?" Bertrum asked.

"Don't answer him," Julie said.

"Listen, bitch, you're going to do everything I say, and enjoy it," Bertrum sneered. "Can you see her?" he demanded of Jenny.

"Don't answer him," Elizabeth said.

"If you don't tell me, I'll kill your Mommy," Bertrum said, pointing the gun at Julie.

"Not if I can help it," Elizabeth said.

"Not if I can help it," Sarah said.

"Sarah," Jenny exclaimed.

"Sarah?" Bertrum said. "Who's Sarah?"

"A friend of mine," Elizabeth answered.

"Don't you remember me, Bert?" Sarah asked, sweetly.

Bertrum turned toward the voice, but he couldn't see anyone, or anything.

"Get inside." He pointed his gun at Julie and Jenny.

Mother and daughter climbed the rusty metal steps and went into the doublewide. Bertrum switched on the generator and followed them in.

"In there," he waved his gun at the back of the trailer. Julie held Jenny's hand. They went into the room.

The room was spacious, considering it was in an old doublewide trailer. The walls were white. There was a double bed against the back wall. The mattress was dingy and soiled and without bed linens. Chains were attached to all four metal bedposts. A stainless steel tray with an assortment of surgical instruments rested near the bedside. Photo umbrellas on tripod-stands stood at the corners of the bed. A photoflood was suspended from the wall above the head of the bed and a single bare light bulb hung from the center of the room. Against the back wall of the white room was a wooden table with a computer.

"Welcome to my studio," Bertrum said. Mother and daughter stood near the bed. Bertrum switched on the computer and sat down. "Would you like to see my latest work?" Bertrum smiled.

"No," Julie said.

"I think you'll be quite interested," he said. He clicked the mouse a couple times. A picture of Daniel, naked, filled the screen. Bertrum angled the monitor so Julie could see. She pulled Jenny against her so she couldn't see and looked away.

"Quite dramatic, don't you think?" Bertrum said with pride. He clicked the next picture. "Notice the pain, the anguish. It's part of a series I'm calling, Naked Struggle in Futility." He clicked the next picture.

"You're sick," Julie said. She turned away so she couldn't see the screen.

"I don't usually photograph men," Bertrum said. "But it has been quite well received."

"Disgusting," Julie felt sick, realizing what Daniel had been through.

"In this case, I would agree," Bertrum said, clicking the mouse to the next image of Daniel writhing naked on the bed. "But, there is an erotic quality to torture, whether it be male or female."

"Why are you doing this?" Julie asked.

"Because I'm very good at it," Bertrum said. He double clicked the mouse and then typed a password.

A woman's voice spoke, "You've been a very bad boy."

"I love you, Momma," Bertrum said.

"Access granted," the woman said. "You have one very important message. Shall I read it too you?"

"No." Bertrum clicked the mouse. He read the message. He jumped to his feet, his chair falling backward into the surgical tray. The surgical instruments clattered to the floor.

"Don't do this to me," he said.

"You haven't been careful," the woman's voice said.

"Fix it," he demanded.

"They know you killed me," Elizabeth said.

"Shut up," Bertrum said.

"Who's there with you?" the woman's voice questioned.

"Monson's wife and child," Bertrum said. He turned the monitor toward Julie and Jenny, and then turned it back.

"They know you killed Sarah," Elizabeth said.

137

Bertrum turned toward the voice. "Of course they know that. I tell Momma everything." He thought that would help Big Momma know he wasn't lying.

"Who else is there with you?" the woman asked.

"Your best girl," Elizabeth said.

"No one," Bertrum said.

"Bert, I'm hurt," Elizabeth said, giggling.

Bertrum cringed.

"You're lying," the woman said.

"No he's not," Elizabeth giggled.

Bertrum looked toward the voice, then looked back.

"No, I'm not," he said.

There was no response from the computer.

"I think BAD boy's in trouble," Elizabeth said, giggling. Bertrum couldn't help cringing at the sound.

"You are going to fix it, right?" He was pleading.

"You are being weighed in the balance," the woman's voice said.

"You like my work, don't you?" he said.

"Your work habits have become sloppy," she said.

"No one has ever complained before," he said, desperately.

"I have a complaint," Elizabeth giggled.

"Shut up," Bertrum said. He took a swing in the air.

"You are being weighed in the balance," the woman said again.

"Why? What do you want me to do?" Bertrum whined.

"You will be notified," the voice said.

The screen flashed and went blank.

"You have been found wanting," Elizabeth said.

"You wanted it," Bertrum said.

"I had no idea just how bad you really are," Elizabeth said.

"That's right. I'm BAD," Bertrum let his anger turn to pride.

Julie watched the conversation Bertrum was having. She could only hear one side.

"You're insane," she told him. He was speaking with the voices in his head.

Bertrum turned toward her.

"Take off your clothes," he said. "I'm going to finish my series with a touching family portrait they'll never forget."

"Bad idea," Elizabeth giggled.

"Thank you," Bertrum said. "Take off your clothes," he repeated.

"No," Julie said.

"You go, girl," Elizabeth said.

"Will you just shut up," Bertrum said to Elizabeth. "TAKE OFF YOUR CLOTHES."

"NO," Julie said.

"I should have just said no, too," Elizabeth said.

"You wanted it," Bertrum said.

"I wanted love," Elizabeth said.

"We made love," Bertrum said.

"We had sex," Elizabeth said.

"You loved it," Bertrum said.

"You murdered me," Elizabeth said.

"You deserved it," Bertrum said.

"You deserve this," Julie said. Bertrum turned back toward her as she stabbed him in the chest with surgical scissors. Surprised, Bertrum's eyes opened wide. Julie drove the scissors through bone. Bertrum staggered back and sat on the bed. His shirt bloomed red.

"Tell your Mommy to run," Elizabeth said.

"We should run," Jenny said.

Julie grabbed Jenny's hand and they ran.

Bertrum grabbed the scissors and pulled.

As Julie and Jenny ran out of the trailer, he wailed in pain and rage.

Chapter 32

Detectives Sears and Schwartz were sitting in Jasper Clawson's office. The big man sat behind his desk reading a computer print out. He set the paper down and looked up at the detectives.

"I'll be damned," he said, shaking his head.

"Bad company," Sears said.

"Always on the run," Schwartz said.

"This computer, back east," Sheriff Clawson said.

"Big Momma," Sears said.

"Big Momma," Sheriff Clawson repeated. "She ever make a mistake?"

Sears and Schwartz looked at each other, then looked back at the Sheriff.

"No," they said in unison.

"Damn," the Sheriff said. "I never would have believed it."

"It is pretty unbelievable," Sears said.

"He's been doing it for years," Schwartz said.

"Why didn't we catch him before?" Sheriff Clawson asked.

"He's good," Schwartz said.

"He's very good," Sears said.

"He sure fooled me," Sheriff Clawson said.

"He fooled us all," Schwartz said.

"We won't get fooled again," Sears said.

All three men stood up. Sheriff Clawson wasn't convinced.

"So, if Monson's your guy, who shot him, and why?" Clawson asked.

"Good question," Schwartz said.

"Very good question," Sears said.

"We're going to ask Monson, just as soon as he wakes up," Schwartz said.

"If he wakes up," Sears said.

"Right after we arrest him," Schwartz said.

Sears and Schwartz opened the door of Sheriff Clawson's office.

"That's why you boys get paid the big bucks," Clawson said.

"Yeah, right," Sears chuckled.

"Big bucks," Schwartz laughed.

"By the way," Sears said, as they stepped into the foyer, "where's Deputy Davis, today?"

Sheriff Clawson's defenses rose. "He called in sick. Why?"

"Oh, nothing, really. We just wanted to ask him some questions about his photography," Schwartz said.

"Photo lover's are you?" Clawson said.

"Not really," Sears said.

The two detectives walked toward the exit leaving Sheriff Clawson standing in his office doorway.

"Call us when he gets better," Schwartz said. He opened the door. The little bell tinkled and the two men stepped out.

When the door closed, Sheriff Clawson spoke. "Get Bert on the radio."

"Bert called in sick," Wazulsky said.

"Don't you think I know that?" Sheriff Clawson said. "Do it anyway."

"But…" Wazulsky began.

The Sheriff held up his hand, cutting him off. "Don't be one," he said, disappearing into his office. "I have a bad feeling about this."

Chapter 33

Daniel was reclining in a wicker lounge chair, under a palm tree, on a golden sand beach. The sky was bright blue with puffy white clouds. The water was blue, azure, cobalt, sapphire, turquoise. He couldn't think of any other words for blue. He'd never seen so many shades of blue. He'd never seen water so clear, and blue. Gentle waves broke softly on the sand with a hypnotic rhythm that could last forever. In the distance he could see a much more violent surf crashing against the protective barrier reef. He was completely relaxed.

Stress?

Nope.

Worries?

Nada.

He was lost in the rhythm of the waves. He could stay like this forever. He couldn't remember ever feeling like this. He felt light, peaceful, warm. It was hard to describe.

Joy.

He felt joyful.

His father sat down beside him.

"Feels good, doesn't it?" his father said.

Daniel wasn't surprised to see him, here, on this beach. It felt right.

"It does," he said.

They sat together, in silence. Daniel couldn't tell how long they sat there. Time moves in different patterns under a palm tree on the beach.

"Is this what you want?" his father spoke.

Daniel didn't answer. He felt so peaceful. He couldn't imagine anything else.

"Is this what you want?" his father said, again.

"Why do you keep asking me that?" Daniel said. It wasn't exactly stress. Tension, maybe. It slipped into his voice and found his heart.

Something is missing.

Something was missing. He didn't know what it was.

Was it the same something he'd been missing for a long time? He didn't think so.

What is it?

"You can't stay here," his father said.

"Why not?" Daniel said.

"That's not how it works," his father said.

"Not how what works?" Daniel said.

His father didn't answer.

Daniel was watching the waves break on the sand. They had a definite rhythm. He could feel that rhythm, deep in his soul. It seemed to resonate within him.

Further down the beach, he could see a woman, walking toward them. She was wearing white flowing robes. They trailed behind her in the breeze, revealing a beautifully feminine shape. She was lovely.

She approached.

"Hello, Raymond," she said lightly.

"Hello, Sarah," Daniel's father answered.

"You know her?" Daniel said.

"Of course," Daniel's father said.

"Hi Daniel," Sarah said.

"Hi Sarah," Daniel replied.

He knew he knew her. He felt like he had known her for a long time. He felt like he knew a great deal about her, but he could not remember any of it.

She smiled.

It was a warm smile, a friendly smile, mixed with a touch of melancholy.

He remembered.

"You're dead," he said.

"You're dying," she said.

"No I'm not."

"Yes you are."

"No I'm not."

"Daniel," his father interrupted. "You are."

"No I'm not."

"You can't stay here," his father said.

"Why not?" Daniel looked around. It was so beautiful. He could imagine sitting on this beach, forever.

"When you die, you have to move on," his father said.

"Why is she still here?"

"She still has work to do."

"I'm not dead," Daniel said.

"No," his father said. "You're not."

"Then why am I here?" he asked.

"You have a choice," his father said. "You can move on, or, you can go back."

"Back where?" Daniel asked. He was here. He couldn't imagine anywhere else. His father looked at Sarah.

"They're in danger, Daniel," Sarah said.

"Who?"

"Julie and Jenny."

He remembered.

"You can save them," Sarah said.

He had to go back.

His father smiled at him. It filled him up. He could stay here. It felt so good.

"I love you, son. See you soon," his father said.

See you soon. What's that supposed to mean?

"Hurry," Sarah said.

Daniel opened his eyes.

Chapter 34

As Julie and Jenny bounded down the rusty metal steps of the trailer, they could hear Deputy Davis screaming. If Julie didn't know he was in pain, she would think he was in rage. Or, she would think someone had opened the door to hell and let one of its demons out.

Definitely demons.

She ran, Jenny in hand, toward the Escalade.

No keys.

She veered toward the trees. There was a deer path she could follow into the depths of the forest. Jenny held tightly to her hand as they splashed through the muddy clearing that served as a yard for the rusty trailer.

Into the woods.

Julie looked back to see if they had left tracks BAD could follow. They had. Their tracks created indents in the sandy, muddy ground. Falling rain was turning the tracks into tiny lakes.

Let it rain.

"Keep running," Julie said.

They ran.

Julie had no idea where they were going, but it felt right.

For a while.

They stopped running. Breathing hard. She stepped off the trail and pulled Jenny with her behind a tree.

They were deep in the forest. It was gloomy and quiet, but not disquieting. The trees were enormous. She couldn't see their tops. It was damp on the trail. Occasionally a drip fell on them, but the trees were so thick the rain wasn't reaching them directly. She was sweating, even though it was cool and her clothes were wet.

Jenny whispered, "Where are we going, Mommy?"

"I don't know," Julie whispered. It was right that they should whisper. There was something reverent about these trees.

Julie looked back to see if the deputy was following them. She couldn't tell.

"Why are we whispering?" Jenny asked.

Julie looked up at the tree branches. She couldn't see the sky.

"I don't know," she said aloud.

"I'm cold," Jenny said. Julie shivered.

"Me, too," Julie said.

She picked her daughter up and held her close, for warmth and comfort. Jenny laid her head on Julie's shoulder.

What do we do now?

Jenny was getting heavy. Julie sat them both down and they leaned against the massive tree trunk. The ground was soft and loamy and damp.

"I'm hungry," Jenny said.

It was late afternoon. Julie had no idea where she was. She had no idea where this trail led. She hadn't eaten since breakfast. She knew Jenny had a snack at school, but hadn't had lunch. She stood up.

"Come on," she said. "We're going back."

146

Chapter 35

Daniel heard a growling sound, like a small motor, then something began to squeeze his arm. Tighter. Tighter. He tried to move, but couldn't. His chest hurt. His nose hurt. His throat hurt. Something was pinching his nose.

Oxygen.

He could breathe quite well, in spite of his allergies. He just couldn't move.

"I'm Katie," an alto voice said. "How are you feeling?"

Daniel turned his head toward the voice. A pretty young girl in green scrubs was holding his arm. The growling sound stopped with a sigh. His arm was throbbing. He tried to speak, then tried to gag. He couldn't do either.

"Much better, I see," the girl in green, answered for him. "Your blood pressure is looking much better, too." She smiled.

Daniel tried to smile back. His face cracked. The tube down his throat was taped to his face.

Ouch.

He thought the word as loud as he could.

"On a scale of one to ten, how's your pain level?" the nurse asked.

He couldn't very well answer her, could he? Dentists are the worst. They always ask questions when your mouth is wide open. It's like they want to carry on lengthy conversations when the only thing you can move is your tongue. Now, he realized nurses do it, too. His mouth was taped open and there was a tube stuck down his throat and she was asking him questions. The only thing he could do was blink at her. She got the message and smiled.

"I'm sorry," she said. "You can't talk, can you?"

Duh.

"Blink once if it hurts. Twice if it doesn't."

Daniel blinked once, really hard.

She asked again, "On a scale of one to ten, how's your pain level? Blink the number."

Daniel did a systems check. His head hurt. His face hurt. His arms hurt. But, there was a fire in his chest. He couldn't get beyond his chest. He blinked, and blinked, and blinked. The nurse lost count.

"OK," she said. "It hurts."

Daniel kept blinking.

"You can stop blinking," she said.

A tear blinked out of the corner of Daniel's eye. The nurse dabbed the tear with a damp cloth and then wiped his brow. It felt good. She lifted his hand and placed a small plastic remote in it.

"This controls your morphine drip," she said. "Press the button on the end when the pain gets bad. It should help."

Daniel was anxious to get out of this place, but the pain was overwhelming. He pressed the button. He couldn't feel a difference. He pressed it again, and again, and again.

The nurse smiled at him.

You have very white teeth.

Daniel wasn't sure if she heard him. He wasn't even sure if he said it out loud. He did notice that the hospital bed was floating. He could feel the rippling waves beneath him. He couldn't decide if it felt good, or if he was going to get seasick. It didn't matter. He was floating away. The nurse in green scrubs was smiling at him as he floated away. Wasn't she concerned? It wouldn't be as hard to get out of here as he thought. He just had to float away. Every time he pressed the little button, he got a little higher. He pressed the button and closed his eyes.

Chapter 36

Julie and Jenny stopped at the edge of the forest, watching the trailer from behind a hemlock tree. Late afternoon gloom was beginning to settle into the small clearing. Everything they could see was a little darker. The Escalade was right where Deputy Davis had parked. The trailer was silent and dark. Julie looked for their tracks. She could no longer tell which tracks were theirs. The rain and mud had erased their presence. She tried to determine if the Deputy had followed them. She could not tell. The rain was still falling.

"Listen, sweetheart, I have to go back in there and find our keys," Julie whispered, "so we can go home and get Daddy."

"He's in there," Jenny said.

"Maybe," Julie said.

"He has the keys," Jenny said.

"Probably," Julie said.

"How are you going to get the keys?" Jenny asked.

"Don't ask so many questions."

"Why not?"

Julie smiled, then she sighed. Jenny had a good point. If the Deputy was still in there, how was she going to get the keys?

Maybe he's dead.

She shivered at the thought. She had not intended to kill him when she stabbed him with the surgical scissors. She was just protecting her daughter, and herself. She realized that she, now, was OK if he was dead. In fact, she hoped he was dead.

He's not dead.

She felt, suddenly, prescient. She would like to be wrong. She wanted him dead.

No.

She didn't want to feel that way. But, she did. She would kill him, if she had to. She needed a plan.

"I'm going back inside. You stay here," Julie commanded.

Jenny looked, suddenly, afraid. She was small and very afraid. Julie pulled her close.

"It's OK, sweetie. I'll be back in a flash."

Jenny shook her head. "Take me with you," she said.

"No, honey," Julie said. "I need you to be a big girl and stay right here."

"But I'm not a big girl," Jenny said.

How is it that little children can see the truth through adult-speak so easily? Julie was a better person because she had Jenny.

"Not yet," Julie said, "but you will be."

Jenny looked in Julie's eyes with innocent trust. It brought tears to Julie's eyes. She didn't know how this would turn out.

"I need you to stay here and hide, no matter what happens, do you hear me?"

Jenny didn't respond.

"You stay right here until I come back out," Julie said.

"What if he comes out first?" Jenny said.

"Hide. Don't make a sound, and hide."

Jenny nodded her agreement. Julie steeled herself to the task at hand. She squeezed Jenny's hand then jumped up and ran across the muddy clearing. As quietly as she could, which wasn't all the quiet, she tiptoed up the rusty metal steps of the trailer. She took a deep breath and opened the door.

Chapter 37

When Daniel opened his eyes, he was no longer floating. He felt much better, but he had an intense sense of urgency. It only took a moment for him to remember the reason.

Julie.

Jenny.

He had to find them.

He looked around. He had no idea where he was, or how he got there. He was in a large chamber with marble colonnades. Exquisite paintings decorated the ceiling and the walls. Torches danced in silence against heavy Corinthian Capitols. Five hallways intersected this great hall.

Footsteps on marble. More footsteps.

Sarah entered the great hall followed by 6 other women, all dressed in white. From each hallway, 7 women entered and formed a circle around the grand pentagram in the marble floor. Daniel stood in the center. Sarah stepped forward.

"Where am I?" Daniel asked.

"This is the Hall of the dead," Sarah said.

"I'm not dead," Daniel said.

"We are," Sarah said.

"Why am I here?" Daniel asked.

"You are between worlds," Sarah said.

"Am I dying?" Daniel asked.

"That is still up to you," Sarah said.

"I don't want to die," Daniel said.

"Then don't," Sarah said.

"Why am I here?" Daniel asked again.

"We can not stop BAD," Sarah said. You must do it."

"How?"

"Kill him."

"Are you crazy?"

"Kill him," the women said, as a chorus.

"I've never killed anyone," Daniel said. "Killing is wrong. Right?"

Elizabeth stepped forward. "He killed us. Our blood demands his death."

"Why me?" Daniel said.

"You are an advocate, are you not?" Sarah said.

"I was," Daniel said. "But not for the dead."

"The dead have chosen you."

"What if I won't do it?"

"Then, you will be killed. And, so will Julie and Jenny."

"How do you know this? You can't know this," Daniel exclaimed.

"Look," Sarah said. The marble floor seemed to disappear, leaving Daniel standing in the air. He felt like he was floating, floating, over the Cascade Mountains. He knew this place.

"I know this place," he said.

The trees. They looked up to see him. The trail. He'd been here before. Jenny. She crouched behind an evergreen. He could see her.

"Jenny," he shouted.

"She can't hear you," Sarah said.

"JULIE!" he called out. "Where's Julie?"

Sarah pointed. Julie ran across a clearing. The clearing. The trailer. She ran up the steps and stopped.

"Julie, don't do it. Don't go in there."

His words were in vain.

"She would do it, if she could," Sarah said.

"He's in there," Daniel said.

Sarah nodded.

"She won't kill him, will she?"

Sarah shook her head.

"Unless you choose to kill him, she will die." The scene faded. Daniel stood on the inset pentagram.

"Don't you have some kind of rule against murder, or compulsion, or blackmail, or extortion, or things like that?" Daniel said.

"We who have been murdered demand his death. If you do not do it, then you will stand here with us and we will have no advocate."

Daniel looked around the circle at the women. They were all beautiful, not in a worldly way, but in an intangible, indescribable way. Each woman looked him in the eyes and smiled. They were his sisters.

"I'll do it," he said.

"You'll do what?"

The room disappeared. The women were gone. Daniel opened his eyes. Again.

A large African-American woman, dressed in white, hovered over him.

A nurse.

All this coming and going was disorienting.

"Do what?" the nurse asked.

"I need to go," Daniel said.

"That's good news," she said with a slightly southern accent. "You're going to live. I'll get the bed pan."

"No," Daniel said. He grabbed her wrist. "Not to the bathroom. I need to go...leave."

"Honey," she said, "you're not going anywhere."

Daniel tried to sit up. He was tangled in tubes. He felt his face. He was glad to note that he didn't have any tubes down his throat or up his nose.

"Stop that," the large woman demanded. "Stop that right now." She pushed him back into the bed. When she did, he felt an overwhelming fire consuming his chest. He called out and submitted.

"That's right," she said. "You lie down. Don't move, till I say you can move."

"Julie," Daniel rasped. "Jenny," he whispered.

"Who they?" she asked.

Daniel closed his eyes, as if he was asleep. He could feel the large woman staring at him, assessing his condition. She didn't move. Neither did he. It would take some effort to get out of this hospital. But, he would do it. He had to.

Chapter 38

Julie stared into the trailer. It was dark inside, or nearly dark. It was nearly always dark in these woods. With the perpetual clouds, rain, and trees, sunlight rarely made it this far. BAD had covered the windows for better darkness. She stepped inside. The door behind her wanted to swing closed. She let it. The darkness buried her. She could feel it, pressing all around her, covering her.

Her eyes adjusted. There was some light left. But there was no sound. It was still. Deathly still. He was in here. She knew it. Was he dead? She didn't know. It wouldn't take long to find out. The trailer was not that big. She had stabbed him in his 'studio'. She took three steps and looked inside. BAD wasn't in there. But, it looked like most of his blood was.

Julie was feeling some kind of perverse pride in inflicting a wound that had drained so much blood from him. Then, she realized she was stepping in it. His blood. She gagged. She could see it, blacker than the blackening carpet. It trailed down the hallway. He was down there, dead or alive, a couple of pints low.

Before she followed the bloody trail she looked around the 'studio' hoping he had taken the keys out of his pocket.

Wishful thinking.

Stabbed in the chest with surgical scissors, he carefully removed the keys from his pocket and set them in plain sight so Julie could come back for them.

Right.

No keys, although, she did see a scalpel on the floor.

What kind of sick things was he doing in here?

She picked up the scalpel and held it in her hand like a knife. She was sure it was sharp, but it felt so very small. And, she didn't want to have to use it. But she would, if she had too. And, she knew just where she would stick it.

She stepped out of the 'studio' and wiped her bloody shoes on the carpeting. It was too dark to see if all the blood wiped off.

Probably not.

Slowly, she advanced along the bloody trail through the gloomy trailer. She knew she'd been in there too long. She knew Jenny would be getting worried. She hoped Jenny would stay put. She was such a good girl. She always tried to obey. But, she had her limits. Julie's command to stay there, without her, pushed her limits before she came inside. She needed to hurry. Her feet wouldn't cooperate. Slowly she went.

The blood trail turned into a room down the hallway.

The bathroom.

Julie held the scalpel ready to stab and peered into the room.

He was in there. On the floor. Leaning against the wall. It was light enough that she could see the surgical scissors on the floor next to him. He had pulled them out himself.

I bet that felt good.

His eyes were closed. There was a wad of gauze bandages in his lap. His shirt was torn open and his skin was bloody. She didn't think he was dead. She was pretty sure the keys to the Escalade were still in his pocket. If she was going to get them out of his pocket, she was going to have to kill him.

Keys for a life.

It didn't sound like a fair trade.

I can't do this.

Keys for a life. Julie had to remind herself that there were other issues.

I've never killed anything.

Julie loved small animals, and children. She wanted another baby. She was undecided on capital punishment. She generally voted conservative. She rarely faced moral dilemmas. She believed in God, and love, and her family. She was fiercely loyal.

She took a step forward. He didn't move.

She believed you had a right to defend yourself and your family. She didn't like guns, but wasn't opposed to them. Daniel had taught her how to fire them. She wished she had one now.

She took another step forward.

Is this really self-defense?

She was thinking too much. She knew that. She needed to be in the moment.

I'm going to kill him.

A wave of nausea swept through her.

For Daniel.

She thought he was dead.

For Jenny.

She was waiting just outside.

For me.

Her anger boiled over. In one graceful movement, she raised the scalpel and dropped to her knees.

BAD opened his eyes.

This is war.

She slashed the scalpel with all her strength.

His hand shot, snakelike, through the air. He caught her wrist inches from his exposed throat.

BAD smiled.

"Too late," he wheezed.

Time seemed to stop. They stared at each other, eye to eye, killer and victim. The lines were blurred as to which was which. BAD clarified things.

"You didn't think it would be that easy, did you?"

"I was hoping," Julie said.

BAD slammed Julie's wrist into the wall. The scalpel dropped to the floor and stuck. He yanked her arm and pulled her down. Her face landed in his lap.

Don't scream.

Julie was thinking of Jenny. If she screamed she knew Jenny would come running.

Stay calm.

She could fight him. He was wounded. He was stronger. She was better.

"This could be interesting, if we had a little more time," BAD said.

Julie felt for his leg, for his pants pocket, with her free hand. The keys were in there. She just couldn't get them. Not yet.

She raised her head and pushed off with her feet. The room was small. She had great leverage. She drove her shoulder into his chest. He held a vice grip on her arm preventing her from ramming into him with as much force as she would have liked, but she was angry, and desperate, and didn't have that far to go. Her shoulder hit his chest wound and he hollered.

Pain, and rage.

Two caged animals were fighting for their lives. Both had malice in mind.

BAD was stronger. He threw her off and rolled on top of her. Loss of blood and unfamiliarity with pain slowed him down. As he climbed on top, Julie raised her knee, driving it into his crotch. She didn't have enough room to get the force she hoped for, but she did inflict pain. BAD cringed at the attack on his privates. He swung his large fist and connected with the side of her head as he rolled off of her.

The light left in the small bathroom was dim at best. When his fist connected with her head, lights exploded in her vision. They flashed and sparkled, but didn't illuminate. She couldn't see. But, with the speed of lightning flashes in her vision, she struck him, closed fist and scrambled to get up.

He was screaming.

She got to her feet. Two steps to the door.

He grabbed her ankle and yanked her down. She hit the floor with her knees and elbows. Stunning, stinging pain shot up and down her arms and legs. He scrambled after her and she kicked out.

Julie had played tennis in high school. She was good, not great. At first, she had played because she really liked wearing those short white tennis skirts. But, she had come to enjoy the game and found a measure of success. When she played, although it didn't happen very often, she looked for, longed for, those moments when you hit a perfect groundstroke. The ball bounces and is coming up. You swing the racquet. The ball instantly changes direction and spin and rockets across the net.

Sweetspot.

You can't even feel it. There is no vibration in your elbow, no resistance from your racquet. It is as if the only evidence you hit the ball is the instantaneous direction change and the echoing thud/ping sound you hear but don't feel.

Kill shot.

She knew she had connected. Her heal finished with perfect follow-through. No vibration. No resistance. Julie heard the thud. BAD dropped to the floor.

Advantage Monson.

She turned around. BAD was down, but not totally out yet. Julie didn't want to give him time to recover. She savagely jammed her hand into his pocket and retrieved the Escalade keys. On the way out of the bathroom she thought about the scalpel. She could finish him off, end this.

Jenny.

She ran.

Chapter 39

Detectives Sears and Schwartz were sitting on plastic chairs, eating pastrami sandwiches in a cluttered room filled with computers. Michael Wu's staccato typing played counterpoint to the detectives lip-smacking. The cadence rested with a mouse click, then resumed.

"Find anything?" Sears asked.

"Don't talk with your mouth full," Schwartz said.

"See food," Sears said, opening his mouth.

Michael Wu turned around just in time to see. "Gross," he groaned and turned back to the monitor.

Sears laughed. So did Schwartz.

"Unusual," Michael said.

"You got that right," Schwartz said.

"No, I mean, it is unusual that Mamma can't ID the pubic hair," he said, typing furiously.

"There must be billions of possibilities," Sears said.

"Six-point-seven billion possibilities," Michael said.

"You mean to tell me Big Mamma's got every single person in the world in her database," Schwartz said.

"Not every single person," Michael said protectively.

"Then why's it so unusual?" Sears asked.

"Because, Big Mamma's got just about every single person in there."

"Then it must be one of those people from Tibet, or Shangri-la, or some damn place like that," Schwartz said.

"Highly unlikely," Michael said.

"Why's that?" Sears asked.

"Because Shangri-la is a myth," Michael said.

"Didn't you ever read, 'Lost Horizon'?" Schwartz said.

"True story," Sears said.

"I only read scientific journals and graphic novels," Michael said.

"Literary snob, huh?" Schwartz said.

Michael turned to look at the two detectives, then turned back to his computer without comment.

"Just for fun, type in Bertrum Alexander Davis, and photography," Sears said.

"You want me to type in BAD photography?" Michael said.

"Hey, you're pretty quick," Schwartz said. "Bad photography. That's pretty good."

"You can't be serious," Michael said.

"No, really," Sears said. "Give it a try."

Michael typed in Bad Photography. The monitor started scrolling.

"We got 10 million hits. You're going to have to narrow your search," Michael said.

"Just type in Bertrum Alexander Davis," Sears said.

Michael typed. In moments, the monitor flashed the message, 'Restricted Access. Please enter your password.'

"That's unusual," Michael said.

"Is that because he's in law enforcement?" Schwartz asked.

"No," Michael said. "What's your full name?"

"Why?" Schwartz said.

"I'm going to show you," Michael said.

"Come on," Sears said. "Tell him."

"You tell him yours," Schwartz said.

"He's not asking for mine," Sears said.

"Come on," Michael said. "It's your name, for Pete's sake."

"St. Pete's not that far off," Sears chuckled. "Tell him, Frank."

"Geez," Michael said. "How hard could it be?"

He typed in Frank.

"Middle?" He asked.

Schwartz looked at Sears.

"Tell him," Sears said, smiling.

"Asisi," Schwartz said.

Michael turned around. "You're kidding me, right?"

"He's not," Sears said.

"Frank Asisi," Michael said, smiling. "Francis Asisi Schwartz?" He started to laugh.

Detective Schwartz's face turned red.

"That's his name," Sears said.

"I thought you were Jewish," Michael said.

"My Dad was Jewish. My Mom loved animals," Schwartz said.

Still chuckling, Michael typed in his name. In seconds, Detective Schwartz's picture appeared on the monitor, along with his vital statistics.

"See," Michael said, smiling, "there are links to your service record, commendations, tax returns, medical records, you name it."

"You've got my medical records in there?" Schwartz said. He wasn't smiling.

"Big Mamma knows everything about you," Michael said proudly.

"Your turn," Schwartz said, pointing at Sears.

"No," Sears said. "You made your point. Big Mamma knows everything."

"Come on," Schwartz said. "Do him, too,"

"How come," Sears continued quickly, "if Big Mamma knows everything, she doesn't know about Bertrum Alexander Davis?"

Michael typed Bertrum's name in, again. The same message flashed, 'Restricted Access. Please enter your password'.

"It's not that she doesn't know about him, it's restricted information," Michael said.

"Restricted by who?" Sears said.

"Come on," Schwartz said, standing up, "put his name in there."

Sears stood up. "He's not going to put my name in there."

"Why not? You embarrassed?" Schwartz said.

"No. I'm not embarrassed," Sears said.

The two men were standing nose to nose.

"Guys, stay focused," Michael said.

"Charles Xavier," Schwartz said.

"What?" Michael said.

"Charles Xavier Sears," Schwartz said.

"Feel better?" Sears said.

"You're kidding?" Michael said.

"Maybe," Schwartz said.

"You are, really?" Michael said.

"You should be," Sears said.

"Why?" Schwartz said. "You embarrassed?"

"I told you, I'm not embarrassed," Sears said.

"Alright, I'll do it," Michael said. He typed Charles Xavier Sears into the computer. Sears' picture and info appeared on the screen. "How's that?"

"Good," Schwartz said. "Aren't you going to comment on his name?"

"Chuck?" Michael said.

"No, not Chuck," Schwartz said.

"Go ahead, have your fun," Sears said.

"Charles Xavier?" Schwartz said, waiting for a response from Michael. Michael didn't respond.

"You know. X-men?" Schwartz said.

"I think you guys are letting the pressure get to you," Michael said.

"You laugh about my name, but you're not going to laugh about his?" Schwartz said.

"My name's not funny," Sears said. "Yours is."

"Francis," Michael said.

"What?" Schwartz said, angrily.

"That's his middle name," Michael said.

"What are you talking about?" Schwartz said.

"Charles Xavier," Michael said. "It's Charles Francis Xavier."

"I'll be damned," Schwartz said.

"You ain't no saint, that's for sure," Sears said.

"And I sure as hell aren't some mutant either," Schwartz said.

"Charles Xavier is one of the smartest men in the world," Michael said. "Even without his telepathic powers, he's a scientific genius."

Sears and Schwartz looked at each other. They burst out laughing.

"What?" Michael said.

"Let's just stick to the X files," Schwartz said. "See if you can get access to the Deputy's file."

"Could take a while," Michael said.

"I'm Mulder," Sears said.

"Scully," Schwartz said.

"Not on your life," Sears said. The two men walked out of the cramped and cluttered office. They could hear Michael start to laugh.

"Francis Asisi Schwartz," he said. "That's a good one."

Chapter 40

The door to the trailer flew open and Julie burst out. She jumped off the rusty stairs and landed in the mud at the bottom, sliding and slipping. It had been raining the whole time she had been inside, and it was practically dark. She had no idea how long she had been inside. It felt like forever, in a few moments. Einstein had it right. The perception of time depended on the point of observation.

"Jenny," Julie screamed, splashing across the muddy clearing. "Jenny, let's go. I've got the keys."

She reached the tree where she had left her daughter. Jenny wasn't there.

"Jenny," she screamed frantically. "Jenny, where are you?"

She ran deeper into the trees, into the darkness. It had been raining harder. The ground under the trees was soggy. Large drips were falling on her, each one soaking her already matted hair.

"Jenny!" she was desperate. She was out of breath. She stopped running. Then she heard it.

"Mommy."

The sound was distant. She had been running the wrong way.

"Jenny," she called out. "I'm coming."

She sprinted back towards the trailer, through the trees.

"Mommy."

There she was, standing in front of the SUV.

Good girl.

Julie broke through the trees, into the clearing, in full sprint.

Fifteen yards to the Escalade.

Two-seconds.

There he was, standing on the rusty steps.

"Stop…" he said, not particularly loud.

She was so close. She had fought so hard. She thought she had won. She thought she could get away from this awful situation. His voice cut through the gloom and pierced her heart. He was pointing a gun right at her.

Could she dodge the bullet?

Two-seconds.

Fifteen yards.

She could see so clearly. Jenny was standing there, so small.

She's afraid.

One second and hundredths.

Seven yards.

The game clock was ticking. She'd watched games that were won, and lost, in the last hundredths of seconds. She'd never played in any, until now.

"…or I'll shoot your precious daughter."

BAD was covered in blood, a demon from hell, pointing a gun, at her, at Jenny.

Julie stopped. Dead.

Bertrum Alexander Davis smiled.

Chapter 41

Daniel opened his eyes and looked around. He was in the hospital. It hadn't been a bad dream.

It's a nightmare.

He shook his head to shake off the effects of the drugs. He had such vivid dreams. They were still at the surface of his memory, fading. He had to get out of here. He had to get to Julie and Jenny. He sat up in the bed. Tubing and paraphernalia sat up with him. A wave of nausea and dizziness washed over him. The room was spinning. He told himself it wasn't really the room.

Hold on. It'll pass.

It did.

Slowly.

He looked at his arms. He had IVs in both arms. A heart monitor was attached to his finger. Now he could hear it. The slow steady beeping. That was him. That was his heart.

Slow and steady.

I'll get there.

Too late.

The nausea returned, not for the same reasons.

He was powerless. He felt powerless. Through this whole experience, he realized, he hadn't done anything. It had all been done to him.

I didn't do anything.

That was the problem. He hadn't done anything.

Not true.

He had bought the alarm system.

It was supposed to protect us.

It was passive. It didn't do anything, until it was too late. It didn't stop evil. It just warned you when evil got too close.

Evil was all around. He had just waited until Saruman looked at him.

Daniel thought he had a perfect life. Now, he knew it was an allusion. He had taken too many things for granted.

Too many.

Too late.

The nausea came in waves. Depression came in troughs. Tears came to his eyes.

"Lie down. What you think you're doing," a large African-American nurse commanded. "Don't you know you been shot?"

Daniel knew. He knew the full extent of his sins. Getting shot was only part of his punishment.

He did what she said. He felt better, physically. But he was calculating. Now he was planning. He would not be done to. He would not be passive. He would act. If he could.

If I can.

Oh God. Help me.

The heavens were silent. In his darkest hour, there was no response.

The nurse checked his vitals.

"You a lucky man," she said.

He could hear Emerson, Lake and Palmer singing at his gravesite.

"You think so?" he rasped. The sound of his voice surprised him. He could hear it. He wasn't dead, yet.

"Absolutely," the nurse said. "You're going to live."

"Is that a threat or promise," Daniel said.

The nurse laughed.

"That's a good sign," she said. "You hungry?"

Daniel hadn't thought about it. He checked in with his stomach. It growled. He nodded.

"That's an even better sign," she said. "You'll be outta here in no time,"

"That's the plan," Daniel said. She smiled. She had a nice smile.

"When you feeling up to it, there's some Police wants to talk to you," she said. She put the emphasis on the long O sound of police. Daniel wondered if she was exaggerating her accent just for him.

"Not ready," Daniel exaggerated the rasp.

"That's what I tell 'em," she said. "I'll get you something to eat." For her size, she was quick. Then, she was gone.

Daniel had no idea how long he'd been there. It seemed like months. The clock on the wall said it was 8:30. He didn't know if that was A.M. or P.M. He hoped P.M. It would be easier to get out. And, he would get out. But first, he would have to disconnect himself from the hospital paraphernalia.

He reached his hand up and felt for his chest. The tubing chased his hands. He could feel more pain in his hands than he could in his chest. In spite of the non-allergenic tape, which anchored the IVs to the backs of his hands, it hurt when he moved them. And, the non-allergenic tape was not so non-allergenic. He had blisters all around the insertion points.

Don't they notice stuff like that?

His fingers felt his chest. He could tell that his chest was wrapped. The wrapping surrounded him, front and back, but it didn't hurt. He followed the IV tubing to the source. He had stands with drip bags on both sides of his bed. He had tubes stuck in both hands. He thought he must be in pretty bad shape for how much stuff they had connected to him. He wondered what would happen when he disconnected it. All of it.

He pulled the heart monitor off his finger. The slow and steady beeping just went steady.

Flatline.

He was dead.

Would they come running?

Where's the crash cart?

The noise was actually quite annoying. But, he realized, the monitor wasn't turned up very loud.

What if I was actually dying?

He was annoyed. And relieved. No one came running. He could disconnect and no one would pay any attention.

The large nurse came back, carrying a tray of food.

"If you dead, I'll have to eat this," she said with a hopeful tone. She set the food on the tray and swung it over Daniel's stomach. "What you do?"

Daniel held up his finger where the heart monitor had been. "Sorry," he said, feigning sheepishness.

She took the plastic monitor and clamped it back on his finger. The flatline monotone returned to a slow and steady beep. He wasn't dead after all.

"Now, eat hardy," she said, leaving the room.

"Wait," Daniel called.

She stopped, filling the doorframe.

"What you want now?" she said, sounding surly. Daniel could tell it was put on surliness. Underneath, she was a caring nurse.

"What if I need to go to the bathroom?" Daniel said, holding up both hands. The IV tubing and heart monitor rose too.

"That's why they invented bedpans," she said.

"You really want to clean my bedpan?" he said.

"Nope," she said. "Shift change in half an hour."

"Half an hour," Michael protested. "What if I can't wait that long."

"Good things come to those that wait," she said.

"For instance," he said.

"Ali," she said.

"What?" he said.

"She your night nurse," she said. "She's young and cute and blond. You'll like her. She'll change your bed pan and give you a nice warm bath."

She winked at him.

His cheeks colored.

She laughed and left.

He looked at the dinner tray she had brought him. Since airlines started charging for meals, he wondered if Host International had begun provisioning hospitals. There were four indents with bowls protected from sliding off the tray in turbulence. Fettuccini Alfredo, green salad with a packet of Italian dressing, a fruit cup, a dinner role and a carton of low-fat milk. Probably low sodium. Low fat. Low taste. Perfectly health conscious.

He picked up the plastic utensils and removed the plastic wrap. He spun the fettuccini onto the fork and tried to take a bite. His plastic tubing made it difficult, but he eventually got the fork to his mouth.

"Umm," he mumbled.

The fettuccini melted in his mouth. Garlic. Parmesan. Good. The appearance and presentation wouldn't hold up in any Italian restaurant he'd ever been to, but, he couldn't remember the last time he had real food. While he wasn't sure if this would qualify as real food, it tasted good. It tasted better than good. He ate it all.

His digestive system kicked in. He did have to go. He pressed the nurse call button.

This really is a lot like being on an airplane.

"What?" Large nurse said.

"I have to go," he said.

She pulled the bedpan out of the lavatory and set it on the bed.

"Here," she said.

"No," he said. "I really want to get up and go."

"You want to get up and go?" she said.

"That's right," he said.

"You can't," she said.

"Why not?" he said.

"Short term memory loss," she said. "YOU BEEN SHOT."

He pushed the dinner tray away and swung his feet over the side of the bed.

"I'm not dead," he said.

"Not yet," she said.

He slid off the side of the bed and put his feet on the floor. The plastic tubing followed him, preventing him from going anywhere. His left arm was connected to the IV drip on the other side of the bed.

"I'm feeling pretty good," he said.

"Really," she said.

"Really," he said.

She watched him stand there for a moment.

"All right," she said. "It's your funeral."

She lifted the IV drip off the far side poll and brought it to the near side poll. Daniel sat back on the bed during the maneuver. He wasn't feeling as good as he wanted her to believe.

"What's in the IV?" he asked.

"Meds," she said.

"Really," he said.

"Really," she said.

"Do I really need to have them in both arms?" He held up his hands to show her the blisters forming around the IV catheters.

"You asking for a lot. You know that," she said, inspecting the reddish skin around the insertions.

"What if I need to use both hands," he said.

"What you planning to do in there?" she said.

His cheeks colored again, and she winked. She pulled the IV out of his right wrist and inserted it into the drip line going into his left, as Daniel watched closely. She put both bags on one poll.

"Go for it," she said.

He stood up and held onto the IV stand for balance. He took a step. His legs were stiff. He took another step. She watched him carefully, but didn't offer to help. The bathroom was across the room.

"Maybe I don't have to go, after all," he said.

"You're committed now," she said. "You gots to go."

He felt light headed. He didn't know if he could make it. But, he was committed. He would take the steps necessary to finish this, one way or another. He felt her eyes on him. He tried to pull the back of his hospital gown closed.

"You ain't got nothing I ain't seen before," she said, chuckling.
He gritted his teeth and made it to the bathroom.
"I'll be waiting right here," she said.
"Is that a threat, or a promise," he said, closing the bathroom door.
"A promise," she said. "You call me if you need me."
"No thanks," he said, as he sat down.

Chapter 42

Michael Wu sat at the computer, unaware of his surroundings. It was late. Everyone else in the office had gone home. No one noticed that Michael was still there. He was always there. He had advanced degrees in Biochemistry, Computer Science, and Geology. He was just about finished with a correspondence degree in law enforcement. He hadn't found his niche yet. He was twenty-five years old. He lived at home. But, he spent most of his time with Mamma. For Michael Wu, she was the source of all wisdom and knowledge.

Michael had logged in hours ago. He had access to Mamma. Most of the time his level of access was sufficient for the work he was asked to do. Sometimes, his level of access was inadequate for the work he wanted to do, or, for the information he wished to have. This was one of those times. When he received the message 'Restricted Access'. Please enter your password' he was intrigued. More than intrigued really. His interest was piqued. His curiosity was aroused. By the time Sears and Schwartz left, he was in full hacker mode. He would get in. He would find out who Bertrum Alexander Davis really was. He would find out why Mamma restricted access to BAD files.

Michael was typing furiously. He was looking for backdoors. He knew there were back doors. He used them frequently, when he needed to. He knew that Mamma knew there were backdoors. He knew she knew he was using them. He believed that he had a filial relationship with Mamma. She let him in when he needed to get in. He didn't abuse his privileges. He was a good son. Well, son was maybe too strong a word. He did have a mother and father. He lived with them for heaven's sake. But his true mother, his holy mother was Mamma. Big Mamma. She was big. She knew everything, or so he believed.

Why won't she let me in?

He tried his usual backdoors.

No Luck.

He looked for new backdoors. This was actually quite fun. He hadn't been challenged like this for quite some time. Maybe that was why Mamma was making him work so hard. He needed challenges. He needed to be challenged. Bertrum Alexander Davis was challenging.

The door opened. He was in. He'd never been this deep before.

Holy…

Michael was going to swear, but caught himself. His parents didn't allow him to swear. They were old school Chinese. Obedience and respect reigned supreme. At home, they had always encouraged him to do things. Encouraged may not be a strong enough word. They were the reason he had finished High School at age 12; their encouragement, and his brilliance. But, he was never allowed to swear.

Two times.

He swore two times.

The first time, his father had washed his mouth out with soap. It wasn't really that bad. It tasted bad. But the soap itself wasn't that bad. Michael knew it was sanitary, anyway. He didn't really see the point, though. At six-years-old he knew words didn't come from his mouth. They came from his brain. Anyway, he didn't swear for a long time.

The second time he swore, he was in High School. He was ten. He was getting better grades than all the kids in his school. In fact, he was the youngest Valedictorian HHS had ever had. But, most of the kids made fun of him. He didn't fit in. He had no friends.

When he came home, after one particularly trying day, his Mom asked him to clean his room. He swore at her. He tried the word out on his tongue. He couldn't taste the soap. The word felt good. It was a particularly bad word. His Mom was shocked. When his Dad came home, she told him about it. Michael hadn't looked at his naked butt for a while, but he was sure that if he did, he would still see the scars. He decided that swearing wasn't worth it. Sure, he was angry. He was angry with the kids at school. He was angry with his parents. But he didn't swear. He just didn't.

This might be a reason to swear.

Michael was in. He was way in. He'd never been so in. He had access to information he knew he shouldn't have access to, not even when he knew Mamma was being nice to him.

She must be sleeping.

He had a reason for being here.

Where shall we go today?

He could go anywhere. Do anything. He thought. He was sorely tempted to explore super-secret CIA files. NSA, Homeland security, you name it. He could access it. He wondered how Mamma felt about his being there. Surely she must know. She must have let him in.

Stay focused.

He typed Bertrum Alexander Davis.

The screen went blank.

"NO!" Michael shouted. He slammed his hand against the monitor, as if that could bring the previous screen back. He typed furiously. Nothing.

"Damn it," he said, not even thinking about his word choice.

The screen flashed blue. A status bar appeared.

What the…?

He watched the status bar scroll across the screen. 100%. The screen changed.

Assassin's Creed?

No. The graphics are too good.

A nearly naked woman was walking toward him. She came closer and stopped.

"Welcome, Mr. Wu." She had a pleasantly seductive female voice. "Your avatar has been prepared."

"You know my name," Michael said.

"Of course," she said, smiling. "We know everything about you."

A man opened the door of a nearby building and walked towards the woman. He was barefoot, with jeans and no shirt.

"Who are you?" Michael asked. The male's lips moved. The woman turned toward the man.

"I'll be your…" she paused, then smiled again, "…friend, while you're in our world," she said, sweetly matter-of-fact.

The man was ripped. The woman had a great body.

Perfect people?

The woman held out her hand. The man took her hand in his and then looked right at Michael and smiled.

Michael didn't really have a body like that. He never would. He didn't work out. But, he did see himself like that. Like this. He'd never had a girl friend. He wanted one, a girl friend.

How did she know?

Michael shook his head and looked around. The street was deserted, except for the woman, this woman, holding his hand. It looked like a downtown city street. But it wasn't Seattle. The buildings were tall. The shadows were lengthening. It wasn't the nicest part of town. There was an edge of dirt, decay, everywhere.

"Where am I?" Michael asked.

The woman smiled. Her smile reached deep inside him. Yearning. Desire. Need. She squeezed his hand tighter. They began to walk down the street.

"You're with me now," she said.

Michael looked in her eyes. They were intensely blue. He could see himself reflected in them. He tried, unsuccessfully, not to let his eyes drift lower. She had enough black leather to cover the salient points.

"I'm here for a reason," he said.

"Of course you are," she said.

Michael stopped walking. The woman stopped with him. She looked hurt. She didn't release his hand.

"I need information," Michael said. The woman smiled again, a natural, easy smile.

"Of course you do," she said. She tugged on his hand and they began to walk again.

"Bertrum Alexander Davis," Michael said.

This time, the woman stopped walking. She looked in Michael's eyes. She's evaluating me.

"I'm investigating a case," Michael said.

"Is that really why you're here?" she asked.

Michael couldn't tell if she was pouting or helping.

"Yes," Michael said.

"That's unusual," she said. "Unexpected."

"What can you tell me?" Michael asked.

"Right this way," she said. "If that's what you really want."

He didn't know what she meant. But he could tell she was offering more than information. She pulled his hand and they walked over to a particularly dark building.

"In here," she said. They stood in front of a three-story brick building. The bricks were old. The glass door was tinted. He couldn't see inside. She opened the door for him. He heard a little bell tinkle. He went inside. She followed closely behind.

It was dark inside. Just as he couldn't see in the windows when he was on the outside, he couldn't see out the windows now he was on the inside. His eyes were adjusting. The woman stepped up to a drab counter and pressed the service bell. An old wizened man came out of a back room. The woman and man acknowledged each other wordlessly. The man sized Michael up, then came around the counter and motioned for him to follow.

The woman nodded reassurance and the trio set off.

The man led Michael down a long corridor. The woman followed behind. The corridor was lit by bare light bulbs spaced way to far apart, with such low wattages as to barely provide illumination. You could see the light bulbs, but you couldn't see the way.

They passed a number of closed doorways, until the man stopped abruptly. He took out a set of keys, fumbled through them, found an odd shaped key and inserted it into the lock. Turning the lock, then the doorknob, he opened the door.

Yellow light poured out, orangish-yellow light. The man motioned for Michael to step inside. Michael hesitated.

"What's in there?" he asked.

"What you're looking for," the woman said.

"How do you know what I'm looking for?" Michael asked.

"Mamma knows," she said.

"I have a bad feeling about this," Michael said. The woman smiled at him.

"Isn't that what this is about?" she said.

"I'm investigating a case," Michael said.

"What's the worst that could happen?" the woman said sweetly.

"I don't know," Michael said, shivering in the cold draft coming from the room. Michael wished he had a shirt on. He felt...naked.

"You're using valuable resources," the man said, speaking for the first time. His voice was remarkably young sounding for his withered body. He put his hand against Michael's back. Michael could feel the energy pulsing from the point of contact. It began in his lower back and traveled up and down his spine. The man shoved Michael into the room.

He was in. He was way in.

This is bad.

As Michael looked around the room, the spine tingling sensation spread throughout his body. As the images around him began to resolve, the tingling sensation grew to a consuming pain. At first, he couldn't believe what he was seeing.

Shock. Horror. Words were inadequate.

He was being carried deeper and deeper inside a mind of irredeemable filth, by an irresistible current of filthiness. Unspeakable acts of depravity were occurring all around him, in real time. He couldn't take his eyes off the visions of raw, naked, carnal debauchery.

He was disappointed. He had hoped for something more. Deep inside, he had hoped for some kind of enlightenment. What he found, this far in, was hopelessness. He tried to retch. His body began to shake. He realized, way too late, that, this far in, he couldn't get out.

This is BAD.

He would have liked to call Sears and Schwartz. They would definitely want to know. He smiled to himself. St. Francis couldn't save him now. He lost consciousness beneath the surface of an overwhelming wave of despair.

Chapter 43

Bertrum Alexander Davis was good at what he did. He smiled, in spite of the pain. Good was a relative term. He was disappointed to be leaving this part of his life behind. But, they would fix it. He hoped.

When he joined the secret society, he had done so, he thought, to contribute, to lead. The cause was great, and he was born to lead. He knew it. He would do things others would only dream about. And, they paid him well to carry out, then photograph their dreams. Within the organization he had found sanctuary. Within that sanctuary he had found opportunity. From opportunity he had developed artistry. Artistry provided notoriety. Notoriety within a secret society was a bad thing. Bertrum liked that. He did BAD things.

He looked in the rear view mirror. The woman and child were securely bound. He wouldn't make the same mistake twice. He rarely did. Never three times. He had this time. He had under estimated the Monson's. All of them.

Now, it was personal. He would punish them for their insolence. He would make them pay for his mistakes. His clients in the society would pay him for his vision. His secret oaths would protect him. They would cover up what would soon be a very public exhibition of his talent.

He felt free. He was a master of the great secret. He could do anything he wanted to do. And, he wanted to do some very bad things.

"Hello, Bert." Elizabeth sat in the passenger seat of the Escalade.

Bertrum swerved slightly. He was startled, a bit unnerved.

"Just like a bad penny," she said. "Although, I'm not really sure where that expression comes from."

Bertrum stared straight ahead. His grip on the steering wheel whitened his knuckles.

Elizabeth giggled.

"Aren't you going to talk to me?" she asked, sweetly. "Aren't you glad to see me?"

She giggled again. The sound rankled in Bertrum's ears. She knew it. She couldn't help it. She laughed out loud.

"Shut up!" Bertrum commanded. "Shut the hell up."

"Oh Bertie, you're so funny," she said, giggling.

He took a swing at her. His closed fist passed through her and hit the seat back. She laughed out loud, again.

"You can't get rid of me, Bert," she said. "We bonded, that night."

"You bonded," Bertrum said.

"You killed me," she said.

"And I'll do it again," he said.

She giggled. "That's funny," she said.

"Shut up," he said.

She watched him. He could feel her watching him. He stared straight ahead, beginning to perspire. She looked into the back seat.

"We're not going to let you do it, anymore," she said.

"Do what?" he said.

"What ever evil, sick, twisted plan your demented little mind is dreaming about," she said.

This time he laughed. "I can do anything I want," he said.

"Could," she said.

"Can," he said.

"Not anymore," she said.

"Watch me," he said.

"We are," she said.

Three women appeared in the road in front of him. It startled him. He swerved to avoid them, nearly hitting an on-coming truck. Elizabeth giggled.

"We won't let you do it," she said.

Three more women appeared in the road ahead. Bertrum griped the wheel tighter and drove right through them.

"See," he said. "You can't stop me."

"We won't," she said.

"Then what are you going to do?" he asked.

"We're going to drive you mad," she said, giggling.

She was annoying. Her giggles were infuriating. He knew she knew it bothered him, drove him crazy. She disappeared, but her giggles continued. He could still hear her, but he couldn't see her.

"Shut up," he hollered.

The giggles became a laugh. The laugh became a cackle.

I need some earplugs.

"It won't help," she said, from the seat beside him.

"What won't help?" he said.

"Ear plugs."

"You can read my mind?" he asked.

She giggled. "Maybe."

The sound of her giggles was like the screeching of fingernails on a chalkboard. It pierced his soul with tiny needles. It made his skin crawl. No matter how many times he heard it, he could never get used to it. She knew it. She did it again, then disappeared.

"We're going to haunt you, Bert," she said, from somewhere beyond.

"I don't believe in ghosts," he said.

"You should."

The voice was tiny. It came from the back seat. He looked in the rear view mirror. It was the little girl. She was sitting up, on the seat. He thought he had put duct tape on her mouth. He thought he put duct tape on her Mom. They were both sitting up, watching him.

Giggles.

He looked at the passenger seat. Nothing.

He looked in the rear view mirror. Mom and daughter were bound and lying on the floor. He was losing it. He felt his chest wound. It hurt, bad. He had lost a lot of blood. He couldn't believe he had let her get so close.

A woman, no less.

She had stabbed him.

"Damn it," he said out loud. "Damn them all."

He knew he needed medical attention. He knew his clients, the society, would provide it for him. Mamma would take care of him, he hoped.

They owe me.

He had given them his best years. His best work.

They know me.

He was famous, in an anonymous circle.

They love me.

He wasn't totally convinced, but he knew where he could go.

Giggles. She was back.

"Stop it," he said.

"I never really left," she said.

Slowly, she started unbuttoning her blouse. He tried to keep his eyes on the road in front of him. She smiled. He couldn't. He could tell she didn't have a bra on, underneath. She was beautiful. He wanted her.

"I know where you can go," she said, breathlessly.

"Where?" he said.

"Hell," she said, smiling sweetly beside him.

"Not without you," he said, reaching over to touch her.

She disappeared.

"Of course," she said, giggling.

The tires on the Escalade began to sing. He had drifted into the emergency lane and was heading off the road. He turned the wheel. The Escalade shuttered and swerved. He was fishtailing across both lanes. He was lucky, this time. There was no oncoming traffic. He smiled. He was an expert driver. But, he was losing it.

He would get medical attention. It would help. They might think he needed mental attention. They would be wrong. He just needed to get rid of these ghosts.

Chapter 44

She was waiting for him when he came out of the bathroom.

"Don't you have better things to do?" he asked.

"Nope," the large nurse said. "You the most important thing in my life."

"Right," he said.

She helped him back into bed. He let her help him.

She reconnected his IV tubing and monitors and tucked him in.

"Thanks, Mommy," she said.

"I ain't your Mamma," she said. "I'm going home."

"Me too," he said.

"You ain't going no where," she said smiling. "Ali, she be here soon. She'll make sure you snug like a rug." She winked and was gone.

Good.

He didn't mind her. She had a good heart. She seemed like a good nurse. But, he needed to go. He needed to be gone. He had to. He only had a few minutes before Ali got there.

He sat up and pulled the IV tubing out of the catheters stuck in the backs of his hands. He swung his feet over the edge. He was feeling much better. He could tell they hadn't been giving him as much morphine. His senses were sharper. He could feel the cool breeze on his backside as he made his way to the door. He realized he probably wouldn't make it very far with his bare butt blowing in the breeze. He had to find some scrubs.

He paused in the doorway to his room. He was breathing hard. He knew he had to do this. But, he was becoming painfully aware of his own mortality. The lack of morphine also increased his pain awareness. His chest hurt. He was lightheaded and nauseous.

So what.

The nurse's station was empty. The nurses were tending their patients one last time before shift change. They'd return in moments for paper work. Now was the time.

He stepped out of his room and walked down the deserted hallway. No bells sounded. No buzzers went off. His backside was totally exposed and he was free as a bird.

Halfway down the hallway he found what he was looking for, the supply closet. He stepped inside and closed the door.

Scrubs.

Hospital scrubs. He was hoping for better. The kind the doctors wear. These were the disposable pseudo-cloth kind they give to people to put on over their clothes. He had no clothes. He put them on over his bare skin.

Better than mooning everybody behind me.

His chest and shoulder were wrapped tight in gauze dressing, making it difficult to get the shirt over his head and arms. After struggling for a few minutes he did it. He pulled a flimsy green head covering off the shelf and put it on. He found the smallest size shoe coverings and put them on his feet. He hoped he didn't have to walk very far in them. For good measure, he pulled a mask off the shelf and tried to put it on. He couldn't tie it in the back so he twisted it around and tied it in front. It was too loose. He slid it around and just let the mask part hang like a medical necklace. He hoped he looked like a doctor just come out of surgery.

He cracked open the door and peeked out. The hallway was still empty. He slipped out the door and continued down the hall. He made it out of the unit and found the elevator common area. He pressed the down button. A bell rang. The doors opened. An attractive young girl in green scrubs stepped out. He could see her badge. Ali Hunt. She smiled.

He looked down at his feet and stepped into the elevator. He pressed the main floor button. She looked back at him. The doors closed. His heart was pounding in his chest. His heart was pounding in his ears. His heart was pounding in his temples. He leaned against the wall for support. He heard a beep and the door opened revealing a different floor and a different world.

He stepped out of the elevator. He was near the emergency entrance at the back of the hospital.

Good.

He walked down the hallway. There were quite a few people waiting, staring with blank, greenish faces. He didn't have to work hard to avoid making eye contact. He walked through the automatic double doors and was outside. He made it. Now what.

It was raining.

His paper-based scrubs weren't going to last long in this weather.

A car pulled up and a young man jumped out. The man hurried around the car and opened the passenger side door. He struggled to help a young woman out of the car. She had a very large belly and was grimacing. The man looked pleadingly at Daniel. Their eyes met.

"Help me, please," the young man said. "Our baby...". The woman groaned.

Daniel turned and shuffled quickly back inside.

"We need some help here," he commanded. He was trying to think of all the hospital shows he had seen and what the TV ER people would say. He couldn't think of a single thing.

"Get some people out here, right now," he shouted.

A sleepy looking girl with a badge pinned to her sterile blue smock ambled out from behind a plastic window.

"What's going on?" she asked.

"We've got a pregnant woman in the last stages of labor, bleeding badly. She needs immediate attention." Daniel felt pretty good about his situation assessment skills. The woman woke up instantly. By now, the young man and pregnant woman were coming through the door.

"Help," he called out, trying desperately to help the young woman through the door.

The blue smocked girl slammed a button on the wall. "We have a situation," she shouted as the exam room doors opened. Scrub clad bodies began to scurry. A wheel chair was found for the woman. The young man and the young woman were whisked through the doors. Daniel stepped back against the wall and watched. No one seemed to notice him. The exam room doors closed, but the chaotic shouting continued, muffled behind the doors. Daniel went back out through the automatic double doors. The car was idling, passenger door and driver's door still open.

Daniel closed the passenger door, walked around the vehicle and got in. He pulled the driver's door closed, buckled his seat belt, put the car in gear and drove away.

Just like that.

He was a car thief.

I'm just borrowing it.

He felt guilty.

The needs of the one outweigh the needs of the many.

He suddenly felt very heavy. The drugs in his system were wearing off. His chest was hurting. The seat belt strap pressed against his dressing. The car had an unpleasant, pungent odor. The passenger seat was stained with various bodily fluids.

The poor girl.

He hoped she was OK. The lights of oncoming cars hurt his eyes. He was glad it was dark.

He would return their car. He was sure they wouldn't notice for quite a while. He rolled down the driver's window part way to get some fresh air. The smell inside the car was making him nauseous.

He passed a police patrol car. His heart rate, which had moderated from hospital escape rate, immediately reached maximum training speed. He didn't have his driver's license. He was dressed in scrubs, driving a stolen car, and the passenger's seat was covered in blood. He pulled the surgical hat off his head.

This won't look good.

The patrol car drove past. Air escaped his lungs. He hadn't realized he'd been holding his breath.

It started to rain again. He couldn't find the windshield wipers.

What kind of a car is this?

He didn't recognize the symbol in the center of the steering wheel. It was a foreign car. European.

Probably French.

He fumbled around with various switches and buttons. The windshield wipers banged across the glass in high speed.

He twisted a knob. The blades slowed down.

Metal scratching glass. Rubber flapping in the breeze. He'd have to replace the wiper blades. He'd have the car detailed. The young couple would thank him.

He turned onto his street. He was going home. He couldn't wait to see Julie.

She won't be there.

He drove past his house. Mrs. Thorson's asleep.

Wishful thinking.

He didn't know what else to do. He hadn't planned his escape that far in advance. He knew Julie and Jenny wouldn't be there. They hadn't come to see him in the hospital. In fact, no one even mentioned them. No one asked about them. He had a bad feeling.

He drove around the block. If he drove past his house too many times, Thorson would notice.

Just one more time.

He turned off the headlights and drove slowly. He wanted to see if anyone was watching his house.

How would I know if they were?

The house looked dark. Empty. Cold.

Where are they?

He pulled into the driveway. He jumped out of the car and pressed the garage door keypad. The door began to raise. He jumped back in the car and drove into the garage, hoping no one was looking. He jumped out quickly and closed the garage door.

He was home.

It was a hollow victory.

He opened the door and went into the kitchen. The house was dark, and quiet. He flipped on the light.

"Hello," he shouted. "Anyone home?"

His words disappeared into the silence. An empty house is a lonely place. Echoes of the life that once was haunt the space between the walls.

"Hello, Daniel." She stepped through the veil.

"Sarah," he said, matter-of-factly.

He wasn't surprised. He was no longer startled by supernatural appearances. He was getting used to it. He seemed to have some ability to comprehend the incomprehensible, the life beyond this life. Sarah had become a part of his life.

She's dead.

He walked past her into the hallway, then up the stairs. She could follow him, if she wanted.

"How are you doing?" she asked.

Daniel stopped, halfway up the stairs. She stood at the bottom, looking up.

"How am I doing?" he said in amazement. "How am I doing? You're dead. I thought you could read my mind. How am I doing?" He turned and finished his climb. He went into the bedroom, exhausted, flipped on the light and pulled off his scrub shirt. He went through the bathroom into the walk-in closet, turning on the lights as he went. He was chasing the darkness away. He dropped his scrub pants. He was naked. She was there. He didn't care.

"I'm truly sorry," she said.

"You've said that," he said, pulling open his underwear drawer.

"I thought I could help," she said. "I needed to."

"I don't want your help," he said, shaking his briefs at her.

She laughed.

He realized his nakedness and put the briefs on.

"I've learned so much, since I've been dead," she said.

He pulled a shirt off the rack and slipped his arm inside.

"Really? Then why don't you go where all the other dead people go?" he said sarcastically.

"I will," she said. "When I finish my mission."

"I thought you had to finish your mission in this life," he said, fumbling with the buttons.

"You do," she said.

"Then how is that you still get to," he said.

"No, I mean, you do," she said. "You do."

"Me?"

"You."

"Right." He pulled on a pair of jeans.

"Seriously," she said. "You have a mission to perform. You have a purpose in life."

Daniel grabbed a pair of socks out of the drawer, picked up his shoes and walked out of the closet into the bathroom. Sarah was standing in the way. He didn't give her time to move and she didn't attempt to. He walked right through her. They both shivered. They both felt something.

"What is it?" he asked. He turned around to look at her. They were standing close.

"I don't know," she said. "I felt…warm."

"No, not that," he said. "What is my mission? You seem to know so much."

"It should be pretty obvious," she said.

"Not to me," he said. "What is it?"

"I can't tell you," she said.

"You can't tell me?" he said, getting frustrated. He sat down on the bathtub edge and put his socks on.

"I can't tell you, but I can help you," she said.

He tied his shoes and stood up. He passed through her once again into the closet. They both felt it.

"Then help me now," he said, turning off the closet light. "Where are they?"

191

Chapter 45

The Escalade came to a stop. The engine went silent. The driver's door opened and closed. Julie looked at Jenny. Sleeping.

Amazing.

They were both on the floor. It wasn't comfortable. Julie's legs had gone to sleep. Her neck ached. Her wrists and ankles were duct taped. She had duct tape over her mouth. Her nose was stuffed up from the dirt on the floor mats. Allergies. She had to fight the panic that she might suffocate.

Jenny was sleeping.

Thank God.

It was still dark outside even though they had been driving for hours

The passenger door opened.

"Get up," Bad commanded.

Julie looked up at him and gave him her most sarcastic glare. He didn't notice.

"I said, get up." Bad reached out and grabbed Julie's hair. He yanked her to a sitting position and then pulled her out of the Escalade. She fell, awkwardly, onto gravel. The rocky ground scraped her elbows and knees.

"Get out," Bad shouted at Jenny.

The little girl obeyed; sleep quickly disappearing from her puffy eyes.

Julie struggled to a sitting position and held her duct taped wrists and ankles out to Bad. He pulled a knife from his pocket and opened it up.

He looked at the blade, then looked at Julie. He smiled. She glared. He sliced the tape between her ankles. The knife was sharp. It easily passed through the layers of tape, also cutting through her jeans and just missing her ankles. He smiled again. She held her wrists out to him. He grabbed them and yanked her to her feet. Jenny quickly moved in behind her.

"Do not speak," Bertrum said.

Julie cocked her head and glared. Her mouth was still taped.

"Do exactly as I say," he said. He reached for her face and ripped the tape off. Julie groaned and put her hands to her face.

"Mommy," Jenny said, clinging to Julie.

"Shut up," Bad said. "Follow me."

He strode quickly across a tree-lined gravel parking lot toward a rundown ranch style house. As they approached the house, Julie could see the shingle hanging from the weathered eve above the door, 'Chelan Valley Animal Hospital'.

"That's appropriate," Julie said.

Bad stopped. He spun around and thrust his opened knife against her throat. His other hand held the back of her head, pressing it against the blade. Jenny clung to her leg, shivering. The knifepoint forced Julie's head back against Bad's large hand.

"I said be quiet." Bad pressed his body against her. Julie kept her eyes open, defiant. Bad bent his head and nuzzled her ear with his nose, breathing deeply. He licked her ear with his tongue. Julie shuddered. He pressed the blade harder into her throat.

"Do you want it to end this way? With your daughter watching?"

"No," Julie rasped.

"Then be quiet," Bad said.

Julie nodded her head, ever so slightly. Bad pressed just a bit. The knifepoint drew a spot of blood. He withdrew the knife and held it so she could see it. He licked the blood from the blade and smiled. Julie felt nauseous.

Bad stepped behind Julie and Jenny and pushed them at the house.

There were no lights on inside. He rang the doorbell.

Silence.

"Nobody's home," Jenny said.

"Shut her up," Bad commanded. He rang the doorbell again.

Julie whispered, "be quiet," to Jenny.

Silence.

Bad rang the doorbell again, twice.

Scuffling inside.

Closer scuffling. Light in the window.

The door opened. A portly man with a large round bald spot held the door open with one hand and held a disheveled bathrobe closed with the other. He was successful with the door hand.

"Do you know what time it is?" the fat man groused. "We don't open for…"

"Master Mahan requires your service," Bad said.

The man froze, momentarily. He looked over the threesome, annoyance changing to anxiety. Bertrum held out his left hand. The man took it. Both men put their right hands on each other's shoulders. Bertrum smiled.

"Come in," the man said. "Quickly."

He held the door open wide with both hands, unconcerned that his bathrobe was wide open. Bad stepped through the door, followed by Julie and Jenny.

"What are you doing here? You should know better than this? Why'd you bring them here?" The fat man switched off the lights. He was about to hyperventilate.

"Calm down," Bad said. "This shouldn't take long." He unbuttoned his shirt.

Outside, the eastern sky was lightening.

Inside, Julie's eyes were adjusting. She could see the blood stained bandages awkwardly taped to Bad's chest. First aid wasn't one of his skill sets. She felt good about that.

"My God," the fat man said. "What happened?"

"I need you to fix it," Bad said. He dropped his shirt on a dreary sofa.

"I'm a vet, not a surgeon," he said.

"I was told you could do this, have done this," Bad said.

"Yes, but…"

Bad pulled his gun and pointed it at the fat man.

"You will do this," Bad said.

The fat man stared at Bad. "What about them?" he finally asked.

"I have plans for them," Bad said.

The fat man looked at Julie and then at Jenny. In the dim morning light, she thought she saw sadness.

"Follow me," the man said. He gathered his robe about his large frame and walked out of the living room. Bad motioned with his gun for Julie and Jenny to follow and the trio left the room.

Chapter 46

Detectives Sears and Schwartz ambled into the forensics office amidst a flurry of activity. It was early, and it was evident from Schwartz's hairstyle that he hadn't had time to take a shower. The paramedics were just preparing to wheel Michael Wu's body out of the tiny office.

"Is he dead?" Schwartz asked, flashing his badge at the paramedic.

"Catatonic," the paramedic replied.

Sears and Schwartz stepped closer to look. Michael's eyes were open. He appeared to be looking at something.

"Drugs?" Sears asked.

"Can't tell," the paramedic said. "They'll run tests at the hospital."

The two paramedics wheeled him out.

A lab coat came out of Michael's office. She had short brown hair and glasses. Schwartz smoothed his hair back. He was captivated by the curves beneath the coat.

"What happened?" Sears asked, giving Schwartz a dirty look.

"You guys should see this," she said walking past them. She opened a small closet door. Inside the closet, a small flat screen monitor rested on top of a DVR. The woman pressed a button. The screen came to life. There were four images, in quadrants, on the screen; the parking lot, the office exterior, the foyer and the interior offices. The interior office quadrant was switching between offices at regular intervals. Sears and

Schwartz could see the paramedics loading Michael's body into the ambulance in one corner of the screen.

"Live shot," Sears said.

"You're good," Schwartz said.

The woman began pressing buttons on a switcher next to the DVR.

"I'm awake," Sears said.

"I was out late last night," Schwartz said.

"Really," Sears said. "With who?"

"With whom," Schwartz said.

"That's what I asked," Sears said.

"Gentlemen," the woman broke in. "Take a look at the monitor."

The quadrant view switched to a full frame view. Michael Wu was sitting at his computer. Two men were looking over his shoulder.

"Hey," Sears said. "That's us."

"We're TV stars," Schwartz said.

"This is the security cam of Mike's office from last night," the woman said.

"Obviously," Sears said.

"What's your name, Sweetheart?" Schwartz asked.

"Personal question," Sears said.

"And I'd like a personal answer," Schwartz said.

The woman ignored them both and pressed fast forward. Sears and Schwartz ran out of Michael's office like keystone cops. A few other co-workers came in and out quickly.

"I've never seen you move so fast," Sears said.

"You should have seen me last night," Schwartz said.

"I just did," Sears said.

The woman pressed play and the speed returned to normal.

"This is time index 11:59 p.m." she said. "Everything appears to be normal."

"11:59. Doesn't he ever go home?" Schwartz said.

"He lives with his parents," Sears said.

"Mike is passionate about his work. He is the smartest man I've ever known," the woman said.

"I see," Schwartz said.

"What do you see?" Sears asked.

"Miss...Lab Coat here, and Mr. Smartest Man have a thing going on," Schwartz said.

The woman pressed pause on the DVR and turned to Schwartz.

"Can I see your ID?" She demanded.

"Why?" Schwartz asked.

"Because I'm finding it hard to believe you're really detectives," She said.

"Why's that?" Schwartz asked.

"Because I feel like I'm trapped in a really bad comedy sketch on SC TV," she said.

"She thinks we're funny," Sears said.

Schwartz flashed his badge.

"Unbelievable," she said and turned back to the DVR and pressed play. "Watch closely."

Michael was typing furiously. He looked up at the screen. He went back to typing. He looked up at the screen.

"I'm watching," Sears said.

"Just a moment," the woman said. "See. Right there."

Michael stopped typing and leaned closer to the screen. His lips moved.

"So what?" Schwartz said. "He stopped typing."

"He's talking to someone," she said.

"How do you know?" Schwartz asked.

"Watch his lips," she said.

"Do you have audio?" Sears asked.

"No," the woman said.

"What's he saying?" Schwartz asked.

"How am I supposed to know what he's saying?" the woman said.

"You're the forensic expert," Schwartz said.

"That doesn't mean I read lips," she said. She hit pause, then rewind, then play, then pause, rewind, play.

"Who does?" Schwartz said. "Don't you have a lip reading expert?"

"No, we don't have a lip reading expert?" she said.

"OK boys and girls," Sears said. "Let's get back to business. What's he saying, and why is it important?"

"Didn't I just ask that?" Schwartz said. "I did ask that."

"I don't know," she said. "We don't have a good shot of his face. But, watch. This is the good part." She let the video run past the previous section.

"See. Right there," she said.

"No, I don't see," Schwartz said. She hit pause, rewind, play. Schwartz leaned closer. They were staring at the monitor, cheek to cheek, leaving Sears to look over and between them.

"Did you see that?" she asked, breathlessly.

"See what?" Schwartz said.

"I can't see a thing. You two love birds are fogging up the monitor," Sears said.

Schwartz and the woman immediately backed away from the monitor. Her cheeks flushed.

"Watch his hand," she said, pressing pause, rewind, play. "There."

Michael Wu reached up and touched the computer screen.

"So what?" Schwartz said. She hit rewind, then play. "Look closely."

Michael Wu repeated the action. It was the same moment in time. He reached up to touch the screen with his hand.

"I'll be damned," Schwartz said.

"You see?" the woman said, leaning in to the screen.

"What?" Sears said. "I can't see it."

Schwartz leaned in to the screen. They were touching. She didn't mind. She played the segment again.

"Watch his hand," she said.

Michael Wu reached up to touch the screen. His hand seemed to disappear into the monitor, up to his wrist. It only lasted for a moment. He sat up straight then fell back against his chair.

"That's how we found him, this morning," she said, straightening up.

"Electric shock?" Schwartz asked.

"Don't think so," she said.

"Was the screen broken?" Schwartz asked.

"Nope," she said.

"What was on the screen?" Schwartz asked.

"Screen saver," she said.

"What'd it look like?" Schwartz asked.

"Just some video game cityscapes," she said. "Michael played a lot of video games."

"Do you think he was playing video games?" Sears asked.

"No," she said, emphatically.

"How do you know?" Sears demanded.

"Because it was just a screen saver," she said.

"Did you hit the space bar?" Sears said sarcastically.

"Pressing a little hard, aren't you?" Schwartz said. He and the woman exchanged knowing glances.

"I'm not the one doing the pressing," Sears said.

"What's that supposed to mean," Schwartz said.

"You know what it means," Sears said.

"Gentlemen," the woman interrupted. "We did look at what was on the screen."

"What was it?" Sears asked. "What'd it say?"

"Restricted access. Please enter your password."

Chapter 47

Daniel was driving for the mountains on I-90 East. He felt like speeding. He felt an overwhelming sense of urgency. Traffic was heavy. He could not believe how slow everyone was driving.

He changed lanes.

He wished that shortsighted government leaders had raised the speed limit to 80 miles-per-hour. He heard there was no speed limit in Montana.

He changed lanes, again.

He was nervous to still be driving the young couple's car. He hoped they hadn't discovered it was missing yet. He didn't want to call attention to himself so he tried to keep his speed at a consistent 72 m.p.h. He couldn't find the cruise control and the Euro-car he was driving was generic enough to be invisible, he hoped.

He hit the brakes and changed lanes again. Traffic was too heavy.

He felt bad for the couple having the baby. He hoped everything went OK. When this was all over, he would have their car detailed and return it to them. For now, it was his only means of transportation. He had no idea where his car was.

Daniel took the freeway exit for Carnation. The two-lane artery was less crowded. Somewhere along the way he would find the capillary leading to the BAD rusty mountain torture chamber.

Hurry up.

He felt frustration building. Road rage. He had a gun.

"Are you prepared to use it?" Sarah said. She appeared in the passenger seat next to him. She didn't seem to mind the stains on the seat.

Daniel swerved, stepped on the brake, stepped on the gas. Someone honked.

"Idiot," Daniel hollered.

Sarah laughed, like music.

"Couldn't you give a little more notice when you're going to pop in?" he said.

"Sorry," she said, smiling.

"Are they there?" Daniel asked.

"No," Sarah said.

"What?" Daniel shouted. "Where are they?"

"Not there," Sarah said.

"You just said that." Daniel thought he would hyperventilate. He pulled into the emergency lane and stopped the car.

"You shouldn't be here," Sarah said with some urgency.

"Oh really," Daniel said, trying to emphasize the sarcasm.

"No Daniel, don't stop here," Sarah said.

"Why not?" Daniel asked.

"I don't know," Sarah said. "Go. Hurry."

Daniel put the car in gear and drove back onto the two-lane road, just as a Carnation patrol car drove past in the opposite direction. Sarah twisted to see if the patrol car turned around to follow him. It didn't.

Daniel looked over at Sarah. She was facing the back seat and listening intently as if someone were talking to her. Daniel looked in the rear-view mirror. A pretty brown haired woman sat in the back seat. Her lips were moving, but he couldn't hear anything. He turned around to see her. The back seat was empty. The roadside turtles began to sing. He swerved back into his lane.

"Lake Chelan," Sarah said, turning to face him. "We need to go to Lake Chelan."

Daniel looked in the rear-view mirror again. The back seat was empty.

"What just happened?" Daniel asked.

"I know where they are," Sarah said.

"Who was that?"

"Elizabeth."

"Elizabeth who?"

"BAD's latest victim. You have to hurry."

Daniel turned onto the highway and stepped on the gas.

Chapter 48

The fat man opened the door into a veterinary surgical room. He switched on the light and a flat stainless steel table glinted with anticipation. The walls were green tile and the floor had a large drain in the center. It was cold inside.

"Wait in here," the fat man motioned to Bad.

"What about them?" Bad asked.

"I have a place for them," the fat man said.

Bad reached out and grabbed the fat man by his robe, yanking him close.

"Be careful, fat man. I have plans for them," Bad said.

The fat man recoiled from the smell of Bad's breath.

"Don't worry," he said. "I won't interfere with your plans."

"In fact," Bad smiled, "I may just use this room."

He held the fat man close, deliberately breathing in his face.

"Do you want me to fix you up, or not," the fat man said.

Bad leered at the fat man then shoved him back.

"Do it," Bad said.

"Wait on the table," the fat man said.

Bad waltzed over to the table and slid his hand lovingly over the shiny steel surface.

"I'll be here," he said. "Hurry back."

The fat man shook his head with contempt.

"This way," he said, to Julie and Jenny.

He led them down the hallway and opened another door.

"In here," he said, switching on a light. Small dogs began to yap as Julie and Jenny stepped inside a kennel.

"Mommy, puppies," Jenny said with sudden delight.

Julie marveled at Jenny's ability to find joy in an instant.

"Don't touch anything," the fat man growled.

Jenny ran over to the cages to play with the excited pups.

"You don't have to do this," Julie said.

The fat man was closing the door. Julie held it open.

"He plans to kill us," she said.

The fat man looked at her but didn't speak.

"He's an evil, psychopathic, rapist, killer," Julie continued. "And you're going to help him?"

The fat man hesitated.

"You don't understand," he said.

"You're right. I don't. You protect and care for animals, yet you're going to let him kill us." Julie held his gaze with an icy stare. "He's going to kill you, too.

"He can't," the fat man said.

"Why not?" Julie demanded.

"They won't let him," he said.

"Who won't let him?"

"Society."

"Society? He spits on society. He does what ever he wants. He's out of control."

"Not society. THE Society. Our secret society," the fat man said. "Once you're in…" His eyes glazed momentarily. "They won't let him do it."

"What are you're talking about?"

"I've said too much, already." The Fat Man turned to go. Julie grabbed the door.

"They can't stop him. And you won't," Julie said. "Help us, please."

"You're beyond help." The FAT Man shuddered, faintly.

"He's more than just bad," Julie said. "He's evil."

"I'm sorry," the fat man said. "So am I. Now shut up and get in there."

The FAT Man stepped through the threshold and closed the door. Julie heard the lock click.

Chapter 49

Bertrum took off his shirt and climbed onto the stainless steel surgery table. He lay down and folded his hands across his chest, deadman casket style. The cold steel table against his bare skin was remarkably comforting, and refreshing. He closed his eyes.

The visions began, again.

He was naked. On an alter. Surrounded by women.

He loved women. He loved to use and abuse them.

He felt his arousal grow.

Elizabeth stepped up to the alter. She looked lovely.

"Nice dress," Bertrum said.

"I'm glad you like it," Elizabeth giggled. The other women ran their fingers across a chalkboard. Bertrum cringed.

Elizabeth pulled a long shiny knife from the folds of her dress. She raised the knife up.

Bertrum couldn't move. He tried. His limbs were frozen.

She sliced.

At first, Bertrum felt cold, coldness in his loins. Then fire. Pain.

Elizabeth giggled.

"He won't be using that again," she said.

The women laughed.

The pain spread down his legs and up, into his chest.

Elizabeth glared down at him triumphantly.

He reached out to grab her by the neck.

"What are you doing?" the fat man said, recoiling.

Bertrum opened his eyes. He felt his crotch. He pants were still on. He still had all his parts. He sat up. The fat man stepped back. Bertrum felt his chest. It hurt. The bandages were missing.

"That's a nasty stab wound," the fat man said.

"What are you doing?" Bertrum demanded. The fat man was holding a hypodermic needle.

"Giving you a local," the fat man said, showing Bertrum the needle.

"No…anesthetic…" Bertrum managed to say.

The fat man looked at Bertrum with curiosity.

"Suit yourself," he said. He put the needle down on a steel tray.

"Suture self?" Bertrum said, closing his eyes.

The fat man looked at Bertrum strangely. "You're in pretty bad shape."

Bertrum opened his eyes and grabbed the fat man's wrist. "Stitches."

"I think I'll start with some pictures,' the fat man said. "See if the knife hit any vitals." Bertrum let go of his wrist.

The fat man pulled a small animal x-ray machine away from the wall and positioned it above Bertrum's chest. He slid some film into a drawer in the table and stepped behind a barrier.

Click.

He stepped out from the barrier, removed the film, put it in a machine that looked like a large printer and returned to the table.

"So," he said, casually, "what you got planned for the woman and the little girl."

"Do you know who I am?" Bertrum asked, his eyes still closed.

"No," the fat man lied.

"Have you seen my work?" Bertrum asked.

"No," the fat man lied again.

"Will you kill to get gain and conceal it from the world?" Bertrum asked.

The fat man shuddered. He'd heard these words before. He knew their intent. He had answered these questions already. He regretted it. He could not take his answers back. He could not undo what he had done.

Bertrum opened his eyes and looked up at the aging veterinarian.

"Yes," the fat man said with great weariness.

Bertrum lay back down on the table and closed his eyes.

"I am a Master of the Secret," Bertrum said. "My plans are my own."

"Yes, but…"

"MY PLANS ARE MY OWN," Bertrum shouted, sitting up again.

"Calm down," the fat man soothed.

Bertrum stared at the Vet with vengeance. He would include this fat man in his plans.

"Calm down," the man said, again.

Bertrum lay back down. He felt calmed. The fat man had that effect. He was probably quite good with wild animals.

The fat man pulled the film from the machine and held it up to the light.

"Looks like you're pretty lucky," he said.

"I have power," Bertrum said. "I don't need luck."

"The knife appears to have gone right through the intercostal space near the manubrium."

"Speak English," Bertrum barked.

"You have a partially punctured lung. That's where most of the pain and pressure is coming from."

"Can you fix it?" Bertrum asked, sitting up again.

A little deeper and you would have real trouble breathing," the fat man said.

"Can you fix it?" Bertrum demanded.

A bit deeper than that and you'd have bled out," the fat man continued.

"Are you listening to me, fat man? CAN YOU FIX IT?" Bertrum shouted.

"You need to go to the hospital," the fat man said. "You need to have surgery to repair the damage."

"DO IT," Bertrum yelled, looking eagerly around the room.

"Are you crazy?" the fat man asked. "I'm a vet, not a surgeon."

"They said you could fix it," Bertrum said.

"They have an inflated opinion of my skills," the fat man said.

"You do surgeries in here," Bertrum said.

"On small dogs and cats," the fat man said.

Bertrum slid his legs off the table and fell to a standing position.

"Dogs and cats," Bertrum said.

"That's right," the fat man said, tentatively.

"That's not all you operate on in here, is it," Bertrum said, wickedly.

The fat man cringed.

Bertrum smiled. He lifted himself back up onto the table.

"We all have our gifts," he said. "Our talents. Some more than others. Others more than most." He lay back down on the table. "Fix me up and I may let you live."

The fat man stood, motionless.

"Try anything…unusual…" Bertrum said, reflectively, "…and I'll demonstrate my own gifts with a scalpel, on you…for you, I meant to say." Bertrum chuckled, then wheezed, in pain.

The fat man still didn't move.

"Come on," Bertrum said. "Let's get this party started. You don't have all day."

The fat man stepped up to the washbasin, turned on the hot water and began to scrub his flabby arms.

Chapter 50

Detectives Sears and Schwartz sat across the desk of FBI Western Region Section Chief Carson Greer. Chief Greer was talking on the phone. The conversation wasn't pleasant. Sears and Schwartz were amused.

"Get back to me when you've got something," the Chief snapped. He pressed a button on the phone. "Lois, get me Sheriff Jasper Clawson from Carnation on the line." The speakerphone squawked in Soprano.

"I'll have fries with mine," Sears said.

"Make mine a combo," Schwartz said.

"Very funny," the Chief said, hanging up.

"Dead end?" Sears asked.

"Road block," the Chief said. "Our guys at Langley can't get in."

"Is that normal?" Schwartz asked.

"Do you secret agent types play together?" Sears asked.

"Sometimes," Chief Greer said. "And no, this isn't normal."

The phone squawked again. Chief Greer pressed a button and picked up the phone.

"Sheriff, Carson Greer, FBI. Can I put you on speaker?" The Chief pressed another button.

"Chief Greer, what can I do for you?" the Sheriff's thin voice drawled.

"Sheriff, what can you tell us about Bertrum Alexander Davis?"

"We can't find him. I can tell you that," Sheriff Clawson said.

"We can't find his service record," Chief Greer said.

"Bert's been a good deputy," Sheriff Clawson said. "Kept a low profile."

"How long's he been working for you?" the Chief asked.

"Two years."

"Where'd he work before that?"

"Don't know," the Sheriff said.

"What do you mean, you don't know?" Chief Greer exclaimed.

"Just what I said. I don't know," the Sheriff repeated.

"Why don't you know?" Chief Greer asked.

"Is this some sort of interrogation?" Sheriff Clawson drawled. "Who you got there with you?"

"Hey Sheriff," Sears said.

"Top 'O the morning, Chief."

"Mutt and Jeff," Sheriff Clawson said.

"Detectives Sears and Schwartz," Chief Greer said.

"We're doing our damnedest to find our boy," Sheriff Clawson said. "He called in sick yesterday. We haven't been able to find him since."

"Why don't you know where he worked before he worked for you?" Chief Greer drilled.

"Suits," Sheriff Clawson said.

"Suits," Chief Greer repeated.

"That's what I said," Sheriff Clawson said.

"Sheriff, we're not in the same room with you. It's a little hard to know what you mean," Chief Greer said.

"I know what he means," Schwartz said.

"So do I," Sears said.

"Enlighten me," Chief Greer said.

"I was told to hire him," the Sheriff said.

"By who?" Chief Greer asked.

"By whom," Sears said. The Chief ignored him.

"Suits," Sheriff Clawson said. "Feds. Guys like you."

"FBI?" Chief Greer asked.

"Looked like it, but no," the Sheriff said. "Said they were from OSI."

"OSI?" the Chief said. "Did you check them out?"

"Do you think I'm stupid?" the Sheriff said.

"He probably shouldn't answer that," Sears said.

"Don't answer that, Chief."

"Well?" the Chief asked.

"They checked out," the Sheriff said. "I had a bad feeling, then. But, Bert's done alright."

"Did you see his service record?" the Chief asked.

"No," the Sheriff said. "They said I didn't need to see his record."

"And you didn't question that?" the Chief asked.

"These aren't the kind of guys you question, if you know what I mean."

"OSI?" the Chief repeated.

"That's right," the Sheriff said.

"What's that stand for?"

"Office of Special Investigations."

"Never heard of it," the Chief said.

"Check 'em out," the Sheriff said.

"Don't worry, I will," the Chief said.

"Good," the Sheriff said.

"Good," the Chief said.

"Bad," Sears said.

"I agree," Schwartz said.

Chief Greer pressed a button on the phone and the speaker clicked off.

"That's the biggest load of crap I've heard in a long time," he said.

"I've heard bigger," Sears said.

The Chief picked up the phone.

"Lois, get me the director of the Office of Special Investigations." The phone squawked. "I don't know. Do some investigation." He slammed down the phone. "I think we're going to join this investigation."

"Good," Sears said.

"Bad," Schwartz said. "Really bad."

Chapter 51

Julie tried the door handle. It was locked. She tried it again, knowing it was locked. She shook it. The slight rattle of the door was magnified in the shudder, which shook her body. She could feel the tears welling.

"Mommy, look at the cute puppy," Jenny chirped.

Julie wiped her eyes, then her nose. She would not cry. She would be strong, at least for Jenny.

Oh God, help us.

Julie turned around to face her daughter. Jenny had her fingers stuck in the cage of a very cute Cocker Spaniel. The Spaniel was licking her fingers. Julie marveled at her daughter's ability to live in the moment. Jenny took delight wherever she was. Julie wished she could share the moment with her daughter. She couldn't. She knew too much. She knew too little. She had no answers to questions she couldn't begin to frame.

Why?

"He likes me," Jenny said.

Julie tried to smile. She looked around the room, searching for some means to escape. There was none. The walls were lined with cages. The cages were filled with animals. The door was locked. The only door. No windows.

No escape.

"Can I play with him?" Jenny asked.

"Sure, honey," Julie said, without thinking.

Jenny unfastened the lock on the cage and opened the door. At first, the Spaniel drew back, away from the door, shivering. Jenny reached into the cage and touched the dog. It wagged its tale. It licked her fingers. It began to pant. Its front paws hung over the edge of the cage.

"Come on girl," Jenny encouraged.

The Spaniel leaped into Jenny's arms. She giggled joyfully. The Spaniel wasn't big, but neither was Jenny. The dog filled her arms and practically swamped the little girl. Tongue and tail and paws and fur. Jenny found her soul mate.

"Can I keep him, Mommy?" Jenny said, amidst the soggy dog kisses. "Please?"

"No," Julie said.

"But Mom, look at her," Jenny said. "She loves me."

"She's just glad to be out of her cage," Julie said.

Julie watched her daughter hold the Spaniel. They were fast friends.

"Her name is pearl," Jenny said.

Julie was looking around the room for something, anything that might help them escape. "That's nice," she said, absently.

In the movies, this room would have a window, or an oversized air conditioning duct. Julie would have Special Forces spy training to handle any situation. She would crack open the window or climb into the duct and escape before the evil villain knew about it. She would move to a small island in the Caribbean and home school her daughter and they would live happily ever after.

Daniel.

There was no happily ever after this.

Oh Daniel.

She could see him lying there in the driveway. His eyes were open, apologizing.

He was always apologizing. Julie realized that most of the time he didn't have anything to apologize for. She just made him feel like it. She wanted him to apologize. She wasn't sure what for.

The force of this vision, Daniel, bleeding, was overwhelming. It pressed on her. She couldn't breathe. She couldn't stand. She slid to the floor. She was crying.

The Cocker Spaniel climbed onto her lap. It began licking her tears, her face. She didn't mind animals. She liked cats. Dogs had bad breath.

"She likes you," Jenny said, sitting by her Mother.

Julie wiped her face. It was sloppy wet.

"How are we going to get out of this place?" Julie said to Pearl.

The dog's floppy ears stood up. Her bushy tail swished back and forth. She looked Julie right in the eye. Julie had the distinct impression the dog understood her need and had an idea.

"I don't speak dog," Julie said.

The Spaniel licked her face.

"Sorry," Julie said.

Pearl hopped off her lap and ran to Jenny. Jenny held the dog's jowls between her hands. No words were spoken. Her daughter and the dog were staring at each other. Unmoving. Julie watched with fascination.

Telepathy?

"She wants us to open all the cages," Jenny said.

"Right," Julie said. "She told you that."

"She did, Mommy," Jenny said. "Really."

Other dogs, in other cages began to bark. There were also cats, meowing.

"There must be sixty cages in here," Jenny said. "If we let them all out, the place will be trashed." The noise level was increasing dramatically. The animals had a sense something was happening.

Pearl ran back and forth from Jenny to Julie, whining.

"She wants us to hurry," Jenny said.

The past several days had been surreal and supernatural. Normally Julie would not have believed that her daughter could actually understand and communicate with animals.

Why not?

Pearl ran to the far corner of the room and barked. Jenny followed her. Julie followed Jenny. Behind a stack of large steel cages was a door.

Pearl whined.

"Mommy, a door."

Julie looked closer.

It was a door.

"Open the cages," Julie said.

"Oh boy," Jenny exclaimed.

The bottom cage in the stack held a black dog. A BIG black dog. Julie didn't know her breeds, but this was not a dog she would want to meet alone. If she saw this dog on the street, she would cross to the other side to avoid it. This was the kind of dog that gave dogs bad names. This dog was the kind of dog that would bite you, just because.

Jenny opened the cage. Julie stepped back.

What kind of a Mother am I?

"Be careful," Julie said.

The dog didn't move. It was a big black lethargic dog.

"Come here, boy," Jenny said.

The dog's tail slapped against the cage once. It raised its head.

"Come on, boy. You can do it," Jenny said.

The dog rose to its feet and wobbled out of the cage.

"How long have you been in there?" Julie said.

The dog was taller than Jenny. She put her arms around it. Its tail began to wag in earnest. The dog looked taller. It was gaining energy from Jenny's hug.

Julie undid the latch on the next cage up. Golden Retriever. There was a nameplate on the cage.

Molly.

Molly whined and fussed and pawed and clawed. Golden's rarely lack for energy. Molly was no exception. Julie pulled open the cage door. Molly leapt out and hit the floor, sliding and scuffling for balance. She immediately nuzzled Jenny, pushing against the big black mutt. Jenny put her arms around both dogs.

The next cage was stacked on the other two, at eye level. Julie looked inside. A little dog bared its teeth and yapped.

Chihuahua.

Julie expected the skinny dog to bark with a Spanish accent. She reached into the cage to grab the dog. It cowered in fear, quivering in the back of the cage. Julie pulled the dog out of the cage and set it on the floor. It joined the other two dogs.

Julie pulled the cages away from the wall to gain access to the concealed door. Without the dogs, the cages weren't that heavy, and they weren't secured in place. Julie tried the doorknob. It turned. She pulled. The door opened. It was dark inside. She reached in and flipped a switch against the wall.

No hope.

No escape.

Illumination revealed the room was a tiny supply closet, equipped with mop, bucket, basin and cleaning supplies.

Now what?

Jenny was talking to the three dogs. She jumped up and began to open the other cages. Some dogs jumped out. Some dogs ran out. Some dogs didn't move. Most dogs began to bark and yap. They followed her around the room. On the opposite side of the room were the cat's cages. Jenny opened their cages.

Some cats hissed. Some meowed. Some arched. Some watched, unimpressed by the dog cacophony. A few jumped out of their cages and onto cabinets or shelves. The noise grew and grew.

They're going to hear.

"Jenny, come here," Julie said, over the noise.

Jenny ran over to her Mother. "Isn't it great, Mommy?"

"Get inside," Julie said, practically shoving Jenny into the supply closet.

Julie got inside and tried to pull the cages back in place. They wouldn't go all the way back.

It'll have to do.

The big black dog came over to the door and tried to nuzzle its way in.

Jenny took the big dog by the jowls and said some words Julie could not hear above the cacophony. The big dog turned and trotted away. Julie pulled the door almost closed just as the main door opened. The big black dog's deep angry bark reverberated above the noise. The other animals growled and howled and hissed. The animals charged for the door. A voice called out.

"What the…"

The animals swarmed the fat man, knocking him down. Dogs were biting and cats were scratching. Once he hit the floor he didn't have much of a chance. Julie looked away, pulling the door tighter.

The noise rose to a swell.

The man screamed.

The tumultuous noise receded. Then it was gone.

Silence.

Julie's heart was beating in her chest. She could hear it, in the darkness.

"Mommy?" Jenny said. Julie could feel her little girl clinging to her leg.

"Yes, Sweetheart," Julie whispered.

"What happened? Where's Pearl?" Jenny asked. Her small voice in the darkness was hopeful.

"I don't know," Julie said, honestly.

"Can we go see?" Jenny asked.

Julie pushed the door open just a crack. She couldn't see much. The room was still. The outer door was open. She pulled the inner door closed.

"Let's just wait here for a little longer," Julie said.

When you're afraid, darkness can taste better than light. Julie was fighting her fear. Adrenaline had kept her going. Holding the door closed would not keep the fear away. Darkness breeds fear. Her fear was growing.

"I don't like it in here," Jenny said.

"Shhhh," Julie whispered. She listened. The room was silent. The darkness made sounds she could only feel.

She pushed the door open, slightly.

Silence.

She waited.

She pushed the door again. The door met the metal cages. The sound was enormous. Julie knew he could hear. She pulled the door closed.

Maybe not.

She pushed the door open again. She would have to push the cages to get out. It would make noise.

Now or never.

Never.

"Mommy. I have to go to the bathroom."

Now.

Julie pushed against the door. The room was small enough that she could use the wall as leverage.

Bench press.

Julie was never really strong, but she was fit, athletic.

The cages resisted.

She pushed harder.

The metal began to slide on the tile floor. The sound was hideous. Fingernails on chalkboard hideous. Julie shuddered. The demons were screaming.

Just enough.

The door was open just enough for them to get out. The flickering green fluorescent lighting was better than blackness. By just a little.

Julie took Jenny's hand and stepped out of the closet. She stood there in the empty room expecting something to happen.

Nothing did.

The door was open. There was blood on the floor near the door, but no body. The blood was smeared into the hallway.

Julie gagged and turned away. She turned Jenny away.

"Mommy, I have to go," Jenny said.

"So do I," Julie said.

She took Jenny's hand and led her out of the room.

"Watch where you step," she said.

They walked down the hall, boldly. Julie found the bathroom and they went in together. Julie locked the door. Jenny went first. Waiting for her daughter, Julie realized she hadn't gone to the bathroom in a very long time. She thought her bladder was going to burst. She pinched her legs together. Jenny didn't seem to be in much of a hurry.

"Hurry up," Julie said clenching.

When Julie sat down she gave thanks for simple things. Relief. Literally.

The toilet flush was powerful, and loud. Julie knew it gave away their presence. Remarkably, he hadn't come looking for them.

She opened the bathroom door and looked out.

Nothing. No one.

Cautiously, she walked down the hallway. The surgical room door was open. She looked inside.

Empty.

Together, they peered around the corner into the living room reception area.

Julie recoiled when she saw him. The fat man. She covered Jenny's eyes and held her back.

His clothes were torn. His body was mangled. His blood was pooling beneath him.

Apparently he was not well liked by his charges.

The front door was open. The animals were gone. Julie could smell...

Toast.

Her stomach growled.

Fifteen feet to freedom.

Then what?

"Don't look at him," Julie said, taking Jenny by the hand.

They stepped into the room. The smell of toast grew stronger.

"Would you like some breakfast?" BAD said.

Julie froze. Ten feet to freedom. She measured the distance with her eyes.

"Don't bother," BAD said. "I would just have to shoot you." He was sitting at the kitchen table, reading the paper. He picked up a handgun and waved it for their benefit.

"How can you eat with him lying there, like that?" Julie said.

Bad took a bite of toast.

"I'm hungry," he said. "You must be, too."

"You disgust me," Julie said.

Bad sopped his toast in runny egg and took another bite.

"I was going to kill him anyway," Bad said. "They just did a better job."

"They?" Julie said.

"The dogs," Bad said. "They didn't like him much, did they?"

Julie was trying to edge her way around the body, towards the door.

"He must have been a pretty lousy vet. But, he did a nice job with my stitches," Bad continued. "It still hurts, thank you very much. But, I feel much better."

"You don't look it," Julie said.

Bad smiled.

"I like you," Bad said.

"You don't know me," Julie said.

"What did you see in him?" Bad said.

"Who?" Julie said.

"Hubby," Bad said. "Your love interest."

Bad scooped dripping bits of poached egg into his mouth.

"Really," he said with runny food in his mouth. "He couldn't have been good in bed. Although, I don't think I have tased anyone more times than him, so maybe he did have some staying power."

"What do you plan to do now?" Julie asked.

Bad wiped his face with a napkin.

"Time to go," he said, standing up. "Let's get in the family tank."

Jenny looked up at Julie.

"Where are we going, this time," Julie said.

"Back to Seattle," Bad said. He waved the gun at them and they went out the door. Bad closed the door behind them.

When they got in the Escalade, Bad duct taped their wrists and ankles, but didn't tape their mouths.

"See," he said. "I'm not such a Bad guy." He laughed at his own joke. "In fact, when the time comes, you'll find I'm pretty good."

Julie suppressed the urge to throw up. As Bad drove out of the parking lot, Jenny leaned over to rest her head on Julie's lap.

Stay alive. For Jenny.

Chapter 52

Daniel pulled into the gravel parking lot of the Chelan Valley Animal Hospital.

"It looks more like a run down house than a hospital," Daniel said.

"They're not here," Sarah said.

Daniel stopped the car. Abruptly. It slid in the gravel.

"What?" he said.

"They're not here," Sarah said.

"I heard what you said," Daniel shouted. He was upset. "You said you knew where they were. You're supposed to be helping me. Now, you tell me they're not here."

The front door of the animal hospital was open. Daniel jumped out of the car and raced to the entrance.

"Daniel, wait," Sarah said to no effect.

Daniel disappeared inside.

The sun was nearing mid-day. The air was clear. The sky was bright blue above greenblack evergreens. The light inside the animal hospital living room entrance was dim. When Daniel dashed inside, it took a few moments for his eyes to adjust. Then, he gagged.

"No," he said, sickly. "No. No. No."

In the middle of the room a mutilated body was draining the last of its precious life fluids. The smell was nauseating.

"I told you to wait," Sarah said, appearing in the dim light.

"You told me they were here," Daniel scorned.

"They were here," Sarah said.

"And now they're not," Daniel said. "Why didn't you tell me that?"

"I can't know what's going to happen," Sarah said.

"You didn't tell me what did happen," Daniel said. "Why not? Maybe we could have caught them. Intercepted them. Something."

Sarah looked Daniel in the eyes. Her gaze was intense. He couldn't look away, yet, he could see through her.

"I," she began, "was…watching you."

"Don't do that," Daniel said. He picked up the phone and dialed 911. "Just leave me alone."

"911 operator. Please state your emergency."

"There's been a murder," Daniel said.

"Please state your location," the operator said.

"I can help you," Sarah said.

"Chelan Valley Animal Hospital," Daniel said.

"What is your name?" the operator asked.

"I don't want your help," Daniel said.

"Excuse me," the 911 operator said.

"Not you. I wasn't talking to you," Daniel said.

"You need my help," Sarah said.

"Is there someone with you?" the 911 Operator asked. "Are you in danger?"

"No," Daniel said. "Yes," he said.

She thinks I'm crazy.

"You should be looking for Bertrum Alexander Davis," Daniel said and hung up. He made a feeble attempt to wipe his fingerprints from the phone. He'd seen criminals do that on TV. It probably didn't work.

I am crazy. Or I'm going crazy.

"No you're not," Sarah said.

"Stop that," he said. "I'm leaving."

"Where're you going?" She asked.

"I don't know," he said. "To find my wife and daughter."

Daniel left the house and got in his car. It was empty. He waited for her to appear.

She didn't.

Good.

He didn't really mean it.

He could hear a siren in the distance.

Pretty good response time.

He didn't want to be caught for a murder he didn't commit. And, he didn't want to be caught before he had accomplished the murder he wanted to commit.

They're gone.

She's gone.

Daniel was alone.

He started the car and drove out onto the highway. He tried to drive casually.

How do you drive casually?

Slowly.

He took a deep breath.

A Chelan County Sheriff drove past, lights flashing, siren wailing.

He took another deep breath. His heart was racing.

Maybe they haven't reported the car stolen.

The Sheriff's patrol car didn't stop. It didn't recognize him.

Maybe I'm invisible.

Ever since he had left the hospital he had been wondering about that.

Now what?

"Now what?" he said out loud.

"Where do I go now?" he shouted. He hoped she was listening. He hoped she would tell him.

He was answered by the rattling engine of his stolen car.

He had no idea where to go.

They're alive.

He knew they were alive. He couldn't give up. He had to find them.

How?

"I don't know."

If you talk to yourself, are you crazy?

"Only if you answer."

You're crazy.

"Who're you talking to?"

I'm losing it.

"I need to get some help."

"I'll help you," she answered.

She was there, beside him, in the passenger seat. He could see her, but he couldn't feel her.

She smiled.

It was an odd sensation. He was glad she was there. He reached over to touch her.

Nothing.

"Am I going crazy?" he asked.

"No," she said.

"How do you know?" he said. "You're dead."

"I know where they are," she said.

Chapter 53

Carson Greer drove up the rocky fire road in a black FBI SUV. It felt good to get out of the office. It felt good to drive the black SUV. It gave him an apocalyptic sense of mission.

He missed his days doing fieldwork. If you were good at what you did, they promoted you. If you were really good, they found you a desk.

Unfortunately.

Greer felt like most of the agents in his division would never find their way behind a desk. That was not a good thing. But Greer was good. When his secretary Lois gave him the name of the Director of the Office of Special Investigations, he recognized the name.

Marvin Steinmetz.

No address.

The phone number listed, D.C. area code, rang through to a service.

Carson went to school with Steinmetz back in the day. Steinmetz had been in the class just ahead of him. He didn't know him, but he'd heard of him. Spy school, he liked to call it. FBI training at Langley.

Carson bumped into him every once in awhile. But not for a while. What was he doing?

CIA?

Black opps?

Domestic spying?

When George W. invaded Iraq, a lot of special ops guys went in. Carson seemed to remember hearing that Steinmetz had been one of them. When they didn't find any WMDs, George W. created a lot of jobs for independent security contractors like Blackwater. Some guys made a lot of money, all tax-free.

What most people, most all of the people, didn't realize was that George W. created even more jobs at home for these same contractors. The Federal Government spent billions, literally, billions on domestic spying.

Under the Patriot Act umbrella, domestic spying was a lucrative business. The threat of terrorism would never go away. Terrorism itself may never materialize, but the threat of terrorism was here to stay. The government wanted to know everything about everyone, all the time. If you wanted to attract attention, try to hide.

Bertrum Alexander Davis.

He must have some pretty powerful friends.

Marvin Steinmetz.

Carson didn't think he'd call back. The message he left was friendly enough. He was the Western Regional FBI Section Chief. His rank deserved a response. Something told him the subject matter would not allow it.

BAD was invisible.

Carson motored up to a rusty old doublewide trailer planted in the middle of a mountain forest.

"They must have had a hell of time getting this up here," he said.

Carson sat behind the wheel of the SUV. He felt safe. The SUV was bullet proof. It was Kevlar reinforced to stop armor-penetrating rounds. He felt safe.

He lied.

There was something spooky about the place.

Firemen run into fires.

Policemen run toward gunshots.

FBI investigate the hell out of stuff. But, they also run into trouble.

There's no trouble here.

The place was quiet.

Then why do I feel so weird?

Carson had a sixth sense. It had served him well. He'd learned to listen to it. It didn't speak much behind the desk. He hadn't heard it for a while.

Maybe I'm just rusty.

He wasn't rusty. He knew that voice. He trusted that voice.

He got out of the SUV and drew his gun.

The place was quiet. Dark. Dank. Wet. It was raining.

He heard an engine sound.

Sears and Schwartz.

The jury was still out on those guys. They acted like Inspector Clouseau mixed with Colombo. Both seemed to solve the crime, but you were never really sure how.

Once he'd found where Davis lived, he exercised professional courtesy in inviting them to come along. He didn't want to feel foolish, standing behind the door of his SUV with his gun drawn at an empty doublewide, so he put his gun away and waited. He tried to look casual. He didn't feel casual. He was on edge.

It took a remarkably long time for Sears and Schwartz to get there. They didn't have the luxury of a government issue black SUV. He could hear the engine of their police issue Crown Victoria laboring over the rough and muddy road.

When they finally made the small clearing, the 400 horsepower Crown Victoria was covered in mud. There was no way anyone in the Snoqualmie Mountains didn't hear them coming. This actually made Greer feel better. If there was someone in there, he would have seen some sign of movement.

The big Ford engine shut down.

Greer thought how remarkable it was that a sound, which hadn't been there, could so fully fill the clearing, such that when it was no longer there, you missed it.

Ticking metal joined the syncopated rhythm of raindrops. Greer didn't mind the raindrops. He wore his hat.

Two car doors opened. Greer looked away from the doublewide.

"Gonna need my rainfly," Sears said.

"You bring s'mores?" Schwartz said.

"Good night for ghost stories around the campfire," Sears said.

"You boys sure make a lot of noise," Greer said.

"Scares away the ghosts," Sears said, smiling.

"You look like you seen one," Schwartz said. "Whadda we got?"

"This is Davis' place," Greer said.

"You came up here alone?" Sears said. "I thought you government types had rules against that sort of thing."

"I didn't get this information in the usual way," Greer said. "Thought I'd use some unusual methods."

"Hey, you're the boss," Schwartz said.

"We're just a couple of gumshoes," Sears said.

"You guys have read way too many Raymond Chandler novels," Greer said.

"True stories," Schwartz said.

"Right," Greer said. "You ready to go inside?"

"I was born ready," Sears said.

"I have to stop being ready, just to get ready," Schwartz said.

Greer pulled out his gun and sloshed toward the trailer.

"You think you're gonna need that?" Sears asked.

"No," Greer said.

"Good," Sears said, pulling out his own gun. Schwartz looked at him funny.

"What?" Sears said. "He did it first."

"Guns don't work on ghosts," Schwartz said mysteriously.

"Shut up," Greer said.

He climbed the trailer stairs. There wasn't room on the landing for all three men. Greer stood at the top. Sears stood on the steps. Schwartz stood at the bottom.

Greer rapped on the door.

"Open up, FBI," Greer shouted.

"Subtle," Sears said.

230

"I think we've been promoted," Schwartz said.

Greer pushed on the door. It was flimsy doublewide metal. It wasn't locked. It wasn't even closed. Or, the latch was broken. When he pushed, it opened.

"FBI," Greer said again. "Anybody home."

It was dark in the clearing even though it was day. Full sun rarely ever made it this deep into the forest. Moss hung on all sides of the trees.

It was darker inside the trailer.

"You first," Sears said.

Greer drew his gun and went inside. Sears and Schwartz looked at each other. Although they talked a lot, they didn't need to speak to communicate. It was obvious Greer was expecting something. They drew their guns and went in after him.

Greer swept the room with his gun.

Empty.

Sears and Schwartz spread out. They weren't FBI, but they knew the drill. There wasn't much cover inside. They were exposed.

Move fast.

Eyes open.

Secure the premises.

Greer went left. Sears went right. Schwartz watched their back.

There were dark stains on the floor. They looked damp. The room was empty.

Bathroom. Blood. Empty.

Bedroom. Empty.

"Nobody home," Sears said, coming back down the hallway.

"The lights aren't even on," Schwartz said.

"In here," Greer said.

Sears and Schwartz joined Greer in…the studio.

Photographic lights were set up at the corners of a metal-framed bed. Handcuffs and chains were attached to the metal bed frame. A steel tray with surgical instruments was overturned near the corner of the bed. Surgical instruments were strewn across the floor. It looked like somebody performed surgery on an unwilling victim. Blood covered the corner of the bed and floor. A small desk with a computer sat across from the bed. It looked like it could have been the set for the movie Misery.

"What do you make of that?" Greer said.

"You're the FBI guy. What do you make of it?

"Somebody likes to play doctor," Schwartz said.

"And not just on TV," Sears said.

"The blood's been here for a while," Greer said.

"Let's get CSI out here," Sears said.

"We'll handle it," Greer said. "FBI does a better job."

"Can't argue with that," Schwartz said.

"You can, but it doesn't do any good," Sears said.

Greer's cell phone rang.

"What?" Greer said, flipping the phone open.

Schwartz's phone rang.

"What?" Schwartz said, imitating Greer.

Sears' phone rang.

"Detective Sears," Sears said.

The three men looked at each other. They'd all gotten the message at the same time. Greer walked into the other room for as much privacy as the doublewide could offer. Sears and Schwartz closed their phones and followed him. Greer was annoyed.

"I hear Lake Chelan's nice in the fall," Sears said.

"Never been," Schwartz said.

"Want to go?" Sears said.

"No," Schwartz said.

"Me neither," Sears said.

"Out of our jurisdiction," Schwartz said.

Greer flipped his phone.

"My guys are on their way. They'll be here in about an hour," Greer said. "I guess you got the news."

"You ever watch the X-files?" Schwartz asked.

"Yeah," Greer said. "I loved that show, until it started getting too weird."

"Any of that stuff true?" Sears asked.

"No," Greer said.

"See," Sears said. "I told you."

"The truth is out there," Schwartz said.

"I'm Mulder," Sears said.

"I'm Mulder," Schwartz said. "You're Scully."

"I'm not going to be Scully," Sears said.

"Gender issues," Schwartz said.

"I'm going to Lake Chelan," Greer said. "You boys wait here till my guys arrive." Greer walked out of the trailer. Sears and Schwartz followed him.

"Do we look like FBI?" Sears said.

"I don't think so," Schwartz said.

"Don't touch anything," Greer said, getting into the black SUV.

"How do we get one of those?" Sears said.

"Join the FBI," Schwartz said.

"Not a chance," Sears said as they watched Carson Greer drive away.

Chapter 54

Bertrum drove slowly down Alaskan Way, past the historic Seattle waterfront. He warned the woman and the girl to be quiet and look like tourists. Ferryboats leaving the docks disappeared into roiling clouds ominously approaching the city. It was raining, with the promise of violent rain coming.

Bertrum was not sight seeing. He drove past the famous waterfront piers, past the construction sites where the homeless live and into the industrialized but decomposing terminals and warehouses where the longshoremen move the mass of maritime trade.

Giant cranes rose above the filth like Gundams in a Japanese sci-fi movie. The Gundams moved rusted steel containers like legos. Every imaginable cargo came and went with a speed and efficiency that baffled Homeland Security.

Bertrum felt a certain solidarity with the foul-mouthed, foul-minded longshoremen he drove past. They were big, burly, rough men loitering about for their next job. They didn't care what it was or where it was going. If it paid, they'd move it. If it paid well they'd keep quiet. If you crossed them, they'd kill you. Bertrum felt empowered.

He brought the Cadillac Escalade to a stop behind a weathered building on the fringes of the terminal district. He was well up the Duwamish River, out of the way of most of the legitimate shipping traffic. This was where they brought the rusty broken barnacle encrusted ships. Some would sail again. Most would not.

"We're here, honey," he said.

Julie and Jenny were asleep in the back. Bertrum had a momentary twinge of regret. Not for Julie or Jenny. Not for what he was planning to do. His regret was for their sleep. He hadn't slept in a very long time. He was afraid to sleep. He was afraid of the visions. He was afraid of the women.

Sleep was over rated.

He felt good. He didn't need to sleep. Red Bull. Jolt. No doze. Speed. Speed.

His drug of choice. Now. Meth brought on the visions. When he took speed he felt such clarity. He could see forever. He could run forever. He could live forever.

"You're gonna crash," Elizabeth said.

Bertrum jumped at the sound of her voice. He looked around but could not see her.

"Get out of the car," Bertrum commanded. He threw open the door and leaped out. "I'm not going to crash."

Julie and Jenny sat up, sleepy eyed. Bertrum opened their door.

The smells of the docks assaulted his nose; creosote, diesel, acetylene, rotting fish and low tide. Bertrum's solidarity with the longshoreman blew away in the putrid air.

"Nobody lives forever."

Bertrum spun around, trying to catch site of her. She wasn't there.

He heard her giggle.

Bertrum was furious.

"Get out of the car. Now," he shouted.

Julie and Jenny slid out of the Escalade.

"I have to go to the bathroom," Jenny said.

"Inside," Bertrum said. "Hurry up."

Bertrum didn't bother to cut the duct tape from their wrists. He pushed them toward a rusted steel door next to a large corrugated roll-up. A sign by the door said, 'Division Offices.'

"Which division?" Julie asked.

"Western," Bertrum said. "Duh."

Bertrum opened the door. The trio stepped over the elevated metal threshold, into the darkness.

"I have to go to the bathroom," Jenny said again.

"This way," Bertrum said.

The inside of the warehouse was huge. There were a couple of dim bulbs hanging high above like stars in the night sky. They gave only a hint of illumination. Bertrum led them on a circuitous path amidst nets, ropes, damaged dinghy's and broken crankshafts. Everything was damp with mildew. The smell outside was mixed with the scent of airborne mold.

As the trio moved through the seeping paraphernalia, the yellow glow of an office window revealed the hulk of a rusty fishing boat, resting ingloriously on blocks.

"In there," Bertrum said.

He opened a door next to the office window. Sickly greenish fluorescent light flooded into the vast expanse of the warehouse. The trio stepped into the built out hallway and the door closed behind them, stopping the leakage of light.

"Bathroom's there," he said. "Hurry up."

Julie opened the bathroom door and a sickening stench flooded out. Julie suppressed a gag reflex. The room was filthy. Disgustingly filthy. Jenny looked up at her Mom, questioningly.

"We'll wait," Julie said. She closed the door.

"Suit yourself," Bertrum said. He opened a door on the other side of the hallway. Yellow light spilled out. "In here."

Julie and Jenny stepped over the threshold. Bertrum followed.

Across the room, a huge man with olive skin and a black beard was consuming a pornographic magazine. His boots were next to his metal chair and he had his stocking feet up on a steel table. His thick socks had holes in the toes. He looked away from the magazine with some effort. Bertrum closed the door and strode over to the man.

"Master Mahan requires your service," Bertrum said.

The big man stood up. He was taller than Bertrum, by several inches and much heavier. Not fat, but heavy. Bertrum held out his left hand. The man took it. Both men placed their right hands on each other's shoulders. The big man's arms were huge, tree trunk huge. Steroid huge. Bertrum felt the weight of the big man's arm pressing down on him.

"What is wanted?" the big man said. They released their strange embrace.

"I desire an audience," Bertrum said, "with Mama."

"Good luck with that, Bra," the large man said.

"Do you have access?" Bertrum asked, annoyed.

"Yah, we got access," he said, "but that don't mean you can get in."

"I can get in," Bertrum said, sitting down to the computer.

"Take them to the room," Bertrum said.

The big man looked at Jenny, then at Julie. His eyes were hungry. A smile twisted a corner of his mouth.

"Gladly," he said.

Bertrum stood up and grabbed the big man's thick arm. "They're mine," he said. "Don't touch them."

The two men glared at each other.

"If you want to live," Bertrum said.

The big man shook off Bertrum's hand. "This way," he said, opening the door.

Julie, Jenny and the big man went through it.

"Bye, honey," Bertrum said. "I won't be long."

The door closed. Bertrum sat down to chat, with Mama.

Chapter 55

Daniel stood under the eve of a RadioShack waiting for the rain to slacken before he made the twenty-foot dash to his car. He held a newly activated pay-as-you-go cell phone in his hand. The battery was warm.

Pretty good plan.

The rain wasn't going to slacken. Daniel looked up at the sky. He didn't have to look far. He broke for the stolen car, hitting the unlock remote on the way. He opened the door, slid inside and closed the door in one fluid motion.

Ouch.

He felt like he pulled out all of his stitches. His fluid motion on the outside was inhibited by his wounds on the inside. And, he was soaked.

There are different kinds of rain in Seattle. Sometimes it just drizzles. There is a constant feeling of moisture in the air. It isn't so much that the rain is falling as it is surrounding. Other times, it rains. Rain falls. The falling rain can be a trickle to a flood. Still other times, it isn't so much raining as it is soaking; almost as if the land was covered under a layer of water. Moving around was more like doing water aerobics. The moisture was penetrating. This rain was the penetrating kind.

Daniel sat in the driver's seat, draining. He could feel the moisture clinging to his hair begin to drip down his neck. It was cold, and annoying. His wet dog smell blended with the pungent staleness of the pregnant woman's effluence.

I hope they had a healthy, happy baby.

He called 4-1-1 on his new phone.

"Seattle Police department," he said to the operator.

"If you are experiencing an emergency you should call 9-1-1," a professional sounding female voice intoned.

"I'm not experiencing an emergency," Daniel said. "Well, I am, but not one I can tell you about."

"Which division?" the annoyed voice said on the other end.

Daniel felt certain the operator was trying to make him feel stupid for not knowing the information he was calling to find out.

"I don't know," he said. "Headquarters, I guess."

"There is no number listed for 'headquarters," the voice said.

"What numbers are listed?" Daniel said.

"Deputy Chief of Staff. Special Operations Bureau. Field Support Bureau. Criminal Investigations Bureau."

"That's the one," Daniel said.

"Which one," the voice said, making Daniel work for the information. He wondered if he paid for the 4-1-1 call as one charge or if he paid by the minute. Probably both.

"Criminal Investigations," Daniel said.

"Hold for the number," the voice reprimanded.

A recorded female voice came on the line, friendly and perky. "The number is: 206-684-5485."

Daniel didn't have anything to write with. He tried to memorize the number.

206-684...

He was interrupted by the perky voice.

"For an additional 75 cents your call will be connected. Press one if you would like to be connected now."

Daniel wondered if the girl speaking to him recorded all the numbers randomly and the computer put them together or if she recorded every number in the phone book.

He pressed one.

"Thank you for using Sprint Connect," the perky voice said.

He felt better. Fulfilling the desires of a recorded female 4-1-1 voice helped make the world a better place.

"Seattle P.D. Criminal Investigations." This voice was not nearly as perky. "How may I direct your call?"

"I'd like to speak to Detectives Sears and Schwartz," Daniel said.

"Which one?" the voice said. Daniel couldn't tell if it was male or female.

"I don't know," Daniel said. "You decide."

"I can't decide for you," the voice said. "Choose your poison."

"Sears," Daniel said.

"Detective Sears is not in right now. Would you like his voice mail?"

"If you knew that Detective Sears was not in right now, why'd you ask who I wanted to talk to?" Daniel said, frustration building.

"I'm not a mind reader, sir."

"Okay," Daniel said, "give me Schwartz."

"Detective Schwartz is not in right now. Would you like his voice mail?"

"You're kidding, right?" Daniel said.

"No, sir."

"Unbelievable," Daniel said. "Okay, give me his voice mail."

Daniel heard a click.

"This is Schwartz. The truth is out there, and I'll find it. Go ahead, make my day."

BEEP

"Uh, Detective Schwartz...this is Daniel Monson. You're probably looking for me. I'm not dead. I know where he's taken my wife and daughter. Call me back at...oh...what is the number...I'm using this new disposable cell phone...I don't know the number...just a minute...let me look."

Daniel fumbled with the phone. He pressed some buttons. The call disconnected.

"Damn," Daniel said. This was one of those times that called for a swear word.

"You need to hurry," Sarah said, appearing beside him.

"I am." He started the car and zoomed out of the parking lot. He could barely see through the rain sheeting on the windshield.

"Turn here," she said.

He switched on the wipers and the world clarified. He made the turn. He was driving through what appeared to be a really old shipyard. Everything was rusting in the moisture above and the black-green water below.

"Are we supposed to be here?" Daniel questioned.

"I'm not," Sarah said.

Daniel drove slowly. It was getting darker. The heavy sky rested on the water. Sodium vapor streetlamps winked on casting a hellish orange glow that was swallowed up in damp fog.

"Here," Sarah said. "They're inside."

Daniel slowed to a stop.

Now what?

End this.

He heard her voice in his mind. No words were spoken. He watched this woman sitting next to him. Her skin was translucent, transparent. Her eyes were bright and penetrating. He had gotten used to having her with him. He didn't need to speak for her to know his mind. From the moment he saw her his life had changed. He wondered what her life had been like before she died.

Empty.

Why?

I never found what I was looking for.

Daniel had. He'd just taken them for granted.

Sarah smiled, sadly.

"They're inside," she said, out loud.

Daniel wondered if she really said it out loud, or if she just moved her lips for his benefit.

Sarah laughed, like music.

"You're stalling," she said.

He pulled the car out of the lane and shut it off.

"Time to slay the dragon," he said, without mirth. Sarah nodded and was gone.

Or be slain.

He opened the car door and stepped into the cold and the fog and the rain.

Chapter 56

Detective Schwartz sat close to the brown haired woman in the cramped forensic computer room. Their shoulders touched as she moved a mouse and typed commands. Schwartz took a sip from his Starbucks cup. He watched her fingers intently. They were long and supple and fast. Unbelievably fast.

"How're you two love birds doing?" Detective Sears came in with a box of donuts.

"Hi Chuck," the woman said.

Sears growled a greeting.

"I don't think he likes it when you call him Chuck," Schwartz said.

"That's his name," the woman said.

"He prefers Charles," Schwartz said.

"Yeah, right," the woman said.

"Donuts?" Sears said.

Schwartz reached into the box and took one.

"You're going to eat one of those? Seriously?" she said.

Schwartz had the donut in his mouth. He took it out.

"Whipped," Sears said.

He put it back in his mouth.

"I never really believed all those stereotypes about cops and donuts," the woman said. "I thought you were different."

"I am different," Schwartz said.

"You got that right," Sears said.

"I just don't know if I can be with a guy that eats donuts," she said.

"You didn't mention that last night," Schwartz said.

"To much information," Sears said.

"I didn't know you ate donuts, last night," she said.

"I don't like where this is going," Schwartz said.

"Nowhere," Sears said.

"You got that right," the woman said. Her fingers never stopped typing.

"Gotcha," she exclaimed.

Schwartz jumped.

"Good one," he said. "You really had me going with the donut thing."

"Bertrum Alexander Davis," she said. "I found him."

Sears leaned in closer to the monitor. The woman continued typing.

"What do you got?" Schwartz asked, leaning closer to the woman.

"Keep your mind on the job, Frank," Sears said.

"I don't know what you're talking about," Schwartz said.

"Sure. Sure," Sears said.

"Boys, stay focused," the woman said.

"He's focused, alright," Sears said.

"I found him," the woman said again, triumphantly.

"So, tell us what you've got," Schwartz said.

The woman hit the return key dramatically and stopped typing.

"I know where he is," she said.

The computer screen changed to a shot of the world from space.

"Google Earth," Sears said. "You can see my apartment building from space."

The view began to zoom in. The trio watched in fascination. North America zoomed into the Pacific Northwest. You could see the Cascades, the Olympics, Puget Sound, Seattle, Eliot Bay, the Terminal District, warehouses.

"That's pretty interesting, but what do you have on BAD?" Schwartz asked again.

The woman didn't respond.

The view continued to zoom into a specific warehouse. The view changed from an actual photograph to a 3 dimensional wireframe view, inside the warehouse.

"That's interesting," Schwartz said.

"You sure this is Google Earth?" Sears said.

"There's a lot more data coming in that my computer can't even begin to understand," the woman said.

The view stopped zooming. A wireframe body was standing up inside the building.

"That's him," she said.

"How do you know?" Sears said.

"I know," she said. "I went in through the back door. This is some kind of super locator program. I've never seen anything like it. But, I know it's him."

"What's he doing?" Schwartz said.

"I don't know," she said. "My computer's too slow to process all the available data."

"I thought you had a fast computer," Schwartz said.

"I do," the woman said.

"So?" Schwartz said.

"So what?" the woman said.

"Then why can't you process all the data?" Schwartz said.

"You'd need a really fast computer, super computer, NASA like computer, to process all this data," she said.

"The truth is out there," Sears said.

"Where is he?" Schwartz asked.

She began typing again. The view changed from wireframe to line code. "Terminal district. Warehouse 66."

"You're amazing," Schwartz said.

She smiled.

"You're amazing," Sears mocked. The woman's cheeks colored.

"Shut up, Chuck," Schwartz said.

"I thought you said he doesn't like it when you call him Chuck," she said.

"He doesn't," Schwartz said.

"Let's go," Sears said.

The two men got up and left the room.

"Wait just a minute," the brown haired woman said, following them out. "I'm coming with you."

"You're kidding," Sears said.

"No, she's not," Schwartz said.

"You're going to let her?" Sears said.

"Look." The woman held out an iPhone. "I found this mobile tracking app. You boys need my help."

"Was it the serpent, or the apple that tempted Eve?" Sears said.

"Very funny," she said.

"The apple," Schwartz said.

"What if he moves, while you're en route? I can tell you exactly where he is."

"She's got a point," Schwartz said.

"That's what the serpent said," Sears said.

"You're wasting time," she said.

"Another good point," Schwartz said.

"You really like her," Sears said.

"Good point," she said, smiling at Schwartz.

"We're wasting time," Sears said.

The trio walked out of the room.

"Tin man," Sears said.

"Scarecrow," Schwartz said.

"Brainless," Sears said.

"Now boys, be nice," the brown haired woman said and she linked arms with both detectives.

"What's your name anyway?" Sears asked.

"Glinda," the woman said.

"It figures," Sears said.

"Follow the yellow brick road," she said, looking at her iPhone.

Chapter 57

"This way," the big man said and he lumbered deeper into the warehouse.

Julie didn't move. Jenny looked up at her, questioning. Julie put her finger to her lips. Julie was hoping the brute wasn't as smart as he looked. He didn't look very smart.

He stopped. And turned around.

"This way," he said again.

"No," Julie said.

The big man clenched his fists. His face turned red.

"Bitch," he said.

"Sometimes," Julie said.

"I break your face," he said.

"He'll kill you," she said.

The big man's face turned purple.

"This isn't your fight," Julie said.

"He wants you," the big man said.

"Why?" Julie said.

The big man's eyes consumed her. He licked his lips.

"Don't you want me," Julie said, seductively. Jenny starred up at her Mom. Julie ignored her. She had to. She would play him. Dangerously.

The big man took a step toward Julie. "You will come with me," he said.

His eyes were cloudy, hard to read. Julie took a step toward him.

"There's time," she said. "He'll never find out."

"What about the girl," the big man said.

"Let her go," Julie said. "She's too young."

"Not for some," the big man said.

A wave of nausea washed over Julie. She wanted to gag. She was in the depths of hell. These people knew no light. They had no redeeming qualities. She had little hope of surviving, but she would not let them have her daughter.

"Let her go," Julie said again, moving closer to him. She gestured behind her for Jenny to stay. "She has no value here."

"She's already been sold," the big man said.

How do they do it?

She would be sick.

I can't be sick.

Julie pressed up against the big man. He smelled like stale tobacco. She couldn't look at his eyes. She focused on his mouth, on his dirty beard.

"Let her go," Julie said, tears quivering her voice.

Don't cry!

She kept her eyes lowered. She didn't want him to see her struggle.

He breathed on her.

Alcohol. Tobacco. Garlic. Gum disease. Rot.

Her body spasmed. She turned her head away and threw her arms around him to hide her revulsion.

She had nothing to bargain with. No skills. No training. No preparation to deal with the events of the last few days. She was not Angelina Jolie. She wasn't beautiful. She was not a super spy. She didn't know Kung Fu. She knew this Neanderthal could kill her. She knew that BAD would kill her. She hoped God knew her name. She hoped he would forgive her for what she was doing. She wondered why, on this once beautiful earth, he would let this happen.

She had nothing to bargain with. But they wanted her body.

She had been taught that one of the purposes of mortality was to gain a body. She had been taught that her body was sacred. She tried to take care of her body. Daniel loved her body.

Daniel.

Grief mixed with nausea.

The trade wasn't fair. It wasn't right. But, for Jenny, she would make it.

"This way," the big man said. He pushed away from her.

Julie turned around to Jenny.

"Hide," she said, "in the warehouse."

"Mommy?" Jenny said, tears in her eyes.

"Hide, Jenny. Run and hide. Someone will come for you."

Jenny turned around and followed the brute. Her body shook. The tears spilled out. The big man opened a door for Julie. She looked back at her daughter, still standing there, so small, so alone, so precious.

Run, Jenny, run. Julie mouthed the words.

The big man yanked her into the room.

Chapter 58

Daniel turned the rusty knob of the man door expecting it to be locked.

It wasn't.

He looked back to see if Sarah was with him.

She wasn't.

He knew he had to go through that door. He didn't want to. He had to.

He pushed the door open and stepped over the threshold.

It was dark inside. He couldn't see.

The metal man door clanged shut behind him. He jumped. The sound echoed through a cavernous darkness.

So much for surprise.

He took his handgun out of his overcoat and held it out in front of him like he'd seen them do in the movies. The gun felt small, small and heavy. He would have felt silly if he wasn't so scared.

As his eyes began to adjust, he could see he was in a very large warehouse. A distant glow gave just enough light to see there were broken pieces of boats all around him. Everything looked old and rusty and broken.

Holding his gun out in front of him, he began to navigate a narrow path between the rusting machinery.

Deeper. Deeper.

The floor was damp. He stepped in occasional puddles. He passed coils of ropes and torn nets. Gigantic rusted boat anchors pulled the oppressive darkness above down upon him.

He could see a sickly yellow glow up ahead. He made his way toward it. Eerie shadows took solid form as he drew closer. He thought he heard voices. He could hear water dripping. The wetness made him cold. He passed a large barnacle encrusted boat resting on massive steel blocks. Shadows turned giant propeller blades as he drifted under the boats stern.

The light was brighter, but no healthier. He could see its source. A window.

Maybe the warehouse foreman's office.

He crept carefully up to the side of the window and looked in.

BAD was in there. He was staring at a computer monitor. Daniel couldn't see what he was looking at. But, BAD was weeping. Daniel could see the tears streaking his face.

Why is HE crying?

Daniel pulled back quickly, from the window. He didn't think BAD saw him. Daniel thought he looked too distraught to see him.

There was a man-door near the window. Daniel wondered if it went directly into the office or if it opened into a different room. He tried to picture the room he had just seen. He didn't think the door opened into the same room.

He turned the doorknob, slowly, with his left hand and held his gun out with his right hand. He pulled the door open, a crack.

Hallway. He could see light at the other end.

Daniel pulled the door open wider and slipped through.

Another door to his right.

The office.

Bad was in there.

Now what?

"Shoot him," Sarah said.

Daniel jumped. His heartbeat spiked. He lost his breath. He was going to scream at her.

Her lips never moved.

She had spoken to his mind.

Daniel screamed at her, inside.

"Hurry," he heard. "Kill him now, while you can."

Daniel looked at her. She was barely visible. But, she had changed his life. In a bad way. He didn't say it, but he thought she could hear it.

Do dead people have an agenda?

He wondered.

Holding his gun at the ready, he opened the office door and went in.

Chapter 59

Carson Greer was flying across the Cascade Mountains in a black Bell Jet Ranger. Noise cancelling headphones allowed him to get lost in his own thoughts.

He had the full resources of the FBI at his disposal. Most of the time he used them for FBI business. Sometimes, he used them for personal business. Occasionally he used them for Mamma's business.

He didn't mind using government resources for personal business. That was just how it was, one of the perks. He enjoyed his job as FBI regional director, most of the time. He was pretty good at the politics. That's how he got to be regional director. He was pretty good at the politics. That's why he would only be a regional director. He was OK with that. He could come and go as he pleased. He got to leave the office whenever he wanted. He had his hand in a number of investigations. And, he did like the X-files. Literally. Mamma made that possible. He knew things the Director of the CIA didn't know. He knew things the Director of the NSA didn't know. He'd done things they would both want to know. Mamma orchestrated things that Mulder and Scully wouldn't believe. He didn't believe it, at first.

Most of the time, he could figure it out. Sometimes, he couldn't. But, when Mamma spoke, everybody jumped. On the way up, they asked how high. And, it went pretty high up. As far as Carson could tell, Mamma was all the way up. If not, he was pretty sure she was in charge anyway.

Mamma spoke. Carson jumped.

Another cleanup job.

Sometimes, Mamma's boys got out of control. Unlimited power and limited accountability did not always provide complete invisibility.

For the most part, Mamma let her boys play. They could do anything they wanted. They were bound by oath. Secret oath. Ancient oath. Mamma's boys took these oaths seriously. If they didn't, they died. As long as the boys stayed within the bounds Mamma set, they were free. When they strayed, Mamma would punish them. If they disobeyed, Mamma killed them. She was ruthless. She was selfish. She was powerful. And, she was invisible, except to those who knew.

Bertram Alexander Davis had strayed. He'd been disciplined. He'd disobeyed. That was bad.

Carson Greer was cleaning up behind him. It was messy. It was the mess that provoked Mamma. She did not like messy. Clean up or die. Pretty simple message. Bertram didn't get it. Or, he couldn't do it. Sometimes that's how it worked. Too much freedom, too much power made it difficult to bend to Mamma's will. Some, like Bertram, thought they were above, or beyond, or exempt from Mamma's will. Others, like Bertram, thought they were Mamma's favorites. Carson knew Mamma had no favorites.

Bertram was dead, or soon would be. So, would Daniel Monson, his wife, his daughter, the two bumbling detectives, and anyone else Carson could find who was involved in anyway with this ongoing mess. It was messy. Carson would clean it up. It would disappear. No one would ever know it had happened. Unless they had access to the X-files. But, the reason they became X-files was because they were unexplainable. Carson could explain many of them. But, he would become one of them, if he ever did.

Carson looked out the window of the Bell Jet Ranger. The Pacific Northwest was beautiful. The snow covered Cascades sloped ruggedly down to the fingerlike tendrils of Puget Sound. Carson wondered how such beauty became blanketed in such corruption. Secret corruption. Black green mountains, covered in steel gray fog, a mist of darkness.

How did he ever get involved?

Power.

He had risen to the level of his displacement. He had power. He used to want more power. Now, he just wanted to have a nice life. He wanted out. But, once Mamma lets you in, she won't let you out.

He was good at his job. He had navigated the shoals of FBI politics and had only used his relationship with Mamma on occasion. He realized early on that the more you used that relationship the more Mamma watched you. Mamma realized that he had climbed as high as he was going to climb, long ago. Now, she used him. She used his position. But, even Mamma didn't abuse him or his position. When something happened that required cleaning up, Carson got the job. He could make things go away, disappear, drown.

"Where would you like to put down?" the pilot spoke in his headset.

Carson had a panoramic view of Eliot Bay. The ceiling was low. They were flying lower, below the cloud cover. It was raining, and darkening. Lost in thought, Carson had completely missed the aerial view of Seattle. He loved the city, when the sun was shining. That happened about two weeks every year, mostly in July. This was September. The sky was gray. The water was black, or green.

"There," Carson pointed to a large warehouse dry dock in the terminal district. There was a helipad right next to it.

Convenient, Carson thought. They may not even know we're coming.

He had radioed ahead from Lake Chelan and called on his most trusted guys to meet him there. They were probably waiting, out of sight, for his arrival.

The helicopter set down. Carson nodded to the pilot, ducked his head and got out. The helicopter was off the ground and gone before Carson had taken three steps.

He sought cover behind the pillars of a giant crane. His cell phone rang.

"Greer," he said.

He nodded, then disconnected. He stepped out from his cover and strode, purposefully toward the giant building where his target was breathing.

Two men, in jeans and jackets joined him, materializing out of the fog and mist.

"Do we have eyes inside?" Carson asked.

"No," one of the men said.

"Do we know the layout?" Carson asked.

"Not really," the other man said.

"How many are in there?" Carson asked.

"Not sure," the first man said. The trio stepped up against the stained cinderblock wall of the building.

"Do you know the objective?" Carson asked.

"No," the second man said.

Carson smiled. "You both look like Mamma's boys."

The two men smiled back. The trio made their way to a man door on the waterfront side of the building. The two men took up positions on either side of the door.

"Kill them all," Carson said, "quietly. Then burn it down."

"This should be fun," the first man said.

Carson pulled out his gun, opened the door and went in. The men followed him with military precision.

Chapter 60

The room was dark as Julie went through the door, and cold. Julie could feel the cold and damp, penetrating. The big man pulled a lever and lights came on. The room was a sound stage. The walls were black. Lights shone down from a grid above. Julie was pretty sure the room was well insulated. She was pretty sure no one would hear her scream. The big man latched the door so no one could come in.

How do I get out?

There was a bed in the center of the room, bathed in light from above. Julie looked around, for a weapon, for anything that could help her in this situation, for anything that could help her out of this situation. She was in survival mode. She would not give in. She would not give up.

"Get on the bed," the big man said.

Julie didn't move. She held her arms across her chest against the cold.

The big man walked over to a tripod with a video camera and aimed it at the bed.

"What do you do here?" Julie asked.

"What's it look like?" the big man said.

"Pornography," Julie said, shivering. She wasn't even sure what all the things surrounding the bed were, but she knew they were for sex. Twisted, sick, sex.

"I prefer to call it reality TV. And you're going to be the star," the big man said, sneering.

"He'll kill you for doing this," Julie said, strolling casually away from the bed.

The big man was adjusting settings on the camera. "No, he won't."

"Yes, he will," Julie said. "He's ruthless and vengeful. He will kill you."

The big man shrugged. "Not this time."

Cables and paddles and stands and clamps cluttered the studio wall. Julie was searching for something she could use against him. She was stalling for time.

"Why not this time?" she said.

"Get on the bed," the big man commanded. "I need to check focus."

Julie kept searching for a weapon.

"What are you planning to do?" she asked.

"Do I have to spell it out for you?" the big man said, fiddling with the camera.

"I was hoping you had some spark of humanity in you and you would help us. Let us go," Julie said. She picked up a small metal rod, ten inches long. It looked like part of a stand.

It'll have to do.

"GET ON THE BED," the big man shouted.

Julie turned around, holding the rod behind her back. Slowly, defiantly, she walked to the bed and sat on the edge.

"I'm not going to do this," Julie said.

"What was all that offering yourself to me, out in the hallway," the big man said.

"Strategy," Julie said.

"Strategy. Really," the big man said. "This could be interesting."

"I'm not going to do this," Julie said again.

"I am," the big man said, sneering. "You can just come along for the ride."

He pressed a button on the camera. A red light came on. A large monitor near the bed lit up. Julie could see herself in the monitor.

"Look at the camera," the big man commanded.

The Julie in the monitor wasn't looking at her. She was watching that Julie. As Julie turned toward the camera, she could feel the monitor Julie looking at her.

"Good," the big man said. He made some final adjustments on the camera. "Now, take off your clothes."

Chapter 61

Daniel pointed his gun at Bad.

"Don't move," he said.

He didn't.

Daniel wasn't sure what he had expected, but this wasn't it. Bad just sat there, staring at the computer and weeping.

Breakdown?

"Shoot," Sarah said.

"Where are they?" Daniel said.

"It's over," Bad said, turning slowly toward Daniel. "My life is over."

"Shoot him now," Sarah said, "while you still have a chance."

"WHERE ARE THEY? WHAT HAVE YOU DONE WITH THEM?"

Daniel took two steps closer to him.

"You want to know. You want to see," Bad said. He wiped the tears from his eyes. "Oh yeah. I had plans. Your wife, she's a looker. I was going to do her, and do her and do her…"

"SHUT UP!" Daniel screamed.

"Shoot him," Sarah said.

If Bad would have moved, would have made some attempt to attack Daniel, he probably would have shot him. But, he just sat there. Daniel held the gun steady, his finger on the trigger, pointed at Bad's head.

"You want to see her?" Bad asked, wiping the tears from his eyes. He swiveled the monitor toward Daniel and pressed a button on the keyboard. The image on the monitor changed. Julie was there, sitting on a bed. The rest of the room was dark. She appeared to be looking right at Daniel.

Daniel's breath caught.

"Julie," he called. She couldn't hear him. She said something. Daniel could see her lips move, but couldn't hear.

"It's so much better with sound," Bad said.

Something obscured the image. A large bearded man approached the bed. Julie stood up. The man was huge. He slapped her across the face.

"Julie," Daniel hollered. He took two steps closer to the monitor, closer to Bad.

In the far reaches of his thought process, he knew he shouldn't have done that. He knew he couldn't do anything for her where he was. He had to get to where she was. It was impulse. It was compulsion. He was drawn to her. He had to help her. At the speed of thought, he knew he made the wrong move.

Bad was up. He was moving. He was charging toward Daniel.

Daniel could see him coming. He knew what his intention was. There was only about four feet and 130 million atoms between them. It would only take 1 second.

"You should have shot him," Sarah said. "You still can."

Daniel realized that when he saw Julie on the monitor he took his aim off of Bad.

Bad idea.

Daniel laughed at his own joke.

He changed his aim.

He realized that he could think much faster than he could move. The big man on the monitor ripped Julie's shirt. Daniel pulled the trigger.

The sound was deafening.

Bad was relentless.

Daniel hoped that his shot would stop him. It didn't.

The bullet ripped into Bad's leg, but he didn't go down. Before Daniel could squeeze the trigger again, Bad crashed into him.

Chapter 62

Sears, Schwartz and the brown-haired woman, Glinda were standing in the rain next to their brown Crown Victoria when they heard the gunshot. It wasn't loud, but it was clear. The rundown dry-dock warehouse was huge, but, apparently not well insulated.

"Gun shot?" Glinda asked.

"Fire cracker," Sears said.

"It wasn't snap or crackle," Schwartz said.

"That can't be good," Sears said.

"They still in there?" Schwartz asked.

Glinda looked at her iPhone. "Yep," she said, admiring the sophisticated tracking app.

"They still alive?" Schwartz asked.

"Too soon to tell," She said.

Sears and Schwartz pulled their .357s from shoulder holsters beneath their worn trench coats.

"Call for backup," Sears said.

"No time," Schwartz said. "You stay here," he said to Glinda.

"No way," she said.

"You're not going in there," Schwartz said.

"I am too," she said.

"You don't have a gun," Schwartz said.

"I don't need a great, big, gun," she said sarcastically seductive.

"What are you going to do, wave your great, big, wand at them?" Sears said.

"Come on," Schwartz said. "Lay off."

"Well?" Sears said. "What is she going to do?"

"I don't know," Schwartz said. "Moral support."

"Moral support?" Sears said. "Since when do you need moral support?"

"Boys," Glinda broke in, "I've got skills." She held up her iPhone.

"I didn't know the iPhone had a working handgun app," Sears said.

"I can tell you who's in the building and where they are, within one meter," Glinda said.

Sears and Schwartz looked at each other.

"That could come in handy," Schwartz said.

"I might have to get me one of those iPhones," Sears said.

"Can I come? Can I? Please, Daddy?" Glinda said.

"Geez, Louise," Sears said. He turned toward the building.

"Come on, Baby," Schwartz said.

"I'm gonna gag," Sears said.

The trio headed toward the nearest entrance. Sears and Schwartz held out their guns. Glinda held out her iPhone.

"Don't let that thing get wet," Schwartz said.

Glinda smiled. "I use protection."

Schwartz smiled. "So do I."

"I know," she said.

"T.M.I.," Sears said.

They reached the entrance.

"Ladies first," Sears said, motioning for Glinda to go through the door.

"Not this time," Schwartz said.

"My hero," Glinda said.

"I am gonna gag," Sears said. He pulled open the door and stepped into the darkness.

Chapter 63

Julie took the shot to the face, partly in defiance, partly as strategy. She had to let the big man get close enough that she could use the metal rod to greatest effect. He hit her hard. She screamed. It hurt. Lights flashed in her peripheral vision. She staggered back against the bed and sat down involuntarily. The big man was quick. He grabbed Julie's blouse and pulled her to her feet.

"Take off your clothes," he growled.

He grabbed her blouse and yanked hard, ripping the thin fabric. Buttons popped off revealing her bra. The big man sneered and grabbed for her bra. That was when she struck. She slammed the metal rod into his eye socket.

He hollered. His hands let go of her bra and covered his face.

Julie slammed her knee into his groin.

The big man screamed and doubled up. Julie brought the metal rod down on the base of his skull. The big man crumpled and fell to the floor.

"Those self-defense classes really do work," she said. "Angelina Jolie, eat your heart out."

Julie pulled her torn blouse across her exposed chest as best she could and slipped out of the studio in search of Jenny.

Chapter 64

Carson Greer heard the gunshot. The dry-dock warehouse was huge, maybe 100,000 square feet, maybe more. The gunshot came from the other end. He motioned to his men to keep their eyes open. They answered back with a similar hand motion. They were systematically securing the place.

What a nightmare.

There were a thousand places, a million places someone could hide. Fortunately, for Greer, it looked like the place hadn't been occupied for a while.

There was junk everywhere. Nautical junk. Relics of rusted boats broken beyond repair. He didn't have the manpower, or the time to find Bertrum Davis if Bad didn't want to be found.

Who fired the shot?

Probably Davis. He was an expert marksman with a military background. Law enforcement had given him his most recent cover to use and abuse his victims.

Who was he shooting at?

Greer knew the warehouse wasn't empty. But, he didn't know how many Mamma had inside at any given time. Not many, he thought. The fewer the better when the real purpose of the warehouse was pornography and human trafficking. If he had more men, he could just burn the place down and watch the exits.

He had the firepower, but not the manpower.

Greer shrugged. He accepted the good with the bad. The good, he could pretty much do whatever he wanted. He could have whatever he wanted. The bad, you could buy anything in this world, and people with lots of money did.

A door opened 30 yards from where Greer and his men were looking. They crouched down and prepared to fire.

A woman peered out the door.

Greer held up his hand to stop the men from shooting.

The woman was attractive. Her blouse was nearly torn off. Greer noticed his men noticing.

Monson's wife. Has to be. This might be fun.

Greer wondered if she had fired the shot. He didn't think so. She didn't have a gun. But, he wondered if someone, Davis maybe, had paid the price for getting a bit too friendly. She didn't look that tough, but, you never know.

The two men looked curiously at Greer. They had their orders to kill everyone inside. Greer knew they were wondering what his plans were for the woman.

He didn't have any plans for her. At least he hadn't had any plans for her. The torn blouse inspired a change of plans.

"Kill everyone. Leave her to me," Greer mouthed.

The men smiled and nodded. They could have their turn, too.

The lethal trio made their way to the open door. One man went inside. A brutish man was lying on the floor, unconscious. Greer looked inside and gained a new respect for the woman. He didn't know how she had done it, but, she had been effective. This guy was alive, but was out of commission. Greer nodded to his associate. The man rolled the brute over and fired a silenced shot into the back of his head. A pressure pop preceded a rapidly expanding pool of dark liquid beneath the dead body.

Next.

A yellowing glow coming from an office window provided the next stop for Carson Greer and his men.

Chapter 65

"Where are they," Schwartz whispered.

Sears, Schwartz and Glinda were slinking through the semi-darkness amidst the rusting rumble of former sea going paraphernalia.

"40 meters west," Glinda answered.

Forty meters didn't sound like a long way, but there was an ocean of obstacles in the way.

"How many?" Schwartz asked.

"Three," She said.

"No problem," Sears said.

"But," Glinda added, "that's not all. There's two more 30 meters south, and there's one 15 meters north. Not moving."

"Dead?" Schwartz asked.

"Can't tell," She said.

"Which ones are the bad guys," Schwartz asked.

"Don't know," Glinda said.

"Don't you think when they made that app it would have been important to add that feature?" Sears said.

"What? Bad guy detector or dead guy detector? " Schwartz said.

POP.

PING.

"Both," Sears said.

A bullet ricocheted off a giant rusted anchor. Sears and Schwartz dropped and rolled behind it.

Schwartz grabbed Glinda and pulled her down with him.

"Drop and roll," he said, angrily. "Drop and roll. If you're going to hang with us, you've got to act fast."

"My iPhone," she said.

"What about your iPhone?" Schwartz said.

"I dropped it," she said.

From their vantage point behind the giant steel anchor, they could see it was sitting in a puddle in the middle of the cluttered asphalt thoroughfare.

"Oh no," she said. "It's wet."

"Another feature," Sears said.

Sears and Schwartz looked at each other and nodded. Years of partnership eliminated the need for words.

"Stay here," Schwartz said to Glinda.

"Hide," Sears said.

"Yeah," Schwartz said. "Stay here and hide."

"No way," Glinda said. "I'm coming with you."

"No iPhone. No gun. No come," Schwartz said. Impulsively, he leaned over and kissed her on the mouth.

"I am going to gag," Sears said.

"Just like in the movies," Schwartz said.

"Except you're not Brad Pitt and she's not Angelina Jolie," Sears said.

"And you're not Sundance," Schwartz said.

"He died, didn't he?" Sears said. "I'll stick with Mulder."

"You're Scully," Schwartz said.

"No way," Sears said.

Both men jumped up and ran, in separate directions.

"Be careful," Glinda said.

POP. POP.

PING. PING.

When the ricochets stopped, she scrambled out into the open, grabbed her iPhone and scrambled back behind the giant anchor.

"Now what?" she said, looking around for a place to hide. Shaking the water off her iPhone and wiping it on her pants, she noticed it was still working. She didn't have a gun, but she could tell where everyone was, including Sears and Schwartz. She didn't need a gun to help after all. Her iPhone would do just fine.

Chapter 66

Bad crashed into Daniel's chest before he could aim or get off another shot. He drove Daniel back against the wall with a horrible growl. The blow knocked Daniel's breath out. Bad slammed Daniel's hand against the wall and his gun fell to the floor. He tried to resist. He tried to punch. He couldn't breathe. Bad was too close. Bad punched him in the stomach. He wanted to double up but couldn't.

The door to the office burst open and a man dressed in black burst in. He had a black beanie on. As Bad pummeled him in the stomach, Daniel's eyes met the man in black.

Cold.

The man in black had a job to do. He was doing it. There was no morality in his gaze, just determination. He a long handgun pointed right at Daniel.

POP. POP. POP.

The gun was remarkably quiet.

Silencer.

Daniel felt like he was in a movie, maybe one of the Bourne movies. But, he wasn't Jason Bourne. He could see the bullets heading toward him. Slowly. He stared into the man's eyes.

No regret.

No remorse.

He had a job to do.

Does it hurt to die?

"Not really," Sarah said. "It's the living that hurts the most."

"What are doing here? Why aren't you helping me?" Daniel said.

"You're helping me," Sarah said.

1.2. 3.

The bullets struck Bad in the back. His body jerked. The force of the bullets drove him into Daniel with even greater force. Daniel expected to feel the bullets pass through Bad and into him. He expected to die.

Maybe I'm already dead.

Bad stopped pounding him in the stomach. He clutched Daniel's shoulders. Daniel looked up. The gunman's eyes were cold. Bad began to slide down, his fingers releasing Daniel's shirt.

The gunman nodded and took aim for one more shot.

BOOM.

"Freeze."

The gunman slammed into the door jam, then crumpled to the floor.

Bad did too.

"You're supposed to say freeze before you shoot," Sears said, appearing in the doorway.

"I always get that mixed up," Schwartz said, joining Sears and kneeling to examine the lifeless gunman.

"How's it going, Monson?" Sears said. "Long time no see."

Daniel stood against the wall. He didn't speak. He couldn't. Bad was bleeding at his feet, on his shoes. The gunman was dead in the doorframe and these clowns wanted to know how he was doing.

Fine.

Just Fine.

The office window exploded.

Daniel could see the safety glass spinning and twirling and glinting in the greenish fluorescent light of the office.

A bullet ripped into the doorframe above Schwartz's head. Wooden splinters took flight.

"Get Down," Sears shouted. He dove into the room.

Daniel slid down against the wall. Bad's weight against his feet slowed his descent. Daniel's weight against Bad's body streaked the floor with blood.

Sears hit the ground, rolled and popped up, shooting.

1. 2. 3. 4.

Daniel counted the shots. They were loud. They hurt his ears. Wood and drywall exploded all around him, above him, near him. Schwartz rolled into the room and together Sears and Schwartz overturned the only piece of furniture in the room, a steal-case desk. The computer on the desk crashed to the ground.

"Evidence," Sears said.

"Facebook," Schwartz said.

5. 6. 7. 8.

Sears squeezed off the shots with military precision.

Strange.

Daniel couldn't see who Sears was shooting at. He couldn't hear the gunshots coming at him, only the impacts.

"We've got to get out of here," Sears shouted.

"Good idea," Schwartz said. "Where shall we go this time of year?" Schwartz fired off four shots while Sears reloaded.

"Somewhere a little warmer," Sears said.

Return fire penetrated the desk and punctured the walls all around them.

"Hell?" Schwartz said.

Sears fired back. "Already there."

"What did you do to piss these guys off?" Schwartz asked Daniel.

"Wrong place at the wrong time, I guess," Daniel said.

"Did you kill that woman?" Sears asked.

"No," Daniel said.

"Did he?" Sears pointed at Bad.

"Yes," Daniel said.

"How do you know?" Schwartz asked.

"She told me," Daniel said.

"The dead woman?" Sears said.

"Yes," Daniel said.

"Right," Schwartz said. He pulled the trigger. Nothing happened. "Well, that pretty much takes care of that."

"Didn't you bring extras?" Sears asked.

"I didn't expect to be in a war," Schwartz said.

Sears tossed Schwartz a clip. "I'll cover you. You get him out of here."

"You been watching too much TV," Schwartz said.

"He's a material witness," Sears said.

"Nobody's gonna believe a wacko that talks to dead people," Schwartz said.

"He can leave that part out. Right, Danny boy?" Sears said.

Daniel hadn't been called Danny boy since he was a boy. His Dad used to call him that. He still missed his Dad. A lot. He wondered what his Dad would do in this situation.

"Sure," Daniel said.

"See," Sears said.

"Maybe," Schwartz said. "What I don't get, though, is who are these guys? Who is it they're mad at?"

"Everybody," Sears said.

"Then let's get Glinda and get the hell outta here," Schwartz said.

"My wife and daughter are in here, somewhere," Daniel said.

"Damn," Sears said.

Sears and Schwartz exchanged looks.

"Where?" Schwartz asked.

"I don't know," Daniel said.

"How do you know?" Sears asked.

"He's here," Daniel said, pointing at Bad. "That's why I'm here. They're here. Out there."

"It's a big room," Sears said.

"Glinda'll find 'em," Schwartz said.

"She's really got you whipped, don't she?" Sears drawled.

"Shut up, Chuck," Schwartz said.

Sears looked at Daniel smiling. "He's mad now," Sears said.

"We've got to find Julie, and Jenny," Daniel said.

"Okay, Mom. If you say so," Schwartz said.

"You go first," Sears said. Schwartz nodded.

"Follow me," Schwartz said to Daniel. "Stay close, but not too close."

"How close is too close?" Daniel asked.

"If the bullets go through me and hit you, that's too close."

Daniel wished he hadn't asked.

"Ready?" Schwartz said.

Sears nodded.

"Go," Schwartz said.

Sears fired his gun. Schwartz jumped up and ran and fired his gun. Daniel jumped up and ran, behind him. Sears followed behind, firing his gun. As they ran out of the room, into the hallway, into the warehouse, Daniel was going to tell Schwartz that the bullets the bad guys were using didn't go all the way through Bad's body, so he didn't think they would go all the way through Schwartz's body. He was going to tell him that, when the bullets hit Schwartz's body. They would have knocked him down. Instead, they knocked him back into Daniel.

Daniel caught hold of Schwartz under the armpits and held him up. He didn't mean to use him as a shield. It just worked out that way. Daniel held onto him. Bullets pelted him in the chest. Schwartz groaned and twitched and Daniel held him up, advancing toward a giant rusting anchor he hoped would provide protection from the maelstrom.

As Daniel advanced toward the giant anchor, the bullets in front disappeared. The loud reports ceased at the same instant. Daniel dropped Schwartz and rolled behind the anchor. He looked back to see Sears lying in the thoroughfare.

Chapter 67

Julie could smell the smoke before she could see the flames. Now, she was desperate to find Jenny.

"Jenny," she called out loud.

She wasn't as concerned that they would hear her as she was to find her daughter.

"Jenny," she called again.

"Mommy?" Jenny's head popped up above the deck rail of an aged sailboat. The boat was made out of wood. The wood was rotted.

"Jenny, come quick. We have to get out of here," Julie said, searching for a way to get up into the boat, to her daughter.

Jenny disappeared below the deck rail. Moments later, she scurried from behind the boat and ran to hug her mother. Julie bent down and squeezed the little girl.

In the distance, a new round of gunfire echoed through the massive warehouse.

"Come on," Julie said. "Let's go."

Jenny hesitated. "Daddy's here."

"Daddy's here?" Julie questioned.

Julie thought Daniel was dead. She had tried not to think about it since Bad shot him in their driveway. She had pushed it out of her mind. She didn't want to think about that.

Images of Daniel lying in the driveway, bleeding.

She couldn't let them in. She wouldn't. She had one focus, protect her daughter. She had survived. Jenny was alive. They were together. The possibility that Daniel was still alive, that he was here, was unbelievable.

"Honey, Daddy was…" Julie didn't know what to say, how to say it. The gunfire stopped. The smell of smoke was getting stronger.

"He's here, Mommy. I know it," Jenny said,

"How do you know it?" Julie questioned.

"Sarah told me," Jenny said.

Sarah.

The dead woman.

Talking to my daughter.

Anger swelled in Julie's chest. She grabbed her daughter by the shoulders. They needed to get out of here. They needed to get away from here.

Julie looked in her daughter's eyes. They moistened.

Jenny looked up at Julie with such trust, such honesty.

The eyes of a child don't lie.

The anger in Julie's heart melted.

"Where is he?" Julie asked.

"He's over there."

A woman's voice startled Julie. She pulled Jenny close and turned toward the voice.

A brown-haired woman stepped out from behind the boat's rudder.

"Sarah?" Julie asked.

"I'm Glinda," Glinda said.

"The good witch?" Julie said.

"I get that a lot," Glinda said.

"Where's your wand?" Jenny asked. She was a big fan of the Wizard of Oz.

"Where's your gun," Julie asked.

Glinda held up her iPhone.

"Can you shoot with that thing?" Julie asked.

"No, but it can do magic," Glinda said.

"Do you know where my husband is?" Julie asked.

"Yes," Glinda said.

"Is he alive?" Julie said.

"Yes," Glinda said. "But I don't know for how long."

"Help me find him," Julie said.

Glinda looked at her iPhone.

"This way," she said. Glinda stepped out into the cluttered warehouse thoroughfare. Julie and Jenny followed.

"Not so fast, ladies."

Carson Greer stepped out of the boat shadows.

Glinda checked her iPhone.

"Where'd you come from?" she asked.

"I'm not on the grid," Greer said.

"Come on," Glinda said. "Everybody's on the grid. You look like FBI."

"I am FBI," Greer said.

"Thank God," Julie said.

"I wouldn't," Greer said.

He pulled out his silencer and shot Glinda in the chest. Jenny screamed. The force of the bullet drove Glinda back against the sailboat rudder. Her eyes were open wide. She looked surprised. The iPhone fell from her hand and she fell to the floor.

Julie saw it all, in slow motion. What had happened to her life, to her world? Things didn't get better. They just got worse and worse and worse. She grabbed Jenny and pulled her against her so she couldn't see the dead surprise on Glinda's face.

No child should have to see this.

"I had plans for you," Greer said. "But, I think we're running out of time."

He looked around the warehouse. An eerie orange glow was flickering distantly. The smell of acrid smoke was increasing.

"You're supposed to be one of the good guys," Julie said.

"I am one of the good guys," Greer said.

"And she wasn't?" Julie said.

"She was. She really was," Greer said.

"I don't understand," Julie said.

"You wouldn't," Greer said.

He raised the gun and pointed it at Julie.

"You're going to shoot me right here, with my daughter clinging to me?" Julie said. "Where's your humanity."

"You're right," Greer said. "Get her away from you."

"Good idea," Julie said. "Let her watch her mother get murdered."

"Shut up," Greer yelled. The smoke was getting thicker and the glow was getting brighter. "Get over there, little bitch."

Jenny didn't move. She held tightly to Julie's leg.

"What are you going to do to her?" Julie asked.

"Sell her into sexual slavery," Greer said.

Julie shuddered. She held Jenny tightly against her. She didn't want to die. And, she didn't want Jenny to die. But, there were some things worse than death. In fact, death would be welcome compared to some things.

She moved Jenny behind her. As she did, she saw movement behind Greer. Thirty yards down the thoroughfare she saw someone, ducking in and out of the shadows, getting closer.

She didn't want to give him away. She didn't want to betray him. Somewhere in the back of her mind she felt guilty. If she gave in to it, the guilt would overwhelm her. It was her fault. She hadn't wanted any of this. She had no idea these things could even happen.

Bad things happen to good people.

Why?

Why God?

God didn't answer.

Daniel stepped out of the shadows.

Julie gasped.

"Don't move," Daniel shouted.

Greer pulled the trigger.

Julie dove for cover, dragging Jenny with her.

The bullet traveled at 1,000 feet per second. Greer was only 5 feet from Julie. It took the bullet less than a thousandth-of-a-second to cover the distance. Julie could see it coming, in slow motion.

Strange.

"It's really not so bad."

Julie didn't recognize the voice. But she was pretty sure she knew who the woman was, standing in the shadows.

What's not so bad?

"You know," Sarah said.

No, I don't.

Julie crashed to the ground with Jenny underneath her. She watched Greer turn. He was experienced, and quick.

Daniel didn't move. Julie saw the flame though. It came from the barrel of his gun. Greer was diving, turning, rolling, shooting.

Daniel's shot hit Greer in the chest.

Good shot, hon.

The shot knocked Greer out of the air and knocked the air out of Greer. He hit the ground hard. His gun clattered out of his hand.

Julie wanted to cheer. Daniel was alive. He was here. He was alive.

"You need to hurry," Sarah said.

"Daniel's alive," Julie said.

Sarah smiled.

A loud explosion rocked the floor of the warehouse.

The pressure wave knocked Daniel down.

Hot smoke and ash were filling the air. Jenny was struggling to breathe. Julie knew she should move. She should get Jenny out of there. But, she was tired. She was so very tired.

Chapter 68

"You need to hurry," Sarah said.

"I am hurrying," Daniel said. He was trying to stay in the shadows so they wouldn't see him. Not much further.

"Hurry faster," Sarah said.

He was so close. He could see her. Julie was so beautiful. Jenny was clinging to her, so small, so precious.

Daniel stepped out of the shadows.

"Don't move," he shouted.

He could see Julie gasp.

"I'm alive," he said. His words dissipated in the smoke from Greer's gun.

"No!"

He could hear the word. He said it, shouted it, actually. But the word was slower than the bullet. He could see Julie fall. Greer was moving.

He's pretty quick.

He'd never killed anyone before. He didn't want to kill anyone now. He was just defending his family.

Doing a lousy job of it.

Greer was diving. Rolling. Daniel knew Greer would be shooting at him, momentarily, as soon as he could get his body twisted around and his gun aimed.

"Keep your eye on the ball."

Daniel was 12 years old. He had two strikes already. They had two outs. It was the last inning. They would win or lose right here. Right now. His Dad called time out. The noise went away.

"Keep your eye on the ball," his Dad said.

"He's pretty fast," Daniel said.

"You can do it, Son." Daniel's Dad put his hand on Daniel's shoulder. "I believe in you."

Daniel looked into his Dad's eyes. They were blue, deep blue, and clear.

"Thanks, Dad."

The pitcher threw the ball. Daniel fired the gun.

He hit his target.

Greer dropped to the ground, a rock, rolling to a stop.

A loud explosion rocked the floor of the warehouse.

Daniel thought he heard a scream.

The pressure wave knocked him down. Hot gases rolled overhead like a violent storm, orange and red and black. The air in his lungs went with them.

"Nice hit, son," his Dad said, smiling. "Now, don't forget to run."

"Run," Sarah said.

"Run," Elizabeth said.

Run.

He wanted to. He desperately wanted to.

Run.

His legs were so heavy.

He sucked air. It tasted foul.

He rose up on all fours. Through the smoke, he could see Julie and Jenny.

"Run," Julie said. He could hear her voice, distantly.

"This way," Sarah said, moving through the smoke. Julie was just ahead, holding Jenny's hand.

Daniel tried to keep up. When he stood up to run, he nearly collapsed. The air was hot and toxic. If he stayed low, he couldn't see which way they were going. He was losing them.

Crash.

The warehouse was disintegrating from the inside out.

I'll never make it.

"You can do it, Son." His Dad was cheering for him.

"Come on, Daddy," Jenny was clapping for him.

"Just a bit further," Julie said.

For her, he would do it. For them, he would do anything.

"Over there," Sarah said, pointing to a steel doorway.

He could see it. He could make it. He would get them out. He would save them.

"Come on," he called, turning toward the door. He took one step and stopped.

BAD.

Bertrum Alexander Davis, ghoulish, blood soaked, charbroiled, stepped out from behind a wall of burning pallets.

"Did you miss me?" Bad said. He was holding a fire ax. He should have been using it to get out. Daniel could see he was planning to use it to keep them in. "I left my taser at home, but this should do." Bad slapped the ax handle in his hand like a baseball bat.

"No one said it would be easy," Sarah said.

"No one said it would be impossible," Daniel said.

"Hurry," Julie said.

Daniel looked at his wife and daughter. They were beautiful. They were shimmering through the smoke and heat waves. For them, he would try.

He looked at Bad.

"Bring it on," Bad said.

Daniel walked toward him.

"This is crazy," Daniel said.

"It is, isn't it?" Bad said, smiling.

"Look," Daniel said, "we can all get out of this alive."

"I'm already dead," Bad said.

"No you're not," Daniel said.

"You don't understand," Bad said. "Mamma burned me."

282

"What?" Daniel said.

Boom!

Another explosion rocked the warehouse. Flaming metal began to fall around them.

"Look out," Daniel shouted to Julie and Jenny.

"Look out," Sarah said, standing next to Julie and Jenny.

Daniel turned just in time. Bad took a step and swung the ax.

Good Mechanics.

He probably was a pretty good baseball player.

Daniel sucked in his gut and jumped backwards. The ax missed his flesh but cut through his shirt. The ax head was heavy. Bad's follow-through kept him from swinging again. Daniel leapt forward and crashed into him.

Bad screamed in pain and tried to swing the ax back at Daniel.

He couldn't.

Daniel punched him in the stomach. Bad brought the ax handle up, under Daniel's jaw, connecting with a stunning blow.

Daniel staggered back, sharp white lights flashing in his peripheral vision. He couldn't tell if it was the fire or the impact causing the pain and flashing. He shook his head. It hurt. He looked over at Julie and Jenny. Julie had a sad, melancholy look.

He remembered that look.

A few years ago, as a busy young attorney, he had come home one night, late. Jenny was maybe two. He had come upstairs into the bedroom. The lights were off. He tried to be quiet, to not wake Julie up. He took off his suit and climbed into bed in his underwear, trying not to wake Julie up.

She moved.

She switched on the light.

She had that same look—melancholy sadness.

She was gorgeous, in her lingerie. His favorite nightgown. He could see her beautiful body through the shear fabric. She had been waiting for him.

"Happy anniversary," she had said.

"Anniversary?"

"Wrong answer," she said.

He slapped himself in the forehead.

"Oh no," he said. "I am so stupid."

"Yes, you are," she said. She slipped out of bed and slipped out of her nightgown. She stood next to the bed, completely naked. She took his breath away.

He pulled off his t-shirt.

"Don't even think about it," She said.

She reached down and picked up her flannel pajamas. She slid into them, covering her body quickly. She got into bed and turned out the light.

He stood there by the bed, apologizing.

After a few minutes, she switched on the light. He remembered that look. It was the same look. He wanted to touch her, but didn't.

Now, she had that same look.

"I'm sorry," he said.

"Don't be," she said. "This time it wasn't your fault." She winked at him. The look was gone.

"I love you," he said.

"I know," she said.

He liked it when she said that.

Most couples he knew would say, 'I love you. I love you, too." He knew she loved him. It was obvious to him, everyday. She put up with him, even when he forgot their anniversary, which, he only did once. What was even more meaningful, to him, was to know that she knew that he loved her.

"Look out," she said. He ducked, just as Bad swung the ax over his head.

Boom. Boom. Boom.

Three shots in quick succession.

Bad staggered back, looking more surprised than hurt, and crashed into the burning pallets. His clothes caught fire immediately. He screamed a gruesome, blood-curdling scream, which changed to a gurgle and then a bacon frying sizzle.

"How are you doing, Danny-boy."

Daniel turned around.

"Detective Sears."

"I think we should go," Sears said.

Daniel looked at Bad. His body dropped to the floor in a flaming sizzle. Daniel thought he was going to throw-up. The smell of burning flesh blended with the toxic smoke and flame.

"We can't," Daniel said. He looked over to where Julie and Jenny were standing.

They weren't there. The flames had grown so Daniel couldn't see through them.

"My wife and daughter are in here."

"Listen, Monson, I'm real sorry about that, but there's nothing we can do."

"What do you mean, there's nothing we can do," Daniel shouted. "I haven't come this far to give up now. I'm going to get them out of here."

Daniel started toward where he had last seen them. Sears raised his gun.

"Don't move," Sears shouted.

Daniel stopped. "Shoot me," he shouted back, "or let me save them."

"You can't save them," Sears said.

"I will save them," Daniel yelled.

"Daniel?" Julie said.

"Julie! Come on, let's go," he shouted. "Jenny, come on."

Sears looked in the direction Daniel was looking. The flames were growing. They didn't have much time.

"They're dead," Sears said.

"They're not dead," Daniel shouted. "Julie, come on."

Daniel stepped toward them. The heat was nearly unbearable.

"I will shoot," Sears said, "to save your life."

"Sarah, you have to tell him," Julie said. "He knows you. He knows you're...dead."

"Daniel," Sarah said.

Daniel spun around. Sarah stood by Bad's body.

"Sarah," Daniel shouted.

Sears spun around to look. Bad's body was smoldering on the floor.

"You have to help me get them out of here," Daniel shouted.

"I can't, Daniel. You have to leave, now."

"What do you mean, you can't?" Daniel shouted.

"Please, Daniel, you have to get out of here," Sarah said.

"Not without Julie and Jenny," Daniel said.

Sears looked back and forth between Daniel and the burning body of Bertrum Alexander Davis.

"Let's go, Monson. Now!" He shouted.

Daniel looked back and forth from Julie and Jenny to Sarah. As the flames grew, Bad stood up.

"That wasn't so bad," Davis said, grinning.

"Davis!" Daniel shouted.

"You should have left while you still could," Davis said.

Sears followed Daniel's gaze, but didn't see anyone. "Now this is getting weird," he said.

"Hello, Burt," Elizabeth said.

"Thought I might see you in Hell," Davis said.

"Daniel, you have to go, now," Julie said.

"Not without you," Daniel said.

"She's dead," Davis said. "I'm dead. You're dying."

"Shut up," Daniel shouted.

"I'm sorry," Julie said.

Sears put down his gun and charged toward Daniel.

"I love you, Daddy," Jenny said.

"I love you, Daniel," Julie said.

Sears put his shoulder down and crashed into Daniel's stomach. He didn't have much breath left amidst the smoky air, but what breath he did have was forced out with the impact.

I know.

He should have said it out loud. He would have said it out loud, but he couldn't find the air inside him to make the sounds.

Julie would get it.

As he fell backwards to the floor, he saw Julie smile.

She got it.

"I get it," Julie said.

Daniel didn't see her mouth move.

Strange.

Julie and Jenny dissolved into the smoke as Daniel hit the floor on his back. His head struck cement. White flashes mixed with orange flames. The pain was tremendous, but he hadn't given up yet. From the ground a little air filled his lungs and kept him from passing out. He could see Bertrum Alexander Davis smiling hideously.

Suddenly, a number of other women emerged from the flames to surround Bad.

"I didn't really believe the hype about the 70 virgins," Bad said.

"We're not virgins," Elizabeth said.

"I know," Bad said, and looked at Daniel.

Daniel rolled and threw Detective Sears off of him. The women grabbed hold of Bad and began to claw at him and scratch him and gnash him.

Daniel jumped to his feet. Sears jumped to his feet.

"Come on, Daniel, we have to get out of here. The whole building's going to collapse," Sears yelled.

Bad screamed. The women tore at his clothes. They tore at his hair. They dragged him into the flames. The sounds of his screams merged with the roar of the flames.

"Good bye, Daniel," Sarah said. "I'm sorry I put you through all this."

"I'm sorry, too," Daniel said.

"Thank you," Sarah said, "for doing good."

A loud crack ripped through the air. The flaming beam above Detective Sears broke in half. Daniel charged toward him, knocking him out of the way. The two men jumped up and ran toward the steel man-door. The flames were all around them. The building was crashing on top of them.

Sears grabbed the doorknob of the man-door. His flesh sizzled and he screamed. Daniel ripped off his shirt and wrapped it around his hand. He grabbed the door and turned the knob. The door opened and both men tumbled out into the darkness and rain.

Chapter 69

Daniel opened his eyes and stared up at the ceiling fan above his bed. The ceiling fan wasn't moving. Neither was Daniel. He hadn't been moving for a while now. He didn't really want to move.

It had been a month since the funeral.

To their credit, after the Police dropped the charges, Beck, Strom, Bough, Tem, Feller, Rich and Associates had held his position for him. The company detective had explained the whole thing to Mr. Beck. Beck said they wanted him back. Daniel didn't believe him. But, he had told them he was coming back. They were expecting him back.

He didn't want to go back.

He didn't want to go anywhere.

He traced the blades of the ceiling fan with his eyes. He reached over and flipped the wall switch. The blades began to turn. Dust from the blades made him sneeze. He shivered. It was cold outside. Winter was coming.

Death was coming.

Death had been there before. They were old friends. Daniel couldn't wait.

He reached over and flipped the wall switch. The ceiling fan slowed, slower, stopped.

Daniel used to think he had the perfect life. He used to think about death. He had been afraid of death. Now, he welcomed it. He looked forward to it. He longed for it. He courted it. He would embrace it. If death wouldn't come for him, he would seek it out. It was life he feared now. He wanted nothing to do with it.

The doorbell rang, downstairs.

Daniel closed his eyes.

He tried to dream. He couldn't sleep. When he did sleep, he didn't dream. His dreams were gone.

The doorbell rang, downstairs, again.

Daniel opened his eyes.

"Leave me alone," he said. At least he thought he said it.

I am alone.

When you're alone, sometimes, it's hard to tell if you are talking to yourself or just listening.

He wanted it this way. Now.

The doorbell rang, downstairs, twice.

Daniel sat up in bed and threw the covers off.

The doorbell rang again, three times.

Daniel draped his legs over the side of the bed and let his head adjust to the change in altitude. He felt dizzy, nauseated, hung over.

I don't drink.

The doorbell rang.

"I'm coming," Daniel shouted, hoping whoever it was could hear his annoyance. He got up and went down stairs in his underwear. He looked out the front window to see who was there. Detective Sears stood there, waiting. Daniel opened the door. Their eyes met. The two men shared an experience, a combat like experience.

"You look like hell," Sears said.

"Back at ya," Daniel said.

"At least I put clothes on," Sears said.

"So did I," Daniel said. "Last week."

"Good choice," Sears said. "Can I come in?"

"Why?" Daniel said. "Did somebody else die?"

Daniel could see Sears cringe when he said that. He knew Sears was struggling with the loss of his partner. He felt bad for him. Kind of. He didn't really want to hurt the guy. He didn't really want to hurt anyone. But, he didn't want Sears in his life. He didn't want anyone in his life. He didn't want his life.

"Don't you want to know?" Sears asked.

"Does it matter? Will it change things?" Daniel asked.

"No," Sears said. "But it might help."

The two men stared hard at each other.

"Did it help you?" Daniel asked.

Sears hesitated.

"Listen, Sears, thanks for thinking of me, but I'm late for work," Daniel said.

Sears smiled.

"You going to work?" Sears said.

"You bet," Daniel lied. "Today's my first day back."

Sears looked at his watch. "You're late," he said.

"They won't mind," Daniel said.

"Change your underwear," Sears said. "You stink."

"They won't notice," Daniel said, closing the door.

Sears laughed and pushed back on the door.

"The truth is out there," Sears said.

"Get a life," Daniel said.

"Back at ya," Sears said.

Daniel pushed the door again. Sears pushed back again.

Stalemate.

"What do you want, Sears?" Daniel said.

Sears pulled his card from the pocket of his worn brown suit.

"I know what you're going through," Sears said. "I am, too. If you want to talk about it, I'll listen."

"Thanks, Detective," Daniel said, coldly, "but no thanks."

Their eyes met. Daniel looked away. Sears handed Daniel his card. Daniel took it.

"Bad things happen to good people," Sears said. "That's life."

"Then you die," Daniel said.

"Pretty bleak," Sears said.

"The truth is out there," Daniel said.

"Listen, Daniel…"

"No," Daniel interrupted.

Their eyes met, again. Daniel couldn't read what was in Sears' eyes.

"Sorry for your loss," Sears finally said.

"Thanks," Daniel said. He pushed the door closed. Sears didn't resist. "Me, too."

"You got to move on," Sears said through the closed door.

Daniel didn't respond. He leaned his head against the closed door.

Good idea.

Sears' shoes squeaked.

Daniel watched him go from the front room window.

Sears was right, he decided. He did stink. In fact, his whole life stunk. He didn't want to go back to work. They didn't need him. They'd never miss him. He didn't care anymore.

Daniel knew what he was going to do.

He went upstairs, took off his dirty underwear and got in the shower. He did want to be clean.

Chapter 70

Daniel drove past the smiling happy cow welcoming him to Carnation, Washington. Rain was falling. He'd been here before. He wouldn't be here again. This time, this last time, he stopped at the Carnation dairy for ice cream. The town was famous for two things. He knew one of them. He thought he'd try the other.

He pulled into the dairy. The late afternoon sky was flat gray. He parked near what he thought looked like the entrance, shut off the Honda and got out, into the rain. While he walked into the big white box building, he pulled on his R.E.I. parka. Daniel had a coat for every season. This coat was good for cold wet weather.

What other kind is there?

Daniel hoped to be going somewhere warmer.

He opened the glass door and stepped into a corporate lobby. Behind a reception desk, a large woman, happy and smiling, looked over her black and white jersey glasses.

"Welcome to the Carnation Dairy. How may I help you?" The woman's accent was from somewhere warmer.

"I've heard about your famous dairy and thought I'd stop for some ice cream," Daniel said. He had trouble not matching her drawl.

"Well," she said, stretching the ell out much longer than she needed, "you are in the wrong place, at the wrong time." Her words did not match her plastic smile.

"I've been here before," Daniel said.

"You have," she said. "Then you surely must know we don't serve ice cream."

"What do you serve," Daniel asked.

"Cows," she said giggling. "We serve cows. This is the dairy," she said.

"But I thought Carnation was famous for its ice cream," Daniel said.

"The company. Not the town. Or the dairy," She smirked.

Apparently this was information every knowing person should know. Daniel didn't.

"So," he said, "you don't serve ice cream."

"No sir. We do not," she said.

Daniel didn't know what to say. He had yet to have a satisfying visit to Carnation. He turned and walked out. The happy smiling woman pushed her jersey cow glasses up the bridge of her nose as the door closed.

Daniel hadn't meant to be rude. He was just surprised. He was so surprised he forgot to say thank you. He crossed ice cream off his short list and drove out of the parking lot. He said goodbye to the happy cow.

***

When you live in the Northwest, you get a feel for time of day by the quality of light penetrating the clouds. Daniel could tell it was late afternoon even though he couldn't see the sun. Eighteen percent gray had drifted to fifty percent. The clouds drooling on Mount Si had some mottled definition. Daniel knew he'd get wet before he got warm. In the northwest, late fall meant it got dark early. He wanted to start his hike before it got dark.

Why?

He didn't know. He didn't like hiking in the dark and the rain. Something could happen.

Death comes at night.

Daniel smiled. He wasn't as concerned as he used to be.

He turned on the radio. "Riders on the Storm" was playing. He changed the channel. "Spirit in the Sky" took over. He changed the channel. Billy Joel sang, "Only the good die young." He pressed the button. Roberta Flack, "Killing me softly." He pressed the button harder. Seal sang, "Prayer for the dying."

What are these DJs thinking?

No wonder so many people in Seattle kill themselves in the winter. It wasn't the weather. It was the radio. The thought cheered him up. He turned off the radio.

The trip from Carnation to Mount Si took about twenty-five minutes. As the crow flies, it wasn't very far. Before he entered the deep forest, Daniel could see Mount Si rising up from the army green earth. But, he did enter the deep forest.

Deep and deeper.

The road twisted and wound through old forest sentinels dripping with spidery moss.

Daniel shivered.

He had been through this forest. Last time, he didn't believe in ghosts. This time he didn't see any.

He turned off the state road onto a soggy logging road and drove a quarter mile to the Mount Si trailhead. He parked the Honda in the mud next to the road and got out. He expected to get wet.

It wasn't raining, but the air was moist, and cold, the kind of cold that chilled bones.

Daniel could see the trailhead. The trail was marked with a small forest service sign, Mount Si summit 4.2 miles, 4167 ft. He couldn't see the summit but could feel the rise before him. He was already weary. Thoughts of the 3000 feet of elevation gain made him tired.

The trail led up, into the darkness. Trees covered the entrance to the forest cavern. Daniel closed the door of the Honda, but didn't lock it. The keys were still inside. He buttoned the face guard of his REI jacket against the cold and strode through the cavernous trailhead entrance.

Beneath the evergreens it was quiet. Direct rainfall only reached the ground where the trees were sickly or dying, infested with some kind of fungal rot. Occasionally, large drops of water, which had found their way from the top of the canopy and joined with other drips, fell from the bent fingers of aging watchers, always finding their way down the back of Daniel's neck.

Cold.

It wasn't dark, yet. It was still afternoon. But it was darkening. Under the canopy the colors were graying. Daniel couldn't see the sky. The trail was rising, climbing.

Steeper.

Daniel was sweating, but cold. He was breathing hard and he was thirsty. He thought he would be there already. It was farther than he thought, harder than he expected.

It always is.

Suddenly, the trees disappeared. Daniel stepped from beneath the twisted arms of hemlocks and cedars and Douglas firs onto the bald summit of Mount Si.

The western face of Mount Si drops off, nearly 3,000 feet to the valley below. Daniel stood on the peak and felt the wind batter him as it hit the immovable force of the mountain. The evergreen carpet of valley floor was approaching black. In the distance, there were city lights brightening in the darkening twilight. Above him, but not by much, the clouds were swirling and racing. He reached up to touch them.

He couldn't. They were farther away than they looked.

Daniel thought it would be quiet on top of the mountain.

It wasn't.

The wind whipped against his skin. The noise roared in his ears.

Daniel wanted to see them again, ached to see them again. Somewhere, deep down, deeper than the emptiness he felt, he knew. He was dying to see them again. The thought felt good.

It was life that was bad.

He'd had enough of it.

He stared out over the valley, at the swirling clouds, at the relentless wind and he screamed.

It welled up from inside him, a deep, keening yell. His hands balled into fists. He raised his arms to the sky and screamed. The primal force of his yell shook him to his knees. The sound was without words.

He wailed into the wind and the wind wailed back. Anger for anger. Howl for howl. Cry for cry.

When he could no longer hear his own voice, he realized he was on his back, staring up at the clouds. They were still moving just as fast. There was a time-lapse quality to the way they were skittering across the sky. He could see shapes in them, but they moved and changed and swirled so fast he could never quite grasp what they were.

Just out of reach. Just beyond.

The clouds were heavy with moisture. The wind was blowing hard. But now, Daniel was quiet inside. The furious sound had left him.

Cold.

Empty.

Spent.

But not dead.

Yet.

He stood up, slowly. He was lightheaded. His teeth were chattering. His body was shaking.

"Daniel."

He could hear her voice. He looked around.

"Daddy."

It was just the wind.

He looked down at the valley below. Vertigo made him dizzy.

He realized that he could not just jump off the mountain. The summit sloped downward before it dropped off. He would have to get a running start, or he would end up in the trees. If he could leap out far enough, he could fly.

He turned his back on the wind and walked to his starting point, just below the summit.

He let the sound, the roar, the violence of the wind fill him.

"Daniel."

He couldn't bare the torment. He couldn't listen to the sound of her voice in every breath.

"Death is not the end."

"I know," he shouted. "I'm coming."

He was ready. He could do it.

He would take off into the wind.

"I'm coming."

The sky above was angry gray. He looked to the west, to his flight path. The clouds were swirling.

He took a deep breath. His heart was racing.

The sun came out.

The clouds were still there, but the sun came out.

To the west, the setting sun dropped below the ceiling of clouds and shone on the top of Mount Si.

"Daniel."

He stared at the sun.

Amazing.

Beautiful.

The light was dazzling.

The valley below was dark, but the underside of the cloud cover was brilliant. There was a roof to the world. Daniel had seen it. He knew there was space above, but below the roof, below the ceiling, below the lid, there was light. Reds and oranges and yellows radiating from the setting sun. Shining on the rock, shining on him.

He could feel the light.

He could feel the warmth.

He could feel the love. It took his breath away.

The wind had gone silent.

"Daniel."

Two months ago, he might have called this a spiritual experience. Now, he didn't know. He could feel it deep within, as deep as the emptiness.

Still there.

The hole was still there. The loss was still there. He could feel it. It wouldn't go away. If he went there, the pain was unbearable.

But there was light surrounding it. He could feel the light.

Could he jump into the light? Could he fly? Should he fly?

The light won't last.

He'd come this far. He wasn't going to stop now.

"I'M COMING."

He took his stance like a runner, about to start a long distance race. His heart was pounding. He took a deep breath and closed his eyes.

"Don't."

Daniel stood up straight. He felt the goose bumps rise on his skin. He turned around.

There she was.

"Hey, Babe," she said. "Whatcha doing?" She said it like it was the most normal thing in the world to meet there, on the top of a mountain, never mind that she was dead.

He could barely breathe. He could feel the anger rising from that empty hole. He didn't know there could be so much contained in such emptiness.

"You're dead," he shouted. The wind carried his words away.

She smiled. "You have an attorney's talent for stating the obvious."

He stepped toward her, nearly tripping on the rocks.

"You think this is funny," he yelled.

Her smile vanished.

He wanted to run to her, touch her, hold her. He didn't want to fight with her. He needed her. He wanted her. He could barely see her.

"I'll always be with you."

Her lips didn't move. He heard her voice in his mind. He felt her words in his heart. He felt joy and pain.

He pushed his anger back.

"I'm lost," he said.

"You can't be lost," she said. "You're on the top of a mountain."

"With no where to go, but down." He was serious.

"Don't do it, Daniel."

"Why not? We'll be together."

"You're not done here," she said.

"And you were?"

"I didn't choose this."

"Neither did I." Daniel could feel the anger rising again. He fought against it, but it was so big. He could feel it. He couldn't touch her. He fell to his knees.

"What are you doing here?" He challenged.

"Helping you."

"Really," he said.

"Really."

"I don't think it's working."

She smiled.

The light from the sun was fading. The radiance he felt was from her. She had intense green eyes. He loved her eyes. He didn't want to look away.

"What am I going to do?"

She came to him then, to that place in his heart he kept for her. He couldn't touch her, but he could feel her.

"You'll know," she said. Her words were inside him. He knew it.

The winds would blow. The storms would rage. But he knew it. She filled that place in his heart.

It hurts.

"For a while," she said.

"How long?"

"Not long."

Daniel didn't speak. It's not that there weren't words to say. It was that in silence, in stillness, he could hear, he could feel Julie touching his mind, his heart.

Daniel knew that death wasn't the end. Death wasn't so bad. Death was just another place, another life. Maybe death was just this place, on another side.

"How's Jenny?"

"Amazing. And busy, and happy."

"I miss her."

"She loves you."

Daniel stood up. "My knees hurt."

"I don't have that problem anymore," she said.

"Not fair," he said.

"I have to go," she said.

Daniel reached for her. "Don't. Not yet."

There was nothing to hold onto. The wind was still blowing.

"Be good," she said, smiling.

"I love you," he said.

"I know."

They both smiled.

"I love you, too." She said.

The sun set. The light was gone. The hole was still there. But the warmth of her spirit would contain the emptiness, for a while, at least.

Daniel looked at the craggy mountaintop. It was dark. He couldn't see the trail and he had a long way to go.

Chapter 71

Daniel Monson thought he had a perfect life. The fears he built walls around, hidden deep inside, found expression.

Death.

Death changed everything.

It happened so fast it made him sick. It made him dizzy. It gave him vertigo.

Running on quicksand.

He knew things now he wished he didn't know.

Death isn't the end.

It's a great wall.

They're on the other side.

He wanted to be there.

"Will you help me?" she asked.

"What?"

Someone sucked the air out of the room. He couldn't breathe.

"Will you help me?"

"Why me?" Daniel asked.

"She said you would."

"Who said I would?" Daniel's heart beat faster.

"She did."

Daniel could spend all his waking life helping lost souls. When he wasn't awake, they haunted his dreams.

I can't help them all.

"I don't know what else to do," she said.

"There must be someone else who can help you," he said. He didn't want to do it.

"I don't think so," she said.

"Why not?"

"She told me you were the one."

He could hear her saying it. She'd said it before.

Daniel smiled. "Who told you that?"

"I don't know," she said, desperately. Her eyes were moist. "She didn't tell me her name."

"And you didn't ask?"

Her tears spilled out.

"No," she said. He could hear the despair creep into her voice.

Daniel slowed down and turned into an asphalt driveway. He turned off the engine.

"What did she look like?"

"She was beautiful. And she had green eyes."

He knew he would help her.

"She was with a little girl."

Daniel could feel it happening. It happened often. The ache he buried each morning was clawing and scratching to get out. It was welling up inside him. It would consume him if he didn't do something. He couldn't give in to it, now.

Maybe later.

He got out of the royal blue Volvo Station Wagon and sucked the cold November air. It kept the ache from escaping. He could breathe again.

He looked at the WWII style craftsman home. It was small, and old. It needed paint. But the yard was neat. As he walked up the driveway in his borrowed deliveryman jump suit, he could see a brown Crown Victoria parked across the street.

He's good.

Daniel knocked on the door. He heard footsteps inside. The door opened. An attractive young woman, girl really, stood there, holding a tiny two month old baby. The baby was beautiful. Daniel felt his eyes moisten.

"Can I help you?" she said with a questioning look.

Daniel handed the woman a clipboard.

"I just need a signature, here and here," Daniel said.

He didn't really need a signature.

"Pink slip's in the glove box. Keys are in the ignition."

The woman had a puzzled look on her face.

"There must be some mistake," she said.

Daniel expected this. He'd done his research. They were good people. He'd made it hard on them.

"Are you…" he pulled the clipboard back, "Kristen Newberry?"

"Yes," she said.

"Your husband named, Andrew?"

"Yes," she said.

Daniel could tell she was a bit frightened. He didn't want that. He smiled warmly.

"Is that your baby, born two-months ago at Mercy?"

"I'm sorry. Who are you?" she asked. "How do you know these things?"

Daniel didn't make eye contact. Too personal, even though he felt like he knew this woman, this family.

"I'm just the delivery guy," he said. "But, you've been given a brand new Volvo Station Wagon, fully paid for, including insurance and gas for a year, tax free."

The girl put her hand to her mouth.

"I don't know what to say…" She said.

Daniel handed her the clipboard.

"Don't say anything," he said. "Just sign here."

She took the clipboard and began to sign.

"Why? How?"

"Don't rightly know," Daniel drawled. "My papers said something about a young couple, new baby, stolen car..."

The baby was fussing.

"It's a nice car," Daniel said. "A family car."

"I don't believe it," she said, stunned.

"No, really," Daniel said. "I drove it over here."

"No," she stammered. "I didn't mean..."

"Go call your husband," Daniel said. "Tell him the good news. He won't have to take the bus to work, anymore."

The woman hugged her baby. She was swaying back and forth. It was a natural motion. She did it without thinking. Daniel remembered when Jenny was a baby. Julie did the same thing.

How do they do it?

"Really?" she said.

"Really," Daniel smiled. "She's all yours."

Tears were forming in the woman's eyes.

"Thank you," the woman said. "You wouldn't believe how hard it's been, since the baby...I don't mean...the baby...the car, I mean."

"Don't mention it," Daniel said.

"Thank you. Thank you. Thank you," she said.

"Don't thank me," Daniel said. "I just work here."

Daniel took the clipboard back with all the paperwork. They'd never know who gave them the car. He turned and hopped off the front porch. Looking back he said, "Precious baby. Hold her close." He winked and walked away.

He could feel the woman's eyes on him as he walked up the driveway. He crossed the street, pulled open the passenger door of the Crown Victoria and climbed in.

"How'd that go?" Sears said, watching the woman peer in the driver's side window of her new car.

Daniel buckled his seatbelt. He felt the warmth of the moment. It was warmer than the cold place he tried to hide.

"Good," Daniel said.

"You're crazy," Sears said.

"Thanks," Daniel said.

"You planning to do this again?" Sears asked.

"Will you help me?" a woman's voice asked. "Please?"

Daniel turned to look in the back seat. She was there. She looked thin. Fragile. She wasn't going to leave him alone.

"Maybe," Daniel said.

Sears watched him, curiously.

Dead spirits that couldn't move on had lots of problems. Daniel knew from experience. He also knew he would help her. He wasn't sure he really had a choice. He hoped it would make a difference.

"She was beautiful," Daniel said to the backseat.

"She's here, isn't she?" Sears said, shivering slightly.

Daniel couldn't tell if Sears was scared, or excited.

"No," he said.

Technically, he wasn't lying. He knew Sears was referring to Julie. Julie was gone. The hole in his heart would not bring her back.

"Then who're you talking to?" Sears said.

Daniel made him wait. Sears held his breath.

He should have been the one to see dead people.

Sears' forehead began to turn purple.

"She moved on," Daniel said.

Sears let out his breath.

"Damn," Sears said.

"Don't say that," Daniel said. "Don't ever say that."

Most of the souls that came seeking help were damned, in one way or another. That's why they needed help.

Sears started the Crown Victoria and looked in the rear view mirror, hopefully.

"Maybe I could see dead people, too," Sears said.

Daniel looked at Sears, then at the back seat.

"Will you help me?" she asked, again. The voice from the back seat was small and forlorn.

"I'll see what I can do," Daniel said.

Purchase other Black Rose Writing titles at www.blackrosewriting.com/books

and use promo code PRINT to receive a 20% discount.

CPSIA information can be obtained
at www.ICGtesting.com
Printed in the USA
FSOW03n0838300815
10403FS